RSVP TO MURDER

*To: Amy
Merry Christmas -
Carol*

RSVP TO MURDER

A Blackwell & Watson Time-Travel Mystery

CAROL POULIOT

First published by Level Best Books 2023

Copyright © 2023 by Carol Pouliot

All rights reserved. No part of this publication may be reproduced, stored or transmitted in any form or by any means, electronic, mechanical, photocopying, recording, scanning, or otherwise without written permission from the publisher. It is illegal to copy this book, post it to a website, or distribute it by any other means without permission.

This novel is entirely a work of fiction. The names, characters and incidents portrayed in it are the work of the author's imagination. Any resemblance to actual persons, living or dead, events or localities is entirely coincidental.

Carol Pouliot asserts the moral right to be identified as the author of this work.

Author Photo Credit: Kevin Lucas

First edition

ISBN: 978-1-68512-385-7

Cover art by Level Best Designs

This book was professionally typeset on Reedsy.
Find out more at reedsy.com

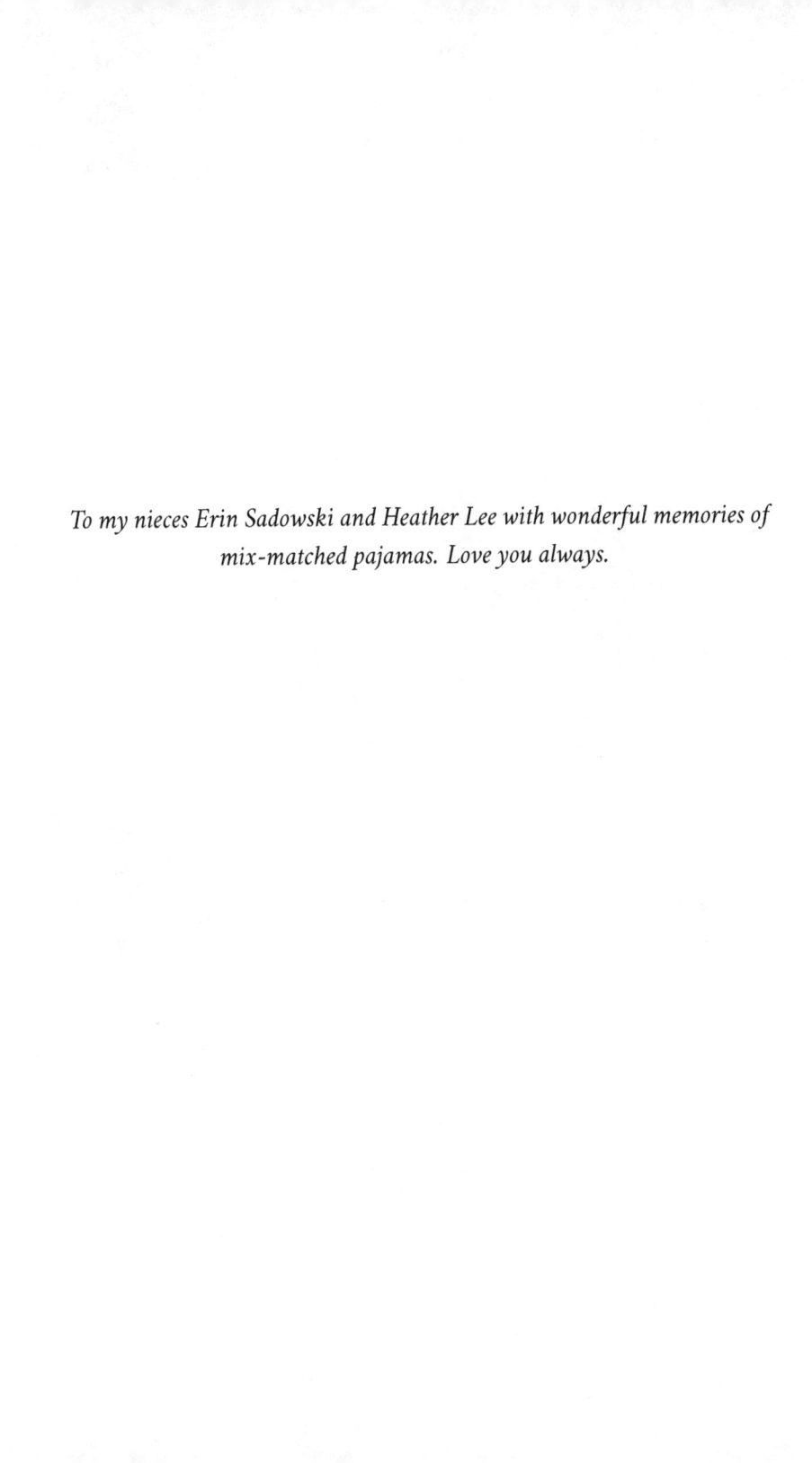

To my nieces Erin Sadowski and Heather Lee with wonderful memories of mix-matched pajamas. Love you always.

Praise for RSVP to Murder

"Carol Pouliot's *RSVP to Murder* is Agatha Christie with a time-travel twist. Pouliot supplies us with just what we crave in a great locked-room mystery: a blizzard, closed roads, dead phone lines, roaring fires, and lots of suspects and motives—all set in a luxurious Adirondack Great Camp in 1934. And then she gives us more. Time-travel! *RSVP to Murder* delivers on so many levels. Snap on your seatbelt and travel with Steven and Olivia to 1934, you won't regret it!"—Tina deBellegarde, Agatha-nominated author of The Batavia-on-Hudson Mystery Series.

"A Great Camp in the Adirondacks serves up a sumptuous setting of plump armchairs, roaring fireplaces, and the heady scent of Christmas pines—all begging to be settled into with this thumping good vintage whodunit set in the 1930s. Outside a blizzard roars, closing the road to the rustic lodge. Inside the host is murdered and a dozen guests, family and servants are snapping at one another's heels—each with a secret to hide. Cleverly plotted with plot-twists aplenty and some time-travel to boot, this immersive mystery is a gem."—Laurie Loewenstein, Silver Falchion finalist and author of the Dust Bowl Mystery Series

"Readers are invited to the glamour of the Thirties, where the rich are putting on the Ritz, until there's a murder to solve. Join time-travelers Blackwell and Watson in the race to the Racines' Adirondack Great Camp to catch a killer. A clever, at times humorous, and a thoroughly unique must for fans of the paranormal and historical. Don't miss it. RSVP today!"—Gabriel Valjan, Agatha-, Anthony-, and Shamus-nominated author of the Shane Cleary Mysteries series

"The Blackwell and Watson Time-Travel Mysteries' latest installment, *RSVP to Murder*, combines the thrilling and "timeless" aspects of Jack Finney's classic *Time and Again* mixed with the wit and charm of a modern, puzzling mystery. Highly recommended for all lovers of time travel, history, romance and wily sleuths."—L.A. Chandlar, bestselling author of the Art Deco Mystery Series

"If you like time-travel, murder, and old English country houses, you'll love *RSVP to Murder*."—Dale T. Phillips, author of the Zack Taylor mystery series

Cast of Characters

- **Gilbert Racine** – Powerful New York publisher of the popular newspaper *The City Chronicle* and fiction imprint *The Racine Literary Press*. Ruthless and driven by the need to succeed, he's made plenty of enemies.
- **Margery Racine** – Gil's wife. Society maven, committee addict, and absent mother. She was once fond of her husband.
- **Julian Racine** – Pampered son of Gil and Margery with questionable talent and a résumé of failed schemes. He's desperate for his father to publish his novel.
- **Irene Racine** – Gil and Margery's daughter. Plain-looking but clever. She's found the love of her life but needs her father's permission to marry.
- **Victor McAllister** – Irene Racine's man-about-town suitor. In love with money, he'd like nothing better than to see her father slip onto the third rail of the uptown subway so he can marry Irene.
- **Harry Racine** – Gil's handsome younger brother. Photographer, explorer, and adventurer. Tired of living out of a backpack and being threatened by deadly insects and wild animals, he's traipsed through his last jungle. He wants a quiet life at the family Great Camp.
- **Commander Jack Racine** – With his matinee idol looks and subtle charm, the middle Racine brother has come home from the

sea. He says he loves life aboard ship but is the Navy man really who he seems?
- **Aunt Emily** – Keeper of family secrets. Does she know more than she's letting on?
- **Gerald Rider** – The clever but discreet butler knows everything that goes on in the Racine household. Information can be dangerous.
- **Doris Buckley** – The easy-going cook consumes gossip for breakfast. But don't accuse her of poisoning the food.
- **Corinne Kelly** – Maid. She used to be middle-class, but after the Crash of 1929 her world came tumbling down.
- **Doctor Lewis Salisbury** – Longtime family physician and friend of Gil. He holds a secret that could bring down the Racine family.
- **Detective Sergeant Steven Blackwell** – Christmas party guest.
- **Olivia Watson** – Steven's girlfriend.
- **Sergeant Will Taylor** – Steven's partner and friend. He has uncovered devastating information.
- **Officer Jimmy Bourgogne** – Everyone's favorite cop. He always knows the right thing to say.

Chapter One

December 31, 1902

New York City, New York

She was marrying the wrong man.
 With a silk-gloved hand, Margery Belleville lifted the bottom of her wedding gown and peeked around the heavy, carved doors into the nave of St. Patrick's Cathedral. Several hundred guests—ladies in expensive finery, wool coats trimmed with ermine and fancy hats with brims reaching out over their shoulders, and tuxedoed men in black silk top hats—awaited the wedding of the decade. St. Patrick's reminded Margery of Notre Dame Cathedral in Paris with its Gothic-style pointed arches and rich stained-glass windows set in lacey webs. The soaring, vaulted ceiling, lit by crystal chandeliers suspended on long rope-like cables, rose hundreds of feet in the air. Light from the chandeliers reached into the far corners of the church and mingled with the glow of candles twinkling in wrought-iron stands. Inhaling the scent of balsam fir from the many holiday decorations, Margery gazed down the long center aisle, where she would soon walk with her father.
 Margery stepped back into the vestibule, her pure-white gown

rustling softly as she moved. She was, at least, happy her parents had allowed her the choice of her wedding dress, if not the groom. Margery and her mother had searched in several shops, nearly deciding to have the dress custom-made when they came upon this elegant, sleek gown. The moment Margery laid eyes on it she knew it was the one. The high neckline draped in soft folds beneath her chin, flattering her face. The form-fitting bodice hugged her curves, yet avoided the dreaded hourglass silhouette, with its yards of smooth satin skirt billowing around her. Margery's unadorned veil revealed topaz eyes and soft lips, but covered her rich auburn hair and cascaded down her back. This was the gown of a modern, independent woman. If only her life matched the dress.

His conversation with the bishop finished, Anthony Belleville joined his daughter. "Are you ready, my dear?"

The organ began Mendelssohn's "Wedding March," and a rumble echoed throughout the nave as the guests stood and turned toward the back of the cathedral. Trembling, Margery took her father's arm.

He must have felt her shaking because her father leaned over and, to Margery's astonishment, whispered, "I know he's not your first choice. But you will be well cared for, and you know Gil adores you. I don't know which man has captured your heart, but you won't lack for anything with Gilbert Racine. The publishing empire he's going to inherit will provide a comfortable, even pampered, life. He's the best choice to keep you in the style your mother and I have provided. I can't bear the thought that you would ever lack for anything, my dearest daughter."

Margery was further shocked when her father wiped a tear from his eye.

It was at that moment when Margery Belleville, soon to be Margery Racine, accepted her fate. She would be a good wife for her successful businessman husband. She would provide him with children and a

CHAPTER ONE

well-run home. She'd bury her feelings deep inside, lock them away in a cupboard, and throw away the key. She could not marry the man she loved. But she might grow to love the man she married.

Margery forced a smile and reached up to give her father a kiss on the cheek. "I'll be alright, Papa. Gil will be a good husband." She patted his hand. Straightening her spine, Margery gave a sharp nod of her head. "I'm ready."

Chapter Two

Thursday, December 13, 1934

Knightsbridge, New York

Steven knocked softly on the spare bedroom door, then eased it open.

"Olivia," he whispered. "Olivia, are you awake?"

Groans emanated from under the pillow, where Olivia lay face down.

How can she breathe like that?

He entered and perched on the edge of the bed.

"I see you're still here." He grinned.

Olivia Watson turned over and sat up, hair tousled, eyes half-closed. Steven's heart skipped a beat. How did he get so lucky to have this woman drop into his life?

"What time is it?" she croaked.

"Seven-thirty. You slept late."

Her face lit up as she became fully awake and realized where she was. "Wow, we did it! I'm still here." She reached out and hugged him.

This had been their most daring experiment so far—riskier than Olivia stepping through the portal that was her bedroom doorway and

CHAPTER TWO

time traveling from her 2014 to Steven's 1934, riskier than leaving the house in his time, riskier than meeting people and becoming part of Steven's Depression-era community.

Olivia had to admit she'd been afraid to fall asleep the past two nights. They'd agreed, however, that they had to know what would happen because the next big step was upon them.

Steven had received an invitation to attend a holiday party at the Adirondack Great Camp belonging to a wealthy newspaper publisher, and his host had told him to bring a guest. Olivia was his only choice.

The question was: Could Olivia time travel to 1934, drive to a location nearly one-hundred miles away, fall asleep there, and wake up still in 1934? Although they'd tried it twice in Steven's house, there was no way to know if the results would be the same at the Great Camp, since Steven's house was also Olivia's home, though they lived there eighty years apart. The last two nights, when she had gone to sleep, Olivia wondered in which century she would wake up.

"I'm going to get breakfast, Olivia."

"Can you give me a few minutes? I want to take a hot shower. It's freezing."

"Sure, I'll finish packing."

A half-hour later, dressed in a heavy wool sweater, corduroy trousers, and thick warm socks, Olivia padded into the kitchen.

"Mmm. The coffee smells like heaven." Olivia loved breathing in the aroma from Steven's percolator as the water boiled bubbled up into the aluminum basket where the ground coffee sat. "And bacon! You're going all out today."

Steven poured a cup and handed it to her. "It's only fifteen degrees out this morning. I thought we should have a hearty breakfast before our trip. Bacon and eggs seemed like the thing to do."

As Olivia leaned against the counter, warming her hands on the cup, she surveyed what had become a familiar sight.

When she'd first spent time in Steven's house, everything had looked so strange. He used a free-standing, white enamel cupboard unit with a small porcelain worktop, while she enjoyed a big steel fridge and spacious granite counters. His pale green, modest kitchen was a far cry from her cheery red-and-white decor. Now, although Olivia felt at home in Steven's version of their house, it still amazed her that beyond the veil of time, unseen but in this same space, sat her red tea kettle and window sill filled with potted herbs.

The only things that sat in both kitchens were Mr. Moto's kitty dishes. When it became obvious Olivia would be spending a lot of time in 1934, she decided to get Mr. Moto used to moving back and forth and comfortable in both eras. It had taken some figuring out and considerable wrestling with the sleek black, emerald-eyed cat, but in the end, she had prevailed. Now, Mr. Moto followed her into 1934 with the ease and grace of a dancer. Olivia always thought it strange that she and Steven needed to physically touch to bring each other into their respective times, but Mr. Moto simply slid into 1934 after them. Maybe cats had some kind of invisible radar system that allowed them to navigate time. Olivia had no idea, but she bought a set of bowls for Mr. Moto at Woolworth's Five and Dime, and he had adapted.

"You be good for Liz while we're gone this weekend," Olivia told her cat as she forked canned salmon into his bowl. "We'll be back before you know it." Mr. Moto wound himself around her leg and meowed, then concentrated on his food.

Olivia took silverware, plates, and napkins from the cupboard and set the table while Steven whipped up a bowl of eggs. He lifted crisp bacon onto paper towels, drained some of the grease, then poured the egg mixture into the frying pan. Olivia made toast and, as she finished buttering his, Steven tumbled scrambled eggs onto both plates. She added strips of bacon, and they sat down to the biggest breakfast she'd

CHAPTER TWO

eaten in a month.

Olivia lifted her cup as if it held champagne and said, "Here's to our first overnight trip together."

Instead of returning the sentiment, Steven frowned. "Are you sure you want to do this? Only spending two nights here might not be enough of a test. What if it's the house or the town keeping you here? I don't know about this, Olivia. Are we making a mistake?"

"I thought you were okay with it. Why haven't you said something?"

"I don't know. What if we've become over-confident? Aren't you nervous that you'll be pulled back to 2014?"

"I guess it depends on when I think about it. One day, I feel confident, and the next, I'm not sure. But this is exciting, and I really want to go." She sighed. "I decided to take some precautions. I tried to imagine what I would do if I woke up in the next century when we were at the Great Camp. I'd be all alone in the mountains in the middle of winter in my pajamas. I wouldn't have any warm clothes or my phone or a way to get to a main road."

Steven relaxed and smiled. "When you went back to your time yesterday, you created one of your back doors."

"I like that you know me so well." Olivia's amber eyes sparkled. "Yes, I packed a bag with heavy clothes and a throwaway cell phone. Then, I drove up to Onontaga and left everything, including my snowshoes, in an empty cabin near the main lodge. If worse comes to worse, I'll have a way to get home—and I won't freeze to death. I told Liz and Sophie…."

"Naturally," he grinned. Steven liked Olivia's best friends, who had accepted him into their circle and seemed to like him as well. More importantly, they kept their time-travel secret.

"As usual, Sophie's scared for me, and Liz took it in stride. They'll come get me if I'm jerked back to my time during the night. I feel better now that I have a backup plan."

"You're sure?" he asked.

"Yes, I've been looking forward to this for weeks. I can't wait to see the Great Camp in all its glory, especially decorated for Christmas. These camps are legendary, you know. I'm excited about the activities they've planned, too." A look of awe crept onto her face. "And the chance to meet a famous newspaper publisher...well, I don't even have words for that!"

"Okay, I appreciate all of that. I wanted to give you the chance to back out if you weren't sure." Steven reached across the table and squeezed her hand, then picked up his last strip of bacon. "So, the weather looks okay right now, but I'd like to leave some extra time because they're forecasting snow. It could easily take us two hours, maybe more. The ice-skating party's at three. If we're on the road by eleven-thirty, we'll have time to stop for lunch and arrive in plenty of time."

"I'll be ready."

Chapter Three

On the Road, Adirondack Mountains

"Couldn't you have reserved a better car than this piece of junk, Victor?" Irene Racine whined. "We'll never make it in this weather."

"Stop complaining. This was the best they had. What's made you so irritable today?" said Victor McAllister, as the heavy roadster, its headlights throwing pale shafts of light onto the snowy road, slid toward the center.

Irene let out a squeal of panic.

He reached over to pat her knee through her thick fur coat. "Hey, we're okay. I know what I'm doing."

Irene's nostrils flared, her lip curled, and she shot him a look.

"Now, let's concentrate on why we're attending this get-together," said Victor. "Do you really think your father will interrupt his Christmas celebrations to listen to you again? You know what he's like during the holidays. And you told me that the last time you broached the subject, he said it had better *be* the last time."

"I know. My father's always been stubborn," said Irene.

"Well, you're Daddy's little girl...."

Daddy's little girl. Irene tuned out Victor, his continued conversation becoming the mere buzzing of an insect on the other side of the car. Daddy's little girl. She relaxed. A small bittersweet smile inched its way onto her face. And she remembered....

Irene Racine's first real memories were of summer nights when she was four years old. Every night while she slept, butterfly wings would flutter against her face, and she'd find herself floating up into semi-consciousness. "You're my little girl," the butterfly would whisper, kissing her cheek, sometimes brushing sweat-drenched curls from her forehead. Irene could always feel herself smiling in her sleep. She knew the butterfly was really her daddy, making sure she was safe. "Sleep tight, my precious child," the butterfly would say.

The second memory was the day after her grandfather died; her father now owned the newspaper. That night, her daddy did not come to check on her. Irene awoke the next morning and touched her cheek. For the first time, she'd felt the absence of the butterfly kiss.

Thus, Irene Racine became a pleaser. Pushing open the heavy door to her father's study, seeing his head bent over piles of files and newspapers, Irene would tiptoe in with gifts chosen especially for him. "Look, Daddy, I found a robin's egg under the chestnut tree in the backyard." "Look, Daddy. See this perfect red maple leaf? It's for you." "Look, Daddy, I got an A on my spelling test."

But Gil Racine, overwhelmed by the crushing new burden of running a major newspaper at the age of twenty-eight, patted his daughter on the head without looking up and mumbled, "Not now, sweetheart." or "Later, Irene." or "Daddy's working now, my dear. Go find Mommy."

Irene wanted to tell him Mommy was never home. She was always somewhere else doing things for other people, strangers that Irene didn't know.

By the time she reached her teens, Irene had changed. She had wrapped her delicate emotions in protective armor and hidden them away. She became

CHAPTER THREE

a loner, a recluse in her parents' home. She made herself scarce, became distant, spent hours in her room surrounded by her books and her sewing cards. She confided in her diary all the things she yearned to tell her father but could not.

When Irene celebrated her twentieth birthday, the act she had so carefully crafted had become real—the mask was no longer an artifice. Irene Racine had convinced herself that she needed no one, that she was better off this way.

And it had worked...until she met Victor.

"...Talk some sense into him..."

Victor's words tumbled into Irene's reverie, intruding like the morning sun through a crack in the curtains. She focused and listened.

"...Wind him around that little finger like you always do. Make him find the time to talk with you. I'm not waiting forever, Irene. It's already been four years. Something's got to change."

"I don't want to lose you, Victor. I *won't* lose you." Irene steeled herself and said, "I'll do whatever I have to. Believe me."

He believed her all right. Beneath that pampered, spoiled facade, Irene Racine was tougher than nails. "Well, you better make it quick. I don't know how much longer I can wait. Maybe we should set a deadline." He glanced at her, rigid and looking straight ahead at the blizzard whirling around them. "How about the thirty-first? Then we'll know where we stand for the new year."

"Don't threaten me, Victor," she said steadily. "And don't you worry. I've got a plan."

"What time have you got, Doc?" Julian Racine asked Lewis Salisbury, who was comfortably ensconced in the leather passenger seat of the Buick Country Club Coupe.

Salisbury spun the calfskin band on his wrist, repositioning his new

11

Bulova. "Two-thirty. We're making good time."

"Yeah, we ought to be there around three. I'm sure my father planned activities for this afternoon."

"He always does." Lewis chuckled. "You know how crazy he is about Christmas."

Suddenly, an enormous eight-point buck jumped out of the storm as if the wall of snow had magically revealed an opening. The deer ran into the middle of the road and stopped. Julian slammed on the brakes. The heavy car slid onto a narrow shoulder toward a snow-filled ditch. Lewis grabbed the strap above his head with his right hand. His other hand flew onto the dashboard to brace himself as the forest rushed at them. Julian spun the wheel to the left, pulling the car back onto the icy pavement in time to avoid diving headlong into the ditch. The deer bounded into the trees on the opposite side of the road.

"Damn!" Julian said. "That was close." He burst out laughing. "I've barely gotten used to winter again. The last thing I need right now is to have to ski the rest of the way to the camp."

Lewis laughed. "No, you've never been much for sports. So, you never said…how was Florida? You got back Tuesday, right?"

"Yeah, it was good. The usual Boca crowd. Met a couple new dames, though. One lives in Boston, so that's not too far to go."

"I'm glad you had fun. By the way, I appreciate the ride today, Julian. The mechanic said my car won't be ready until next week. Lousy timing."

Next week, thought Julian. *By next week, it'll be over. I'll have done what I planned to do. And to hell with the consequences. I'll show him. Not good enough for Racine Literary, am I? You just wait and see.*

Harry Racine hummed to himself as he steered around a slow-moving Amish carriage, the two magnificent horses pulling with ease despite the mounting snow. Wouldn't you know there'd be a blizzard to

CHAPTER THREE

welcome him back from Brazil?

The trip hadn't turned out the way he'd expected, not by a long shot. He could have done without the torrential rains and the damned piranhas in the Amazon River. And those caiman beasts. Talk about prehistoric! Come to think of it, they reminded him a bit of his brother—Gil Racine, the predatory publisher of New York.

Harry remembered when their father died. Gil couldn't wait to get his hands on everything. They already knew Racine Senior was leaving the whole shooting match to Gil, his eldest son. And sure enough, there were no surprises when the lawyer read the will. Harry and his brother Jack inherited some cash, but Gil got the newspaper, the sprawling mansion on Fifth Avenue, and, most important to Harry, Great Camp Onontaga. Luckily, Harry earned decent money selling his photographs because he'd nearly spent his inheritance.

Over the years, Racine Publishing had expanded and become more profitable—after all, everyone read the paper, and considered *The City Chronicle* one of the best newspapers in town. Then, as if that wasn't enough, Gil had branched out. In a remarkably short time, *The Racine Literary Press* had grown to rival Harper, Putnam, and even Scribner.

Harry had decided he'd had enough. This weekend, things were going to change. He wasn't taking no for an answer anymore. He'd wait until Gil had drunk plenty of Christmas cheer, then they'd have it out. Harry wanted Onontaga. Period. He was tired of staying in the noisy, crowded city when he returned home from his travels. He'd had it being relegated to Cabin B when the family came up to the mountains.

Since the Great War, Harry craved solitude more and more with each passing year. He longed for a place tucked away in the quiet stillness of nature, far from the racket and fast-paced life in New York City. He needed a setting where he could relax, where he could wrestle with his demons—stubborn devils that refused to let go. Images that haunted his dreams. Memories no man should have to bear.

Harry sensed his traveling days would be over soon—he'd had enough of those, too. Especially since the disastrous trip to South America. He shook his head, as if the action would dispel the memory. He didn't want to think about it right now. Harry could not let himself be distracted this weekend. He had a goal to accomplish—one goal, one critical objective that had compelled him to choose to endure four days with his family and their guests. He needed to focus on his goal, or the chance to attain it would slip through his fingers. And he could not let that happen.

Harry was determined to spend the rest of his life at Onontaga. It was the least Gil could do. His brother owed him that much after the raw deal he'd gotten from their father.

Harry was older and cleverer now. More resourceful. Either Gil signed Onontaga over to him, or he'd regret it. Harry knew how to be ruthless, too.

An hour into their trip, it started to snow. Steven and Olivia had entered the five-thousand square mile Adirondack Park and were passing Otter Lake.

"Are you hungry yet?" Olivia asked. "Maybe we can find a place to stop around Thendara or Old Forge."

"That sounds good. I could use a break from focusing on the road. This is one of those storms where it looks like the snow is coming right at me. It's making me dizzy."

Steven pulled the jungle green Chevy into the parking area behind the railroad station in Thendara. Olivia knelt on the front seat and reached into the back for Steven's refrigerator picnic basket, another surprising innovation she hadn't expected.

The good-sized basket was lined with tin and contained a small box for holding ice to keep food cold in the summer. In the winter, all they

CHAPTER THREE

had to do was remove the box and put hot food in the basket. The tin radiated the heat and kept things warm.

Olivia spread an oversized napkin on the bench seat to act as a tablecloth. She placed warm, grilled cheese sandwiches on colorful paper plates and set out a container of potato chips and one of dill pickles. "There's hot chocolate in the Thermos," she told Steven as she set two cups on the dashboard. "If we only fill them halfway, they shouldn't spill."

"This is swell," Steven exclaimed. "How do you come up with these ideas?"

"When I was a kid, my parents took me on a lot of day trips in the winter. My mom always brought grilled cheese sandwiches for our lunch. Fond memories." She smiled. "Hang on a second. I want to take a picture."

Olivia reached into her leather tote bag for her new Kodak Baby Brownie. It was a small black cube made of molded Bakelite with vertical ribs on the front, giving it an Art Deco look. The camera fit easily in her hand. She flipped up the frame finder and said, "Cheese." They both laughed as Steven held up his sandwich and wiggled his eyebrows.

"Ha! Good one," she said.

By the time they'd finished their winter picnic, snow covered the windshield. Steven jumped out and pulled his arm through the accumulation to remove most of it. He brushed off some more, then got back in the car and engaged the heavy wipers to push off the rest. Together, they gazed up through the storm at a sky weighed down with pewter clouds. Steven eased the sedan back on the road. An hour later, when they left the partially plowed main road, over eight inches had already fallen. They crawled along the narrow access road to the Racines' Great Camp.

"How can you see where you're going?" asked Olivia. "I can't tell where the road leaves off, and the verge begins. And the trees so close to the road make it seem even darker. It's like we're being swallowed up by the forest."

"To be honest, I have no idea where the road is either. That's why I'm going so slow. I keep thinking that if the car starts to go off the road, I'll feel it, and I can get it back on before it's too late."

"Ugh! The last thing we need is to end up in a ditch. Do you know how much farther it is?"

"According to Gil's directions, it shouldn't be too far."

As the heavy car forged deep tracks in the fresh snow, Steven kept his speed at ten miles an hour. They rounded a bend and saw the outline of the Great Camp emerge in a kaleidoscope of swirling snow. The enormous three-story lodge loomed ahead like a behemoth in one of the science-fiction novels Steven loved to read. Despite the twinkling lights in the windows, Olivia felt a shiver run down her spine.

Chapter Four

Great Camp Onontaga, Adirondack Mountains

Steven rounded the circular drive to the front entrance. As they approached, they could see that Great Camp Onontaga comprised more than one main building. A large multi-car garage sat to the immediate right of the lodge itself. One of a pair of doors had been left ajar, revealing the sweeping fender of an automobile protected from the blizzard. To the right of the garage, several small cabins stretched out along a lane leading into the forest. Olivia noted that the second cabin was where she had left her emergency supplies yesterday, back in her time. Beyond the last cabin stood what appeared to be a small stable—several bales of hay sat piled near the barn door. The entire complex was nestled in the pines along the shores of Raquette Lake.

The main lodge at Great Camp Onontaga was constructed of logs that had darkened over the years. Red trim around the windows and front door drew the visitor's eye above the frames to rustic designs fashioned from different shades of bark. Along the building's foundation, a variety of local stones formed decorative patterns, creating an artistic design and adding to the unique Adirondack architectural style.

Steven pulled up alongside the porch railing and cut the engine. "This is something," he exclaimed. "I couldn't imagine what it was going to look like. Sure is fancy."

A tall white-haired man dressed in a tuxedo opened the front door and stepped onto the porch, where several pairs of skis and snowshoes leaned against the wall near a sled. Steven and Olivia lifted their suitcases from the trunk and carried them up the stairs.

"Detective Blackwell, how are you? I trust your journey wasn't too difficult?" He reached for Olivia's case. "I'll take that, Miss."

Olivia murmured her thanks as Steven said, "Hello, Rider. Not bad, thank you. It's nice to see you again."

Steven and Olivia stomped their feet, knocking snow off their boots, and stepped into a vast room that looked and smelled like Christmas.

Olivia gasped. "Oh, my goodness. How beautiful."

The large room, paneled in a warm knotty pine, was divided into a living area and dining area, the living room portion taking up two-thirds of the space. Plump armchairs and comfortable-looking sofas heaped with pillows and wool throws in red, green, and black Tartan plaid filled the cozy space. A magnificent baby grand piano stood in one corner. Olivia's eyes traveled around the room to lush, fragrant pine boughs draped over the tops of windows, wrapped around a banister, and arranged on fireplace mantles. Separating the dining area to the right from the living room on the left stood the tallest balsam fir Olivia had ever seen inside someone's home. Delicate ornaments, silver garland, and glittering lights bedecked the towering Christmas tree. She gazed up at the angel on top, then followed dark beams that ran the length of the lodge and supported two chandeliers made of deer antlers—one in the middle of the living area, the other centered over the massive dining table. Two stone fireplaces faced one another from opposite ends of the room, each with a roaring blaze, filling the lodge with both warmth and scent.

CHAPTER FOUR

Steven and Olivia removed their boots, adding them to the pile on a colorful rug near a wicker basket filled with ice skates, then padded into the room in stockinged feet.

A husky middle-aged man with salt-and-pepper hair and a hawk-like nose strode across the room, voice booming. "Steven, my boy! Welcome. So glad you made it before the storm got too bad." He enveloped Steven in a big bear hug.

"Same here. Thanks again for the invitation, Gil. This is my friend Olivia Watson."

"I'm happy to meet you, Mr. Racine. Thank you for including me in your party," Olivia said.

"We're all on a first-name basis here, Miss Watson. Call me Gil."

She smiled. "Okay. Then it's Olivia."

"You got it. I want you to make yourselves at home this weekend. Anything you need, say the word. Rider will see to it."

"Steven," said a painfully thin woman as she rushed into the room. "Thank goodness you've arrived. I was getting worried." She brushed a strand of thick auburn hair from her face, then her hand fluttered down by her side, where it pulled at the skirt of her wool dress, giving Olivia the impression that this woman had a repertoire of nervous habits.

"See, Margery? I told you he'd be fine," Gil told his wife, putting a beefy arm around her thin shoulders.

Steven introduced Olivia again.

"You have a beautiful home, Mrs. Racine," Olivia told her hostess. "Everything is so festive. Thank you for inviting me."

"You're most welcome, my dear."

A second man appeared in a doorway at the far side of the room and joined the gathering. This one looked like a matinee idol, had dark hair and an even more pronounced aquiline nose.

"Steven! You made it," he said, vigorously shaking his hand. "And

19

you must be Miss Watson. I'm Jack Racine. We're very glad you could join us this weekend."

"I'm happy to be here. I've really been looking forward to it," said Olivia.

Jack echoed what his brother had said, and they agreed to be on a first-name basis.

"How were the roads, Steven?" asked Jack. "They're predicting over three feet by tomorrow morning. We wondered if you'd come."

"I hadn't heard that. Well, we're here. And it looks like we might not be leaving for a while." Steven shot Olivia a look with raised brows.

"You and Olivia are in Cabin A, Steven. You've got two bedrooms and a living room, your own bathroom, of course, and a tiny kitchen," Gil Racine told him. "Rider's already taken your luggage over. It's the first one after the garage." He pointed to show the direction. "You can't miss it. There's a big letter A over the door." He chuckled. "The fires have been lit, so it should be nice and warm."

"We've decided to cancel the skating this afternoon," Jack said. "Snow's too deep. But if it lets up a bit, we thought we'd go for a sleigh ride instead." He turned to Olivia. "How does that sound?"

"Swell," Olivia exclaimed, the eighty-year-old expression now at the ready as though it were the most natural thing in the world.

"Would you like something to warm you up first? How about a brandy?" Gil offered. Not waiting for an answer, he walked to a drinks cart near the hearth in the living room.

An elderly woman descended the staircase and settled on the end of one of the sofas flanking the hearth. "Pour me a brandy too, Gil," she said.

Steven and Olivia introduced themselves to the new arrival.

"Pleased to meet you. I'm Gil's Aunt Emily," said the white-haired woman as she took the drink from Gil.

Margery settled next to Aunt Emily. Olivia took the opportunity to

CHAPTER FOUR

wander.

This spectacular space was a mix of elegant and rustic design, stunning and homey at the same time. She stopped at the magnificent Christmas tree and thought how Liz would go out of her mind in rapture at the dozens of hand-crafted glass ornaments. Olivia paused at the Steinway baby grand piano, sheet music and books of Christmas carols spread out along the music rack. Sophie would love to get her hands on this beauty, she thought, as she reached out to feel the polished ebony when Jack shouted, "No, Olivia."

Olivia pulled back as though she'd touched a hot stove. "Oh, sorry." Jack hurried over. "No, *I'm* sorry. My brother is a fanatic about his piano. Gil doesn't like people touching it. I should have told you and Steven when you got here. My most sincere apologies. It's no way to treat a guest."

"That's okay, Jack. I should have guessed it was something special." She smiled at him, embarrassed by her mistake.

Gil handed a snifter of Rémy Martin to Olivia and one to Steven. "I'm like a baby with that piano of mine. Just can't stand to share." He shrugged.

After taking a drink from his own glass, Gil Racine gestured to the area above the fireplace mantle. "What do you think, Steven?"

As Steven and Olivia gazed up at a large oil painting, he was transported to an evening one year ago to the gala celebrating the unveiling of his mother's final work of art.

December 1933
New York City

"Evangeline Blackwell and Steven Blackwell."

The butler's deep voice resounded over the sounds of the jazz orchestra, cutting through the crowd of gowned and tuxedoed partygoers.

The music stopped. A hundred people in the ballroom of Gilbert Racine's Fifth Avenue mansion craned their necks to get a look at the guest of honor, applauding as the Blackwells entered the opulent room.

Steven leaned in close and whispered in his mother's ear, "It's an even bigger crowd than last year. Bravo, Maman."

The ballroom was a vision of shimmering Murano chandeliers and glittering gold-leaf trim above creamy white walls. It reminded Steven of Versailles—there were even mirrors placed strategically on several recessed panels. Along the right side of the room, a half dozen portes fenêtres reached from floor to ceiling. When he and his mother attended Racine's annual spring gala, Steven often exited the ballroom via these doors to stroll in the garden on a warm evening.

Gilbert Racine strode across the room. "Welcome! Welcome, Evangeline!" He leaned in and gave her a kiss on each cheek. "They're all dying to see it," he murmured. He turned to Steven and shook his hand. "Good to see you again, Steven."

Steven stepped aside and prepared to follow as Racine led Evangeline to the far end of the room where an easel stood. His mother's latest painting hid beneath a white linen cloth. He didn't know how much the millionaire had paid for this commissioned work, but his mother had said the price would take care of their expenses for the next few years.

"Ladies and Gentlemen, it is my great honor to introduce legendary French artist Evangeline Blackwell."

The crowd applauded again.

As Steven took a crystal flute of champagne—the tiny jewel-like bubbles sparkling as they danced to the top—from a passing liveried waiter, a warm

CHAPTER FOUR

feeling of pride coursed through him. He was so proud of his mother. In the unpredictable and competitive art world, Evangeline Blackwell had left Paris at the turn of the 20th century and had taken New York City by storm. Gil Racine typically bought one or two of her paintings each year and hosted a gala to unveil each one.

"Drum roll, please," Gil said, and the drummer in the far corner complied. "I give you the latest Evangeline Blackwell...," shouted Racine. He pulled off the covering with a flourish.

The oil painting showed Racine's Adirondack Great Camp Onontaga. The near-impressionistic style was reminiscent of western artist Bill Mittag, and attested to both French and American influence in Evangeline's work.

Applause filled the room. Steven heard shouts of Bravo! and Magnificent!

The evening passed in a blur of congratulations, conversation, and champagne. Later at their hotel, Steven and his mother relived her success, as they enjoyed a nightcap before turning in.

"I wonder what he'll ask you for next year," Steven said.

"He hinted at something else to hang at Onontaga," Evangeline replied. "I think maybe the forest and some wildlife. Possibly a deer or two."

Steven smiled as he was falling asleep that night. How blessed they were, he and his mother, to have such a devoted patron. He couldn't know that in a year, they'd both be dead.

Chapter Five

Thursday, December 13, 1934

Great Camp Onontaga, Adirondack Mountains

S teven and Olivia were not in a hurry to leave the friendship and warmth of the main lodge. They settled comfortably on the sofa facing Margery and Aunt Emily—Gil and Jack stood by the fireplace mantle—and, for the next half hour, enjoyed the Racines' fine cognac while conversing with their hosts.

Olivia hadn't realized how close Steven and Gil were, despite the obvious age difference. Steven had gotten to know the newspaperman through Gil's patronage of Steven's mother's paintings. Olivia reminded herself that despite the deep feelings she and Steven shared, it hadn't been a year yet since they'd first met. There was still much about him she didn't know.

The front door banged open, and the third Racine brother blew in, followed by a plain-looking young woman bundled up in an expensive fur—a white wool beret angled jauntily on her dark brown hair—and a tall man with a pencil-thin mustache and heavy eyebrows whom Olivia thought resembled Errol Flynn, an actor in some of the classic 1930s movies she enjoyed. He held the woman's arm as he guided

CHAPTER FIVE

her into the camp. Steven and Olivia rose and followed their hosts to greet the new arrivals.

"Damn! It got colder, and the snow got worse the farther north we drove. I thought we'd never get here. What are we doing in the mountains during a blizzard?" Irene Racine moaned.

"I told you we should stay in town for the weekend, Irene," said the Errol Flynn lookalike.

"You don't know what cold is," Harry Racine said. "When I was on Baffin Island last year, up in northern Canada, it was thirty below, and the wind cut through you like a knife."

Olivia sensed a kindred spirit and had to stop herself from saying *cool*. "How exciting! Do you travel a lot?" she asked as the brawny blond unzipped his heavy jacket and pulled off a knit wool cap. As he moved, Olivia could see the muscles ripple under his wool sweater. If she wasn't dating Steven, she'd go for this guy.

"Traveler, explorer, photographer. Harry Racine, Miss...?"

"Watson. Olivia Watson."

"Well, Miss Watson, it sounds like we might have something in common." He came within inches of her and looked down.

Olivia stepped back and said, "Yes, Steven and I love traveling, don't we, Steven?"

Steven eased through the crowd and stuck out his hand. "Hello, Harry. Nice to see you again."

Harry Racine greeted Steven with a friendly handshake, then made the introductions. "Steven, Olivia, meet my niece Irene and her friend Victor McAllister. We drove nearly three hundred miles, and they pulled in right after me. Funny, huh?"

Everyone said hello.

"Where's my other suitcase?" Irene's voice cut through the chatter. "You didn't leave it at the station, did you, Victor?"

"Rider's getting it," Harry told her.

"Irene, you're here," Margery called. "Gil, we should have hired a car to pick them up."

"Hello, Mother," Irene said, walking to the far side of the room, giving Margery a kiss on the cheek. "It was fine. Victor reserved a car in advance. It was waiting when the train pulled in. Where's Julian? Is he here yet?"

"No, your brother's driving up with Lewis. Wait. Is that a car?"

Everyone turned toward the still-open door as a stunning 1932 Buick Country Club Coupe pulled up. The creamy beige chassis was set off by a black roof and large curved fenders in a classic Art Deco flourish. The deep snow already covered half of the white-walled tires and their sporty-looking wire spokes.

"The gang's all here," said Jack, raising his glass to no one in particular.

Gil and Margery's son, Julian, jumped out of the driver's seat, pushed through the snow around the front end of the car, and climbed the steps as he addressed the butler. "Rider, my bags are in the trunk." He shook hands with his father and strode across the room. He leaned over and kissed Margery on the cheek. "You look lovely as always, Mom." He smiled at his mother's elderly companion. "Swell to see you, Aunt Emily. How are you?"

"Spiffing," she said, grinning at her own use of the young people's vernacular. "It's always good to see you, Julian." She sipped her brandy, her intelligent eyes missing nothing.

Julian stepped to the drinks cart to pour himself a Scotch. As he lifted the cut-crystal decanter, the amber liquid glowed in the light of the fire, making it seem alive.

The sound of a trunk lid slamming drew everyone's attention back to the car outside. A slender man wearing a fedora and a raccoon fur coat entered the lodge with a Louis Vuitton suitcase.

"Hello. Hello. Am I glad to see all of you," Lewis Salisbury exclaimed.

CHAPTER FIVE

"Gil, you may never get rid of me. I might stay here until spring." He set his case to the side. "What a trip! Julian," he called across the room, "pour me a brandy, will you?"

Gil Racine gave the newest guest a bear hug. "I'm so relieved you made it, Lewis." He turned to Steven and Olivia. "This is my lifelong friend, Dr. Lewis Salisbury. Lewis, this is Steven Blackwell and his friend Olivia Watson."

Everyone shook hands and agreed to be on a first-name basis.

"After all, it looks like we'll be living together for a few days," said Lewis.

"And that whirlwind that just blew in is my son, Julian," Gil went on. "Julian, say hello to our guests, Steven Blackwell and Olivia Watson," Gil called out.

Julian turned and waved, smiling.

Jack peered out the door before he closed it. "It looks like the snow's letting up. We can go for a sleigh ride," he said to the new arrivals. "Anyone else interested?"

"I'm not leaving the fire until we go home Monday morning." Irene shivered.

"Not me," Julian said.

"Looks like it's the four of us," Gil said to Jack, Steven, and Olivia. "If you're ready, I'll harness the horses."

"Can I come with you?" Olivia asked. "I'd love to watch."

"Sure, come on along." Gilbert Racine threw back the rest of the brandy in his glass and shook his head as his eyes watered a bit. "That'll warm me up for our ride."

Olivia fastened her jacket and followed her host outside to a small stable at the end of the long row of wooden outbuildings.

"We keep the horses a few miles down the road at a farmer's place when we're in the city. We let him know when we're coming up, and he brings them over," Gil explained.

"That sounds like a good arrangement."

"It is. He takes good care of them, and his kids get to ride them when we're not here. Everybody wins." He pulled open a heavy barn door. "Here we go."

The simple stable, fashioned of rough timber, smelled of horse and hay. Separated in two stalls by a plain wooden partition that rose to their shoulders, two spectacular horses whinnied, snorted, and shook their heads as Gil and Olivia entered. "Hey, boys," he whispered. "How are you? I've missed you." He took two carrots from his pocket. He held out his hand and offered one to the mahogany horse, then entered the other stall and offered the second carrot to the caramel-colored one. The horses chomped noisily and nuzzled the side of Gil's head as he went back and forth between the stalls, spending time with each animal, patting the white splash on their foreheads.

"They're beautiful," Olivia exclaimed. "What kind are they?"

"Percheron draft horses, geldings. You need a sturdy beast to pull a heavy sleigh full of people through the snow."

For the next few minutes, Olivia marveled at the intricacies of the bridle. Gil stood on the left side of the darker horse, raised the apparatus over the animal's back, and settled it in place. It had what looked like dozens of straps going in all directions. One by one, Gil buckled and snapped. As he worked, he looked over at Olivia and said, "Three buckles, four snaps." He grinned. "It's easier than it looks." He put the bit in the horse's mouth and placed the reins over its head. Then, he repeated the process with the other horse.

Gil handed her the reins and said, "Here, Olivia. Lead Caramel over by the door."

"Caramel." Olivia chuckled.

"My daughter named him. She was twelve." He grinned. "This beauty is Dr. Doolittle."

CHAPTER FIVE

"Let me guess…your son?"

Gil chuckled. "Yup. Listen, all you need to do is gently guide him. They each have a side, and Caramel will go to the right. That's right. Good." Gil led Dr. Doolittle to the left. He lifted a rounded metal bar. "Here, hold that end over by Caramel so I can attach it to these straps." When he finished, the bar ran across the front of the two horses. "Now, we back them up to the sleigh in between those long poles. That's it. Easy does it."

Gil hooked the two poles extending from along the sides of the sleigh to the cross-bar on the horses, then led them outside, where they pulled the sleigh down the path to the Great Camp's front porch.

"Your sleigh looks like something Santa Claus will be flying in," said Olivia.

Gil chuckled. "I may have said something like that…once or twice…when the kids were little."

Holding the reins, Olivia remained outside while their host went in to gather Steven and Jack. The horses snorted—their breath visible in the cold air—and threw back their heads. At first, she was uneasy, not used to being around such big animals, then both she and the horses relaxed. She petted their foreheads and whispered words of praise.

Wrapped up in scarves, sitting close together with heavy woolen blankets on their laps, they took off. Gil gently urged the horses along the snow-filled trail into the darkening forest. The trees were thick, the snow white and glistening. Olivia felt like the heroine in an old Russian novel. As the horses trotted forward, the bells on the harness sounded.

"Oh, how lovely," Olivia exclaimed.

"That's twenty-one tone bells," Gil said proudly. "I make sure we get them tuned regularly. Beautiful, huh?"

Steven looked at Olivia. "You know we have to."

Gil and Jack joined in. "Jingle bells, jingle bells, jingle all the way…."

So much for her *Anna Karenina* fantasy.

They sang multiple refrains, then continued with "Deck the Halls" and "The Twelve Days of Christmas."

Jack passed around a Thermos of hot chocolate, and they all took a drink. "I should tell you, Steven and Olivia, every year we have a song fest after dinner. Gil plays the piano, and we sing carols."

"What a wonderful tradition!" Olivia said. "Christmas is my favorite holiday. My family gathers around the tree on Christmas Eve. We open one present, then we sing." A big smile appeared on her face. "When I was little, my mom made hot chocolate, and I was allowed two Christmas cookies."

"I was glad my mother was French because, on Christmas Eve, she served thirteen desserts," Steven said.

"Thirteen desserts!" everyone exclaimed.

"Yes, it's a tradition in southern France—Provence—but my mom carried it on, even though she was from Paris. It's not all cookies and cakes, though. There are dates, candied fruits, nuts. A lot of different things. But for a kid, it's a dream come true."

"I'll say," said Jack.

It was a perfect ride. Before they'd left, Gil had lit two carriage lamps, one on each side of the sleigh. As they glided through the forest, the lamps sketched shadows and caught fleeting shapes that appeared then disappeared in an instant. The wind picked up and blew openings in the clouds, revealing a half-moon whose fingers of light reached down amongst the pines and crept over the snow. Now and then, Olivia looked up and saw hundreds of stars glittering through the tall trees.

As the sleigh flew through the shadowy forest, the horses' hooves sent up sprays of snow that filled the air. They soon reached a spot where Gil turned the team back toward the lodge.

They piled out of the sleigh at the front door and tramped up the

CHAPTER FIVE

steps.

"Cocktails in two hours, everyone," called Margery.

The guests left for their respective rooms or cabins to get ready for dinner.

Steven and Olivia found Cabin A easily and entered the cozy main room. A fire blazed in the stone hearth, which was flanked by two deep club chairs. Off to one side was a small drinks cart and a woven basket filled with small pieces of wood. On the other side, an assortment of well-thumbed novels and stacks of magazines filled a bookcase. A wooden table and two chairs sat near what Olivia thought of as a kitchenette. She peeked around a door to the far right and was thrilled to see a bathroom boasting a clawfoot tub and a simple shower. Two other doors led to the bedrooms, both with smaller fireplaces where crackling fires warmed the rooms. Rider had placed Steven's suitcase on the end of the bed in one room, Olivia's in the other. They looked at each other and grinned.

Chapter Six

At seven o'clock, Steven and Olivia walked along the cleared path to the main lodge. Surrounded by the darkness outside the paned windows, the great room looked more magical than it had that afternoon. Olivia peeked inside before entering. Lights twinkled on the Christmas tree, and candles flickered in the windows and on every surface. The ladies' gowns glittered like the crown jewels—Margery in royal blue, Irene in emerald, and Aunt Emily dressed in silver.

Steven helped Olivia off with her coat, removed his, and handed both garments to Rider. Jack had spied the door opening and hurried to welcome them back. When he got a look at Olivia, his jaw dropped. "Wow! Olivia, I think Hollywood's calling."

Steven had had much the same reaction back in their bungalow. "I'm going to take you to more parties so you can wear that dress again," he'd said, eyes popping.

Dressed in a long, red velvet gown, Olivia was stunning. The draped neckline showed off a thin gold necklace resting on her collarbone. Long full sleeves tight at the wrist covered her arms, but two cut-outs revealed bare shoulders in the back. Olivia had never worn anything so elegant or sexy in her life…and she realized she liked it.

Jack led them to a table laden with canapés—tiny tarts with caviar and crème fraîche, salmon and caviar on crisp grilled potato rounds,

CHAPTER SIX

caramelized figs wrapped with bacon, mushroom, and Parmesan in puff pastry, and tiny toasts topped with shrimp. He pointed to a large cut-glass punch bowl. "Help yourselves. Dinner isn't until eight. Be careful, though; the punch packs a punch." He laughed at his own joke.

Steven made a face and groaned.

"So, Jack, Steven told me you're in the Navy," Olivia said.

"Yep, I'm a Navy man. Enlisted in 1902, when I was twenty-one. Fifteen years later, President Wilson declared war. After the war, the ship I was on had some problems with petty theft and fighting among the enlisted men. I asked my C.O., that's commanding officer, for you non-Navy folks, if I could learn some policing techniques. He thought it was a good idea, so he contacted a friend of his at the B.I., the Bureau of Investigation. That's where I met Steven."

"We trained together for three months, although I stayed for a full six," Steven explained. "All that time, we never knew that his brother had started buying my mother's paintings."

"Yeah, were we surprised when we saw each other at one of Gil's unveilings." Jack laughed. "The Racines and the Blackwells go back a long way."

Gil joined the threesome, accompanied by an elegant-looking man with salt-and-pepper hair. "Steven, Olivia, you met Lewis Salisbury earlier." He turned to his friend. "Steven is Evangeline Blackwell's son."

"I was very sorry to hear of your mother's passing, Steven," said Lewis, then turned to Olivia and complimented her on how lovely she looked. She thanked him and excused herself, leaving the men to talk.

Olivia crossed the room to where Margery Racine and Aunt Emily were seated on a couch, talking. Both held cut-glass tumblers filled with an amber liquid that Olivia guessed was Scotch. Margery's diamond necklace flashed in the fire's glow, competing with the sparkle in Aunt Emily's eyes.

"Mrs. Racine, I wondered if I might take some photographs to remember the weekend. Would you mind?" Olivia asked.

"Certainly, go right ahead. And please, call me Margery. We're informal here."

As Olivia thanked her and left them to continue their conversation, she wished there had been a way for Liz and Sophie to be here. She missed her best friends tonight. Not having them to talk with when she traveled into the past felt strange.

They'd be dishing about all the unusual sights. Olivia imagined Sophie, fashionista that she was, wild about everyone's clothes. They'd gossip about the men—all intriguing. Liz, with her passion for decorating and for all things vintage, would prowl the Great Camp, soaking up every bit of decor. Olivia sighed. Maybe someday she and Steven could figure out how to bring Liz and Sophie along. Wouldn't that be *swell*?

Olivia moved about the room, photographing the men looking debonair in their tuxedos—she'd been speechless earlier when Steven had appeared in his tux—the women elegant in their gowns, the holiday decorations, the camp itself, and the pièce de résistance, the fabulous Christmas tree, of which she took no less than four pictures. Olivia reminded herself to slow down. This wasn't like snapping shots with her cell phone. She'd had to purchase several rolls of film that would need to be developed when they returned to Steven's. But it was all so exciting, and this was the only way she could show Liz and Sophie.

Shortly before eight, over the chatter of conversation, Olivia heard the ring of a silver bell.

"Dinner is served, ma'am," intoned Rider.

Eleven people moved to the dining area, where a long table was draped in white linen and set with heavy silver, sparkling crystal, and gold-rimmed china. Steven caught up with Olivia. He placed his hand

CHAPTER SIX

on the small of her back and guided her to the velvet-upholstered chairs.

"I can't believe this is a camp," she said in a low voice. "The Great Camps are legendary, but I never expected anything like this."

"Gil likes to impress," Steven whispered.

At the table, they saw place cards with everyone's name delicately written in calligraphy. They walked around the perimeter, reading the cards. Gil and Margery would sit at the two ends with their guests along the sides. When Steven spied his next to Margery, he was thrilled to see Olivia's place card on his right. As he pulled out her chair, he leaned over and whispered, "I'm so glad you're here with me."

Olivia had never seen such a feast. It was Christmas dinner with all the trimmings and more. As Rider moved around the table, serving lobster bisque from an antique tureen, Gil Racine made a toast welcoming their guests. Then he made two more—one to his "lovely wife," the other to his "lifelong friend, Lewis."

As the wind raged and the snow piled up outside—it had begun snowing again shortly after they'd returned from the sleigh ride—wine and conversation flowed. Sounds of tinkling crystal and laughter filled the room. Gil's hearty laugh rang out often. He ate and drank and told story after story. Their host was clearly enjoying himself. After the meal, Rider served coffee and a magnificent almond torte piled high with whipped cream.

Olivia leaned over and whispered to Steven, "I'm going to have to skip breakfast and lunch tomorrow if I want to fit in my clothes for the rest of the weekend."

After dessert, the dinner party rose and returned to the living area, where people drifted into small conversational groups. Gil offered after-dinner drinks. Jack added a log to the fire. Olivia strolled to where Irene Racine stood at one of a pair of floor-to-ceiling bookcases, flanking a large window. Instead of sitting on the window seat between the bookcases, she ran a finger along leather spines as she drank from the glass in her other hand.

"Your mother put on an amazing dinner," Olivia said.

"Yes, Mother accepts all the praise. Cook does all the work."

"Well, it was delicious. What's that you're drinking?"

"A sidecar. I hear you're a journalist," Irene said.

"Yes, I was for several years, but I opened my own business five years ago. I do research now," said Olivia.

"Research? For whom?"

"Writers, professors."

"Sounds tedious. Don't you get bored?" asked Irene.

"No, I enjoy it. And I like being independent."

"I go for independent. I can't wait for that. My father treats me like I'm still twelve."

"I think all fathers hate to see their little girls grow up. Do you work, Irene?"

Irene Racine looked like there was a bad smell under her nose. "Work? Good heavens, no." She shuddered. "The only thing I've ever done that even remotely resembles work is when Uncle Harry let me help develop his photographs. And that was only twice. The chemicals he uses wreak havoc with your skin. No, thank you."

The man Olivia had pegged as the Errol Flynn lookalike sauntered by and draped a possessive arm over Irene's shoulders. His dark hair was slicked back. He wore the tuxedo well.

"Olivia, this is my beau, Victor McAllister. Victor, this is Olivia Watson."

Victor took Olivia's outstretched hand and brought it toward his lips. She felt the air move as he air-kissed it. Even without touching, her skin crawled.

"Yes, we met briefly earlier," said Olivia.

"What's this I hear about you being an entrepreneur, Miss Watson?"

CHAPTER SIX

he asked.

Olivia repeated what she'd told Irene about her agency.

"That would never work for me. By the time I finish breakfast, it's afternoon. Then, once I've bathed and dressed, it's already two o'clock before I leave the apartment. Stop at my club to find out the news and gossip of the day. A stroll down Fifth Avenue. Drinks with some pals. Then, it's time to dress for dinner and the evening. Don't know how I'd fit work in."

Olivia had no idea how to respond to this privileged remark. Luckily, she was saved from doing so when Gil called out to get everyone's attention.

"Time for Christmas carols," he shouted. "Because we're in the mountains doesn't mean we're going to drop my favorite holiday tradition." He turned to Steven and Olivia, who had drifted to the piano. "I already know you two can sing!"

Jack leaned over and whispered to Steven and Olivia, "None of us sings very well, but that doesn't stop my brother. He's like a kid at Christmas. We indulge him." He chuckled.

Gil Racine set his snifter of brandy on a small table next to the Steinway and shuffled through the songbooks. "Come on, everybody. Gather 'round." He ran his fingers over the keyboard, from one end to the other and back again. "Let's start with 'Deck the Halls.'"

The guests arranged themselves around the piano—Irene next to her father, her back to the wall, Victor at her side; Olivia, Steven, and Lewis facing them from the opposite side; and Julian, Jack, and Harry at the far end. Margery and Aunt Emily stayed by the warmth of the fire. Everyone joined in good-naturedly and made an effort to keep up with Gil. Olivia was impressed with Jack's voice. She leaned over and whispered, "You're good."

He wiggled his eyebrows and mouthed, "Thanks."

"Terrific," Gil shouted as the song came to an end. He wet his fingertips and paged the songbook. "How about 'Jingle Bells' next? Some of us had a bit of a rehearsal." He laughed.

They got through the first verse and one chorus and were starting the second verse when Gil coughed several times. He stopped playing and pounded his chest. Then he began to choke. He put a hand to his throat. He swayed forward, bracing himself on the fallboard above the keys. He tried to sit straight but couldn't. As he struggled to breathe, a drop of bright red blood trickled from his nose. He turned to his family and friends, brow furrowed, mouth slightly open. He tried to speak. His lips, already a pale shade of blue, moved, but no sound came out.

Later, Olivia would describe it like watching a movie in slow motion. As Gil Racine began to fall, everyone leaned toward him, some trying to grab hold of a part of him.

"Daddy!" Irene screamed. But she was too slow and couldn't reach him as he fell in the opposite direction of her outstretched hand.

Jack and Harry lunged but had nowhere to go, trapped as they were at the far end of the piano.

Olivia froze, her face a mask of disbelief and confusion.

Steven and Lewis, closest and in a position to help, moved quickly but, it wasn't quick enough. They shot out from around the side and made a grab, but both were too late. With a feeble moan, Gil Racine toppled off the piano bench and hit the floor.

"Gil!" Margery shouted, springing up from the couch, intending to set her glass on the table but missing. As she ran toward her husband, the crystal snifter crashed to the floor and shattered in her wake.

"Give him room." Harry pushed people aside. "He needs air."

"Someone get a cold compress," Lewis barked.

Olivia ran to the kitchen.

Lewis kneeled down and loosened his friend's tie and collar.

"Is he having a heart attack?" Irene asked through her tears.

CHAPTER SIX

Lewis put his ear on Gil's chest, then grabbed his wrist to check for a pulse. He put his cheek under Gil's nostrils. "Almonds," he whispered.

Olivia returned with a towel dripping with cold water.

"Maybe it's a stroke," Victor said.

Olivia thrust the towel into the doctor's hand.

"How can that be? He's only fifty-three," Jack said.

Instead of placing the wet cloth on Gil Racine's forehead, Lewis let it go. It fell to the floor with a tiny thud. "It's too late." He looked up at the circle of people, his mouth ajar, eyes wide. "He's gone."

The silence was so complete Olivia thought she could hear snowflakes hitting the window.

Chapter Seven

"What do you mean he's *gone*?" Jack asked, frowning at Lewis.

"What are you saying, Doctor Salisbury?" asked Victor.

Lewis rubbed his hand over his eyes and stood up to face everyone. "He's dead. Gil Racine is dead."

Irene screamed. Margery cried out. Everyone began talking at once. Margery leaned against her son, Julian, and sobbed into his shoulder. Victor half-supported, half-dragged Irene to a sofa, where she collapsed in his arms, trembling and wailing. Her head moved back and forth, as if to negate what had happened.

Having heard the commotion, Rider, Doris Buckley, the cook, and Corinne Kelly, the maid, rushed from the kitchen. All three gasped when they saw Gil Racine on the floor. Rider made to go to his employer, but Steven threw out his arm, stopping him. "No, sir, you need to stay back."

Jack and Harry stood like statues, their eyes wide, mouths agape. Jack recovered first. "Doc, what the hell? You've got to be kidding."

"I wish I were, Jack. I'm sorry," said Lewis.

"Is Irene right? Is it a heart attack?" Jack asked.

"It wasn't a heart attack," Lewis Salisbury said. "I can hardly believe I'm going to say this." The doctor looked around the great room at Gil Racine's family. "But I think Gil was poisoned."

CHAPTER SEVEN

Olivia inhaled sharply and looked at Steven.

"I think so, too. I've seen poison victims. Gil showed all the classic signs," Steven said.

Upon hearing this pronouncement, Margery pulled away from her son and stepped forward, wiping her eyes. She stared down everyone in the room, shoulders thrust back, spine straight, head held high. Olivia was amazed at the transformation—from grieving widow to determined head of the family in less than a minute.

"Steven, I want you to look into this. I know, I know." She waved her hand at him as he began to protest. "You don't have jurisdiction here. But you're all we've got right now. Make it an unofficial investigation. I don't care what you call it. There's over three feet of snow all around us, and it's still coming down. And listen to the wind. We're not getting out of here anytime soon. And no one's getting in, either. I want to know who and what killed my husband. You can find out. When the roads clear and the local police get here, you'll give them the answers they need." She grasped his arm. "Please."

Steven glanced at Olivia, who gave a barely perceptible nod. "Of course, Margery. I'm so sorry. Gil was a wonderful man and a good friend to my mother. I'll do everything I can." He paused a moment. "I agree with your assessment of the conditions outside, but I need to call the local police and report this. For all we know, they may be able to get through the snow. If not, at least I can explain what happened and tell them what you've asked me to do."

"I understand." Margery scanned the room, nailing every person with her flashing topaz eyes. "You all heard me ask Steven. I expect everybody to cooperate. Is that understood?"

Nods and mumblings of "Yes, Mother," "Of course, Margery," and "How can I help?" filled the previously joyful space.

Lewis Salisbury spoke again. "Margery, my dear, I know this is painful, but there are certain things we must do right now. Would you prefer to retire?"

"Yes, thank you, Lewis. I think that's best. Steven, you're in charge. The phone is in Gil's study. Enlist whoever you need to help do whatever it is you have to do. The rest of us will retire for the night."

"I want Lewis, Jack, Harry, and Olivia."

"Margery, get some rest. I have something in my bag if you need help falling asleep. That goes for everybody," added Lewis Salisbury. "My room is upstairs, last one on the left at the end of the hall."

"It's the Black Spruce Room," Margery said. Then, when she saw Olivia frown, she added, "We named all the bedrooms in the main lodge after native trees."

After the others had picked up their drink—Julian grabbed a bottle—and gone to their respective rooms, Steven said to Lewis, Jack, Harry, and Olivia, "Please wait where you are so we don't compromise the scene any more than it already has been. I'd like to alert the police first. We can start when I get back. And whatever you do, don't touch anything."

Steven returned several minutes later. "I spoke with the night desk officer and explained what happened. He told me there was no way they could get through the snow. He asked if I'd keep them updated and told me a Lieutenant John Delaney would be the officer in charge—he's head of their Criminal Investigation Division. I gave him the number here. Now, Olivia, would you take pictures, and would you fellas step back out of the view of the camera?"

Thanks to all the cop shows she watched on TV, Olivia knew to start big and go small. She took shots of the living room from a distance, then closed in on the piano and the area around the victim. Finally, she photographed the body.

"Jack, I need some paper and a pencil," Steven said.

"Right away." He went to the sideboard and pulled a pad of paper

CHAPTER SEVEN

and some pencils from a center drawer. "Here you go."

Steven sketched the scene as he always did when on a case. He folded the drawing and put it in his pocket, then took out the small notebook he always carried with him.

"Doc, what's going on here?" Harry asked. "You can't be serious that Gil was poisoned."

"Of course, he's serious! They think Gil was murdered." Jack stared at Steven and Lewis. "Don't you?"

Both men nodded. "Yes."

"The first thing we need to do is move his body. We've got to keep him cold until the police get here," said Lewis. "Then I think Margery should ask for an autopsy."

"Jack, I noticed several cabins farther down from where Olivia and I are staying. Are any of them empty?" Steven asked.

"Except for Harry, the family is all staying in the lodge," Jack answered. "But Victor is in one of them."

"Yeah, I always stay in Cabin B," said Harry. "It's my home away from home."

Olivia sensed something in his voice. What was it? Sarcasm? Disgust? Annoyance?

Harry added, "Victor's next to me in C."

"Harry uses Cabin D as his darkroom, but E should be available," said Jack. "We can put Gil on the bed and cover him."

"We should keep a small fire going in the living room so his body doesn't freeze," Lewis suggested.

"It's too far to carry him, but there's a sled on the porch," said Harry. "That should help. I'll get it."

"Jack, can you get a blanket to wrap him in, please?" Steven asked. "Lewis, do you have anything in your bag to take a blood sample? And I'd like some of his hair and fingernails, too."

"Yes, I can make do."

43

Ten minutes later, two vials containing the samples Steven had requested were in his jacket pocket. Later, he would give them to the local sheriff. Olivia moved out of the way as the four men wrapped and carried the body to the front entry. They set it down while Harry reached out to open the door. A gust of Arctic wind grabbed the heavy door out of his hand, slamming it against the lodge wall.

"Jeez, that's enough to give you the willies," Harry said.

Rider had been standing quietly off to the side, awaiting instructions. "May I help, Mr. Jack?"

Jack turned to Steven. "Can he clean up now?"

"No. Rider, we don't know where the poison came from," Steven said. "We need to preserve everything. Can you get a box to store the utensils, plates, and glasses that Gil used? His napkin and the liquor he drank, too. Mark it with Mr. Racine's name. Get different containers to store the items that everyone else used. Did you, Mrs. Buckley, and Corinne have the same meal?"

"Yes, sir. Mrs. Buckley always sets some aside for us."

"Okay. Get a separate box and put in everything the three of you used."

"Some of the dishes may be washed already, Detective."

"Would you hurry into the kitchen and stop them from washing anything else?" Steven asked. "And, Rider, put gloves on if you can. Otherwise, use a towel so you don't touch anything that Mr. Racine touched. Don't clean off his plate if there's any leftover food. And, Rider, whatever you do," Steven held the butler's gaze with a stare, "don't go near the piano. Don't touch it or anything around it. As I said, we have no idea how he was poisoned. Do you understand?"

"Yes, sir."

"Rider, you can retire after you're done," Jack instructed. "We won't need you anymore tonight."

The butler gave a little bow, then hastened into the back hallway

CHAPTER SEVEN

toward the kitchen.

The sled worked like a charm. Jack pushed open the door to Cabin E. The four men took Gil Racine's shoulders and legs and carried him into one of the bedrooms, where they carefully placed him on a bed, covering him with the blanket. Harry returned to the living room and got a fire going in the hearth. Lewis told him to be sure it was a small one—they needed the room to remain cold; the blaze should only prevent the cabin from dipping below freezing. Harry placed the grate in front of the hearth and made sure it wouldn't fall over during the night.

"Olivia, I want you to photograph everything here as well. Jack, can we lock the door?" Steven said.

Jack extracted a key from a pine chest and handed it to him.

"Would you fellas mind if I got some preliminary questions taken care of tonight?" Steven asked.

"No, of course not," Jack said.

"Whatever you need," Harry replied.

"He was my best friend. I'll do everything I can," answered Lewis.

"Good. Thank you. I'd like to start with Jack since you arrived before the others. Harry, would you wait in your cabin? And Lewis, can I join you in your room afterwards?"

The men all agreed.

After making a quick stop in Cabin A for Olivia to change into wool pants and a sweater, she and Steven sat across from Jack in the Great Camp.

"When did you arrive at Onontaga, Jack?" Steven began.

"Yesterday, around four in the afternoon."

"Where did you travel from, and how did you get here?"

"I'm on leave all month. I've been in the Far East for the past two

45

years, but after the holidays, I'll have a new assignment. I've been staying at my apartment in New York. I took the train up to Utica, then drove the rest of the way. I'd made arrangements to rent a car before I left the city."

"You keep an apartment even though you're at sea all the time?" Steven asked.

"When our father died, he left the mansion on Fifth Avenue to Gil, as the oldest, but Harry and I each have a large apartment on the upper floors. Because of our jobs, neither of us is there much, although Harry stays more than I do. The maids keep it clean. My father's will stipulated that the apartments are ours for life."

"That's a swell arrangement." Steven made a note. "Did you have supper here last night with Gil and Margery?"

"Yes, and Aunt Emily, too. She drove up with them earlier in the day—the staff came up the day before to get everything ready—and we had breakfast and lunch together today. I see where you're going, Steven. I don't think my brother ate or drank anything that the rest of us didn't."

"Tell me about your brother's marriage. Were Gil and Margery happy?"

"They seemed to get along alright. It was common knowledge that he adored her, but she didn't exactly return the feeling. Oh, I think she liked him well enough, but...."

"What do you mean?" asked Steven.

"It was an arranged marriage."

Olivia forced herself not to let her jaw drop. Arranged marriages were something out of ancient history for her. Then she reminded herself she was sitting with a man eighty years in the past, discussing his brother's marriage thirty-some years before that.

"How was it arranged? Who arranged it?" Steven asked.

"Margery's father and Gil worked it out together. Although, in

CHAPTER SEVEN

fairness, I have to say Margery's been a good wife. She's always stood by him."

Steven made a note, glad he'd thought to bring his notebook. "Except for Victor and Lewis, I know that it's all family here, Jack, but can you think of anyone who'd want your brother dead?"

"I swear, Steven, I have no idea. It's inconceivable. If we were in New York, I'd say sure, maybe. Gil had a lot of business rivals. There are even some writers who feel strongly that he should have published their novel. But something like that doesn't reach the level of murder. And family? We're no different than any other family. We have our disagreements, like everyone else. But no. Maybe Victor. He's pushing to become a part of this family, but he hasn't married her yet. Thanks to Gil."

"Gil was against Victor marrying Irene?" Olivia asked.

"Was he ever! Told her in no uncertain terms that he thought Victor was only after her money, that Victor was a womanizer who'd never change."

"I imagine your niece didn't take that very well," said Olivia.

"No, she didn't."

Back in the main lodge, Steven and Olivia climbed the stairs to the second floor.

"Lewis said the last door on the left," Olivia whispered as they turned the corner on the landing.

Shadows filled the long, windowless hallway, which was lit by sconces. At the end of the corridor, they spied a couple locked in an embrace.

"...don't have to wait...," said a husky voice.

"Not now, Lewis," whispered the woman, gently pushing him away.

Without a word, Steven and Olivia quietly backed up and descended the stairs. At the bottom, Steven gave a low whistle. "Well, there's a motive if I ever heard one."

"With his best friend?" Olivia exclaimed. "That's disgusting."

"Yeah. Let's go see Harry. We'll keep this to ourselves for now. We can talk with Lewis tomorrow."

They went outside and pushed their way through the snow to Cabin B, facing the brutal sub-zero temperature one more time.

At the knocking, Harry Racine threw open the door and beckoned them in. "Come in, get out of the cold. Over here," he said, leading them to a small settee and two comfortable looking leather chairs flanking the hearth. "I've got a fire going. Would you like a drink?"

"Not for me, thanks," said Olivia.

"No, me neither."

Steven and Olivia settled on the sofa as Harry lowered himself into a club chair the color of an expensive red wine.

"So, what can I tell you, Steven? I don't have much to offer. I'm away most of the time. Frankly, I didn't know my brother that well."

"Tell us about your childhood, Harry. What was it like growing up with Gil?"

"I didn't. He was nearly eleven when I was born and was already learning the business. Our father started grooming Gil to take over the company the day he turned ten. Gil once told me that on the morning of his birthday, his governess dressed him in a suit and the kind of little ties kids wore back then. Then Father took him to the Racine Building and walked him through each department and office on every floor, introducing him to the managers. 'You'll be working for Gil one day,' he told them. Imagine how that affects a kid." Harry grimaced.

Imagine how that affects the managers, Olivia thought.

As Harry talked, Olivia observed him with her reporter's eye. Even as tired as he was, and after a good number of drinks, he had that bad

CHAPTER SEVEN

boy look going on. With his dark blond hair and midnight blue eyes, his muscular physique, and the aura of danger all around him, Olivia thought he must have loads of women after him—not only drawn to a beautiful and exciting man living on the edge, but to a man who might inherit millions at the death of his older brother. Yet, the longer Olivia studied the youngest Racine sibling, the more she realized there were great depths to him. More than danger, she sensed sadness, possibly regret.

"You'd be better off talking with Jack about growing up with Gil," Harry concluded.

"Do you have any idea who inherits the publishing company now that Gil's dead?"

"Probably Jack, but I don't know for sure. I mean, it was Father's company, so I'd think it would go from one son to the next in age, right down the line."

"Any idea who the family lawyer is?" Steven asked.

"Keystone and Pierce in Manhattan." Harry looked off into the distance. "I don't have a will. I mean, why would you when you're young and healthy, right?"

"Thanks, Harry. It's getting late. Why don't we talk again in the morning? I'm afraid it's going to be a long, difficult weekend for your family."

Steven opened the door to Cabin A, ushering Olivia into the warm living room. She kicked off her boots, threw her gloves on a chair, and walked straight to the hearth, where she held out her hands to the flames.

"I have to remember to thank Rider in the morning. I suppose he's the one who's responsible for the lights on and the cozy fire. Thank goodness for him! It feels like it's below zero outside," she said.

"I saw a thermometer hanging near the door. I'll look."

Steven returned a moment later. "You're right. Twenty below."

"Yikes! And way over three feet of snow. When you invite a girl for a weekend, you sure know how to arrange things, Steven Blackwell." She laughed.

Steven reached her in three long strides, spun her around, and wrapped her in a hug. He nestled his face in her hair, breathing in the scent of her enticing perfume. "What are you wearing? I like it," he said.

"I googled popular perfumes in 1930 so I wouldn't make a mistake and wear something not invented yet. I figured the women in this family would know their cosmetics. It's called Tabu. Sexy, huh?" She grinned and wiggled her eyebrows.

He laughed. "Well…Here, give me your hat and coat."

"Steven, I haven't even had the chance to tell you how sorry I am for your loss."

"Thank you. You know, despite the twenty-year difference in our ages, I considered Gil a good friend. I always hoped we'd become closer. We talked about getting together more often. He told me about some events coming up in the next few months and invited me to go down to the city to stay with him and Margery. I wish I hadn't waited. Now, it's an opportunity lost." He shook his head and frowned. "I won't get it back again."

They stood pressed together until Olivia sensed he had composed himself. She let go and stepped back.

"I'm beat," she said. "It's been a long day. All I want to do is cuddle up and go to sleep."

"Me, too. And besides keeping each other warm tonight, I have an ulterior motive."

"Oh, yeah? What's that?"

"I'm going to hold on to you till morning to make sure you don't get pulled back to the future."

Chapter Eight

Friday, December 14, 1934

Great Camp Onontaga, Adirondack Mountains

When Olivia peeked out the window Friday morning, she beheld an overcast sky. Winter storm clouds hung low in the leaden firmament, hiding the tree tops and looming over the cabin. It was snowing, though not as heavily as the day before. She shivered as if something cold had trickled down her spine and hoped the weather wasn't an omen of the day that was beginning.

They donned heavy wool sweaters and pants, then walked to the main lodge for breakfast, glad that someone—probably Rider—had cleared a path.

"Speaking of Rider," Steven said, "I want to speak with him and the staff today. We can't overlook them as suspects."

"I suppose you're right," said Olivia. "But it seems like someone in the family would be more likely. All this wealth has to figure into the killer's motive. Don't you think?"

"It'll probably turn out that way. But we can't assume anything. Right now, we have no idea what anybody's motive might be."

Rider had laid out a buffet on the sideboard. Wondering how the man managed to accomplish everything he seemed to do, Olivia headed straight for the silver coffee urn and filled a cup.

One person occupied the long table. Aunt Emily seemed to be enjoying crisp bacon and pancakes smothered in butter and maple syrup. "Good morning," she greeted them. "Come sit by me and tell me all about your exciting lives. I love the company of young people."

If she only knew, thought Olivia, and gave Aunt Emily the 1934 version of her life: graduated from Syracuse University with a degree in journalism, worked for *The Syracuse Journal*, now building a reputation as a freelance writer in Knightsbridge having published two magazine articles so far.

"Impressive," Aunt Emily said. "And what about you, young man? From what Margery said yesterday, it sounds like you're a policeman."

Steven nodded. "I'm a detective."

"Do you like it?"

He smiled. "Yes, I do. I like making sure victims of crimes get justice."

"And what about the crime that happened here last night?" she asked shrewdly. "I may be getting senile, but I'm not likely to forget something like that!"

"As you know, Margery asked me to investigate, if that's what you mean."

"That's exactly what I mean. Are you going to question me?" she asked, her eyes probing.

"What if you and I find a quiet spot after breakfast where we can talk privately?" Steven suggested.

"I'll be there," said Aunt Emily.

As Olivia was digging into scrambled eggs and toast, Lewis Salisbury entered the dining area, looking like he'd aged overnight. "Good morning, ladies, Steven."

Lewis approached the buffet. "Well, well, Mrs. Buckley always does

CHAPTER EIGHT

Margery proud." He poured coffee, served himself a modest breakfast, and joined them at the table. "Are you behaving yourself, Aunt Emily?" he asked, in an obvious attempt at lessening the weight of sadness that permeated the Great Camp.

"Where's the fun in that?" She seemed to catch on and was determined to do her part.

"I've heard stories about your wild youth. Better be careful what you tell these young people. You don't want to shock them," he kidded.

"Best thing for 'em, Doc." And she popped the last bite of pancake into her mouth.

Olivia understood the attempt at deflecting their grief—especially with strangers.

Olivia judged Emily Racine to be in her eighties. She would have come of age during the Victorian Era. Was Aunt Emily hiding her emotions? Was she being stoic, accepting there was nothing she could do to change what had happened? What was the protocol for a woman of her age and background? The Racine brothers' aunt must be tough, having survived the influenza pandemic of 1918 and the sorrows of World War I. Olivia decided that Emily Racine was a strong woman who kept her feelings to herself.

And what about Lewis Salisbury, the doctor who had lost his best friend—but who had possibly won the woman he loved? How do you reconcile those conflicting feelings? So far, Lewis was putting on a brave face.

Lewis looked at Olivia. "I need to get some fresh air this morning. I went out earlier and checked. The forest trail looks good for snowshoeing. Would you like to go?"

"Thank you. Yes, I'd love to get outside today, if you don't mind going with an amateur."

"Not at all."

"Swell." Olivia still smiled to herself when she heard this come out of her mouth so naturally. Current slang had been one of the more difficult things to get used to during her visits to 1934.

As the foursome was about to leave the table, some of the family drifted in. Margery was followed by her son, Julian, and brother-in-law Jack. Everyone offered subdued greetings and repeated the condolences of last night. Olivia observed the newcomers and noted her first impressions. It appeared that Margery had steeled herself to face her new reality and though Julian acted as though no ripples had crossed his pond, Olivia wasn't going to jump to conclusions. People often kept their feelings inside, and she had no idea how Julian might be privately grieving his father's death. Jack was quiet—a distinct difference from his behavior yesterday—and Olivia wasn't sure what to make of that. It could be shock because of the murder, profound grief from losing a beloved brother, or fear that he might have to take on the responsibilities of running an empire.

As Steven led Aunt Emily to the living room area where they settled near the fireplace, Lewis informed the group that he and Olivia were going out for some fresh air.

Margery nodded, then turned her back and picked up a plate at the buffet.

Olivia entered the garage to retrieve her poles and snowshoes from the trunk of Steven's car, then sat on the bottom porch step to fasten them. "I'm ready when you are," she told Lewis.

Feeling like she was inside a snow globe with flakes swirling around them, Olivia fell in alongside Lewis Salisbury.

"We'll take this trail here," he said, indicating the path they had traveled on their sleigh ride yesterday. "It's always perfect. No matter how much snow falls around the property, the canopy of trees blocks a significant amount from reaching the forest floor. We get a good covering, but it's never too deep. It's also a comfortable distance, and

CHAPTER EIGHT

it's not uphill. Good for someone like me, who only wants a leisurely hike."

Returning to the sport after a year was easier than Olivia imagined, and she was pleased the techniques came back to her. They walked without speaking for some time, the only sounds the crunch of the snow under their feet and the chirping of some intrepid, but invisible, birds tucked away in the pines. Olivia breathed in deeply. Despite the horrible events of Thursday evening, she felt peaceful. Was she getting used to murder hanging around with Steven? Olivia shuddered at the thought.

"It smells like Christmas," she said.

"It's all the balsam spruce."

The trail took a sharp turn and narrowed. Here, the trees were thicker. Olivia wished she could identify them.

"Do you know what these trees are?" she asked. "They're really beautiful."

"Eastern pines. And those are Norway spruce," he said, pointing to a cluster of massive firs near the edge of the trail. "And there are a couple of black spruce over there." He indicated a copse of trees heavily laden with pine cones on the opposite side of the trail.

They trekked on.

"Lewis, I want to offer my condolences. I know Gil was your close friend. I can only imagine how you must feel. I have two best friends who mean the world to me. I'm truly sorry."

He stopped, anchoring his poles in the snow. "Thank you, Olivia. To tell you the truth, it's like a bad dream. I can't imagine life without him."

"Irene and Julian must be devastated. I bet Gil was a wonderful father," Olivia said, hoping to glean some background information for Steven.

"He had his moments. Trouble was, he worked too hard, and there weren't many of those." He chuckled. "His business associates would have been shocked to see Gil at Christmastime or on one of the kids' birthdays. He let his hair down when it was a special day, and it was only family. I think he needed to make up for not having that kind of fun when he was a kid. His father didn't allow him much of a childhood."

"I know it will never make up for the loss, but, if it's any consolation, he seemed to really be enjoying himself yesterday." Olivia paused to pull one of her poles out of the snow where it had stuck. She tugged, then moved on. "When we were out here on the sleigh ride, I think he was singing the loudest."

Lewis laughed again. "Yeah, that was Gil. Damn, I'm going to miss him." He swiped his eye with a mittened hand.

They reached the spot where the trail wound through a small clearing. A pale sun poked through an opening in the cloud cover, the beams shooting down through the trees and creating a magical feel to the forest. The tiniest of snowflakes floated in the light, looking like fairy dust.

In this small space, fewer trees blocked the snowfall, and yesterday's accumulation threatened to reach above Olivia's knees.

"This could be rough going, Olivia. I think we'd better turn back," Lewis said.

As they strode along the trail, following the path they'd made, arms and legs in sync, she wondered how she could get more information from the doctor without sounding like she was interrogating him. Luckily, she was saved the conundrum.

"You know, Olivia, I can't for the life of me think of who could have done this," Lewis exclaimed.

"You're sure he was poisoned?"

"Oh, yes. There's no doubt."

"Is there a way you could discover what kind of poison was used?

CHAPTER EIGHT

Maybe we can figure out when he ate or drank it. That might point to someone."

"I've been thinking about that. Let me mull it over this morning. I have some ideas for a test I might be able to rig up."

Margery Racine lingered at the breakfast table after everyone else had gone—to sit by the fire, to rest in their bedroom or cabin, to be anywhere but together, where they would have to talk about what had happened last night.

Rider approached the table. He cleared his throat. "I'm deeply sorry, ma'am. For what happened."

"Thank you, Rider." She looked at him and saw something in his face she had never noticed before. "You know what it's like, don't you? To lose a spouse?"

His eyes closed for a moment, and he bowed his head, then he looked straight at her. "Yes, I do, Mrs. Racine. Yes, I do."

She nodded. "I suppose we carry on."

"Yes, ma'am. Not much else we can do."

Rider checked that there was plenty of coffee on the buffet. There wasn't, so he headed back to the kitchen to refill the silver urn.

At the threshold of the kitchen door, he stopped. A minute wouldn't hurt anyone. And Rider wanted this minute. He stepped away from the door and continued down the hall to his quarters. Opening the heavy door, he felt a peace come over him. This cozy apartment was Rider's sanctuary. Here he could return to the past and remember when his beloved Catherine sat next to him by the hearth. His eyes were drawn to her photograph, and Rider drank in the look of her, remembering the smell of her perfume and the softness of her cheek.

When Lewis and Olivia arrived back at the Great Camp, the sun's brief appearance was a memory, and snow fell again in earnest. They shook the snow from their snowshoes and poles, left their gear leaning against the porch wall, and entered.

Steven had returned to the dining area and was sitting at the table, this time talking with Jack and Harry, who had come in for a late breakfast.

"How was the trek?" he asked Olivia.

"The adventurers are back," said Jack. "I didn't realize you were going. I'd have joined you."

"I don't think any of us will be going out anytime soon. It's snowing again—and hard," Olivia said. "I'll go with you later or tomorrow if you still want to, Jack."

"Swell. You've got a deal," Jack said, sounding more like the man she'd met yesterday.

Olivia wandered over to the piano, wondering if, now that its owner was deceased, someone else would be allowed to play and enliven the time they were going to spend here. She glanced at the Christmas carol books, still piled one behind the other above the keyboard, then gazed down at the keys. *What's that?* She looked closer. *Am I seeing shadows?* Olivia bent her head and looked from several angles. *No, those aren't shadows. Those keys have a blue tinge to them. Oh, my God. I know what killed Gil Racine!*

"Bring me those carrots from the pantry, Corinne," Mrs. Buckley called to the maid, who was up to her elbows in hot, sudsy water doing the breakfast dishes. Rider had topped off the coffee urn in the dining area and was now taking a break at the big pine table at the far end of the kitchen, enjoying a cigarette and another cup of coffee.

Corinne Kelly dried her hands on her apron, crossed the large room, and disappeared in the back. She handed the bunch of carrots to Mrs. Buckley and returned to her washing up.

"Seems funny without Mr. Gil around no more, huh, Mrs. Buckley?"

CHAPTER EIGHT

she said. "What do you think's going to happen to us?"

"Mrs. Racine and the children still have to eat, don't they?" Doris Buckley frowned. "What's the matter with you, child?"

Rider crushed his cigarette and brought his empty cup and saucer to the sink.

"Who do you think done it, Mr. Rider?" Corinne asked, wide-eyed.

"Don't you think about that, my girl. You concentrate on your work. That's got nothing to do with us," Rider said and left the room.

Attempting to control her excitement, Olivia returned to the dining table. "Excuse me, Steven, can I talk to you a minute?" she said, trying to sound casual.

"Sure."

She led him to the piano. Putting her back to the rest of the room, Olivia whispered, "Don't touch the keys. Do you see those dark blue streaks on the white keys?"

He leaned over. "Oh, I didn't notice those last night."

"You know the photography project I just finished researching?"

He nodded.

"Well, I don't remember all the details, but some people use potassium cyanide in photo developing. It comes in a powder form, and they mix it with water. If they accidentally spill it, the liquid will evaporate and leave a residue. The telltale sign of potassium cyanide residue is this Prussian blue color. It's unmistakable."

Steven stared at her. "Gil was wetting his fingers, turning the pages of the songbooks last night. Holy mackerel, Olivia. You know what they said was in Cabin D?"

"Harry's darkroom."

"Exactly. Can you get some pictures of the keys? Take several angles to make sure we'll be able to see the blue streaks in at least one of your shots. I need to speak with Rider." He took a step, then turned back.

"Wait here till I return. Don't let anybody touch anything. We don't know where else the residue might be. It could be on the piano top as well, although I doubt we'd be able to see it on the black."

Olivia retrieved her new Baby Brownie from the leather tote bag she'd left on a chair. She snapped three photographs, then realized she had to change the film. She turned the knob on the camera, winding the film until she saw the end of the paper move past the window. She'd have to wait until she could go into a dark corner to remove the film and load a fresh roll. She returned the camera to her bag.

Steven returned with two large squares of canvas and two pairs of heavy work gloves.

"Where did you get all that?" Olivia asked.

"Rider uses the tarps to cover the furniture when the family is in the city. He has a stack of them in a back room. Put these gloves on, and we'll cover the piano. Don't touch any part of it."

By the time Steven and Olivia had secured the tarps—ensuring the keys were well hidden—and had disposed of the gloves safely, everyone had returned to the great room. Jack and Irene wandered over.

"What's this all about?" Irene asked.

Olivia noticed the pallor in her complexion and dark smudges under her eyes.

Ignoring the question, Steven stepped into the middle of the room. "I need your attention, please."

Everyone stopped what they were doing and turned.

"We've discovered what likely killed Gil," Steven told them.

Olivia heard several gasps and a moan from someone—she thought maybe Irene.

"What?"

"How?"

Steven explained. "It looks like someone dissolved potassium cyanide in something, likely water, and spread it over the piano keys.

CHAPTER EIGHT

The liquid evaporated, and the poison was left on the keys. Not only did Gil absorb it through his skin, but, if you remember, he was constantly wetting his finger to turn the pages of the songbook. He ingested it, too.

"You can see we've covered everything. I can't emphasize strongly enough that you must stay away from the piano. This poison is unforgiving. Even a tiny amount can kill you. I've already told Rider, and he'll warn Mrs. Buckley and the maid."

Olivia saw Jack glare at his younger brother, Harry, who didn't seem surprised at this information.

Chapter Nine

Knightsbridge, New York

"I wonder if Steven and Olivia are having fun," said Jimmy Bou. "I wonder what they're doing. I wonder how bad the storm is where they are."

"Jeez, Jimmy, knock it off, will you?" said Sergeant Will Taylor. "I'm trying to get some work done here. Besides, in a couple of days, you can ask Steven yourself. Why don't you study for your detective's exam? Isn't that coming up next week?"

"I don't need to study anymore, Will. I'm ready."

"Well, find something to do. Go help Ralph and Pete or something."

The phone rang. Soon-to-be Detective Jimmy Bourgogne picked up the black Bakelite receiver. "Criminal Investigation Division. Officer Bourgogne speaking…Steven! We were just talking about you. Are you having a good time?…Yeah, okay…Oh no! How awful. I'm really sorry…Yeah, uh-huh. Okay…I've got some." He pulled the cord connecting the receiver to the telephone base over and around the edge of Steven's desk, sat down, grabbed a pen, and pulled a pad of paper over. "Go ahead. I'm ready…Yeah…Yeah…Yeah, I know what you mean…Okay. What's the number there?" He scribbled down a telephone number. "I'll call you back later. Bye."

CHAPTER NINE

While Jimmy was talking, Will had stopped writing and waited for him to hang up. "What's going on?"

"Somebody murdered Gil Racine last night."

"Murdered?"

"Steven said he was poisoned with potassium cyanide." Jimmy Bou explained what Steven had told him. "He wants us to make some phone calls."

Will rose, circled round to the other side of the desks, and peered over Jimmy's shoulder. He read the notes aloud, "Dr. Lewis Salisbury, Commander Jack Racine, Harry Racine, youngest brother. What's the star by Harry's name?"

"Steven said he's got a darkroom where he develops pictures. According to Olivia, some people use potassium cyanide in the developing." Jimmy screwed up his face. "Are people really that dumb, Will?"

"I thought you said you were ready for the exam. By now, you should know there are no limits to what people think they can get away with." Will looked back at the list. "Margery Racine, Irene and Julian Racine, Victor McAllister, and Emily Racine. That's a lot of people to investigate." Jimmy had written some information next to each name. "And not much to start with."

"Steven wants us to get as much background as we can. They're snowed in, but so far—obviously—the phones are still working."

"Alright, go get Ralph and Pete. The four of us will tackle this."

When Jimmy Bou returned from the Patrol Room with Officers Ralph Hiller and Pete McGrath, Will had wheeled Steven's murder board from its resting place in the corner into the middle of the CID room where it always stood during an investigation.

The chalkboard, set in a narrow wooden frame, was Steven's secret weapon in solving crimes. He believed in the power of organization. During each investigation, the team posted relevant information about all the people involved—victim, suspects, and family, friends, and co-workers of the victim—as well as evidence, motives, and alibis given by suspects. Around the frame, Steven tacked the crime scene photographs.

Will had divided the slate into nine parts and was writing names and the scant information they had in the boxes. He added the initials of the police officer who would investigate each suspect. Several minutes later, when he'd finished, the board looked like this:

GIL RACINE VICTIM (SB) 718 Fifth Avenue, New York City Owner/President of Racine Publishing (The City Chronicle) and Racine Literary Press. Thomas Samuels - VP Racine Publishing. Edward Greenpoint - VP Racine Literary.	MARGERY RACINE WIDOW (WT) 718 Fifth Avenue, New York City Board Member of: The Shubert Theatre Metropolitan Museum of Art Bellevue Hospital The NY Botanical Garden	JULIAN RACINE SON (RH) 718 Fifth Avenue, New York City Writer (unpublished)
IRENE RACINE DAUGHTER (RH) 718 Fifth Avenue, New York City Doesn't work.	JACK RACINE BROTHER (JB) 718 Fifth Avenue, New York City Commander in the Navy. Home on leave.	HARRY RACINE BROTHER (JB) 718 Fifth Avenue, New York City Professional photographer. Travels extensively.
VICTOR MCALLISTER IRENE'S BOYFRIEND (PMG) Address unknown NYC No known job. Wants to marry Irene.	DR. LEWIS SALISBURY GIL'S LONGTIME FRIEND (WT) Queens, NY Has private practice in Manhattan.	EMILY RACINE AUNT TO THE 3 RACINE BROTHERS (PMG) Gil's father's sister Brooklyn, NY

"Okay, fellas. This is what we've got to work with. Steven's going

CHAPTER NINE

to investigate Gil, and he's also going to call Racine's two vice-presidents—Samuels, who's in charge of the newspaper, and Greenpoint, head of the book publishing company." Will pointed to each officer's initials as he talked. "I'll cover the widow and the doctor. Jimmy, you take the two brothers—Jack and Harry. Ralph, take the two kids—Irene and Julian. Pete, that gives you the aunt and the daughter's friend McAllister."

"Steven told me Harry was in the Amazon jungle, in South America, a few weeks ago and last year he went up to Baffin Island. I looked it up in the encyclopedia. That's in the Arctic Circle! He sure gets around." Wonder filled Jimmy's voice, as though Harry Racine had travelled to the moon or Mars. "Steven said to check private men's clubs in New York City. There might be one for people who like adventure."

"That's as good a place to start as any. So, let's get going, fellas," Will said. "We'll have a briefing at five-thirty to see what we've got."

"Sounds good."

"Yep."

"You got it."

As Will was picking up the phone, he couldn't stop a flood of worry from coursing through him.

Steven and Olivia are trapped with a killer. How long do we have to find him...or her?

Chapter Ten

Great Camp Onontaga, Adirondack Mountains

Steven and Olivia donned their jackets, pulled hats over their ears, and wound scarves around their necks. Braced for the weather, they left the lodge and hiked up the path to Harry's darkroom in Cabin D. Snowflakes swirled around them, drifting down so slowly that they appeared suspended in mid-air. Olivia felt several flakes clinging to her bangs and noticed some had settled on Steven's eyelashes. When they arrived at the cabin, Steven opened the door and steered Olivia in before him. She reached to the side and clicked on a light switch.

"This isn't as rough as I thought it would be," Olivia exclaimed.

"I'm surprised he doesn't lock the door with all these dangerous chemicals sitting around. Anyone could get in here." Steven frowned.

A long counter stretched across the back wall with several rectangular metal pans spread out along its surface and bottles of chemicals lined up against the wall. Equipment whose use Steven couldn't identify was neatly stored at one end. There were plastic reels, a large cloth bag, measuring cups, several utensils, a thermometer, a timer, and a pair of scissors. Built into the countertop was a sink with hot and cold running water. Several cotton towels—white with

CHAPTER TEN

a thin red line—were stacked nearby. A clothesline attached to hooks in the walls extended along the left side of the cabin, empty wooden clothespins clipped to it. A red light bulb hung above the counter.

Olivia bent to look under the counter where a low shelf held several containers. "There's the potassium cyanide," she said, pointing to large black letters that read KCN and a skull and crossbones. "I remember the chemical symbols from my research."

"Don't go near it," Steven warned. "It's enough we know it's here. Would you take a picture?"

"When I bought this camera last week, I never imagined these would be the vacation photos I'd be taking," Olivia said with a grimace, as she photographed what was likely the murder weapon.

"Steven, do you have a plan for how you want to investigate this case? You always say that organization is the key for you. No murder board here in the mountains."

"Yeah, we need to get organized. I was thinking about using the other bedroom in our cabin to set up something I can use as a murder board. Any ideas?"

"If we can find some large pieces of paper, like rolls of wrapping paper or wallpaper, we could use the back. I think the walls in our cabin are made of horse hair—they look the same as my grandmother's house. We won't be able to use tacks, but tape might work. I imagine they've got masking tape. Would you like me to take charge of that?"

"That'd be swell. I'm going to call Gil's two vice presidents," he said.

"Sounds good. I'll catch up with you later." Olivia gave him a quick kiss before leaving the deadly contents of Cabin D.

Steven settled at the rustic desk in Gil's study, grabbed the phone, and dialed 0.

"Operator, I need the switchboard at the Racine Publishing Company in New York City." He heard several clicks, ringing, then a woman's voice.

"Racine Publishing, please hold…How may I direct your call?"

"Mr. Thomas Samuels, please."

"One moment, please."

A deep, raspy voice answered. "Hello, Samuels here. Hang on…." The man shouted to someone nearby. "Get the Mayor on the phone and close the door on your way out." He lowered his voice and spoke into the receiver. "Thomas Samuels. Who's this?"

"Detective Steven Blackwell with the Knightsbridge Police Department. Upstate, sir."

"Police? Where upstate?"

"The Mohawk Valley, between Syracuse and Utica."

"Okay, what can I do for you, Detective?"

"I'm sorry to be calling with bad news, but Gil Racine was killed last night."

Steven heard a crash that sounded like something heavy hitting a wall. Samuels' chair, maybe.

"Killed? Was it an accident? We heard you folks got a big storm. Did his car go off the road? My God!"

A wave of emotion overcame him, reminding Steven this wasn't just another case—a friend had been murdered. He pushed his personal grief aside. "No, sir. He was poisoned." He explained what happened.

"Holy hell, this is terrible. How is Mrs. Racine? How can I help you, Detective?"

"She's doing as well as can be expected." Steven cleared his throat, adding a pause before he segued into his main objective for the call. "Actually, I'm calling because Mrs. Racine asked me to investigate until the local sheriff can get here. We're snowed in. I'm hoping you can give me some background information on the relationships Gil had with some of the people who are here this weekend."

"Sure, who've you got?" Samuels asked.

CHAPTER TEN

Steven read off the list.

"Don't know McAllister, but he's got a reputation of being a man-about-town. Only steps out with rich girls. Lewis Salisbury's been a friend of Gil's longer than I've known him. Excellent doctor. I don't think he goes to many social events in town. You know, the circuit—the same people that you see at all the galas, dinners, banquets, and so forth. I met Salisbury a few times at Racine company parties. He was interested in physical fitness and being outside. Of course, he's a medical man, so he would be, right? He always spent most of the evening with Mrs. Racine, Gil's wife. I figured he didn't know many people there."

Steven heard Samuels inhale and pictured him lighting a cigarette. Somewhere in Samuels's office, a clock chimed. Steven glanced at his watch. Eleven-thirty already.

"The only thing I know about Gil's children...," Samuels picked up the conversation again, "...is Julian wants to get his novel published, but Gil didn't want Racine Literary taking it on. That's under Edward Greenpoint's purview. He can tell you more than I can." Samuels exhaled. Steven imagined thick smoke rising to the ceiling, suspected the cause for the publisher's raspy voice, and was glad they weren't in the same room. He realized that Olivia's aversion to cigarette smoke was rubbing off on him, and he smiled. Samuels continued. "Don't know anything about Gil's daughter, Irene. His brothers, I can't tell you much about either, I'm sorry to say. Jack's in the Navy. No idea where. Harry's always off on some wild adventure. He's a photographer. A good one, too. The last I heard, he was in South America, but if he's at the Christmas party, he must be back. They've got some tricky poisons down there. Powerful. Undetectable. Poisonous snakes and frogs. Maybe that's an angle for you."

"I'll certainly think about it. Thank you, Mr. Samuels."

Samuels coughed, then said, "Did you say Gil's Aunt Emily was there this weekend?"

"Yes, have you met her?"

"I have to say it's been my great pleasure. That dame's a corker! She's getting on a bit now, and her memory isn't as sharp as it was, but the stories she can tell you! I'd get her off to the side and pick her brain. The old broad's seen and heard it all. I'd say she's your best source of information, Detective."

"I can't thank you enough, Mr. Samuels. You've given me a lot to think about. I won't take up any more of your time. I'll say thank you again and wish you a very Merry Christmas."

"You, too. I hope you get the bastard. Gil was tough when it came to business, but he sure didn't deserve what he got." And with that, Samuels hung up.

After breakfast, the remaining Racine brothers, Jack and Harry, took their coffee and commandeered the chairs by the living room fire. Although they appeared to have the room to themselves, Jack scrutinized their surroundings, then leaned in close.

"Tell me you didn't have anything to do with this," he snarled at his younger sibling.

"What? Are you crazy?" Harry hissed. "Why would you say that?"

"You heard Steven talking about the blue stain on the piano keys. Who in this family uses potassium cyanide, huh? Who's got buckets of the damn stuff stored away in his darkroom? You, my little brother, that's who."

"The hell with you! Everybody knows about that, and they all know the door's never locked. You could have taken some just as easily as I could, Jack." Harry's eyes sparked in fury, narrowing as he glared at Jack. "Why would I anyway?"

"I don't know. You didn't look surprised when Steven told us about the poison."

CHAPTER TEN

"I couldn't help but think of it," Harry said. "Do you think somebody's trying to frame me?"

Jack whistled. "I hadn't thought about that. You'd better watch your back, little brother."

Olivia knocked on the kitchen door.

"Hello, is anybody here?" A loud bang reverberated, sounding like a heavy pan smashing against something metallic.

"Come on in," called a woman's hearty voice.

Olivia heard the clanging of more cookware. She stepped into the large, well-appointed kitchen. "Hello, my name is Olivia. It's Mrs. Buckley, isn't it?"

"That's me. What can I do for you, dear?" said a plump woman, an apron covering her housedress and a white cap keeping graying blonde curls in place.

"I'm helping Detective Blackwell with the investigation into Mr. Racine's death."

"Investigation, is it? That sounds formal."

"Mrs. Racine asked Detective Blackwell to look into it until the local police can get here," Olivia said.

"I know." The cook chuckled. "I'm just giving you a hard time. Takes my mind off how horrible it is. We all have our ways, don't we?" She slammed an iron skillet on a countertop. "So, what can I get you?"

"I'm looking for some big pieces of paper that we can tack on the wall of our cabin. Detective Blackwell always likes to jot down notes."

"You mean like this?" Doris Buckley pointed to a large roll of brown butcher paper on a stand.

"Yes, that would be perfect. Do you have an extra roll we could borrow? We won't need much and I'll bring back what's left."

"Sure, in the pantry over there." The cook indicated a door at the end of the room.

"Do you have any masking tape?" Olivia asked.

"Drawer at the end," said Mrs. Buckley as she took a large package wrapped in the same brown paper from the icebox. *"Boeuf bourguignon* tonight. A nice hearty meal for the cold weather, you know?"

"I loved your dinner last night, Mrs. Buckley. It was delicious."

"Aren't you nice? Mr. Harry loves my cooking. No matter where he travels, he always tells me he's never had better food anywhere in the world." Clearly, Doris Buckley had a soft spot for Harry Racine.

"It sounds like he loves adventure," said Olivia.

"Oh, he's always been like that. Even as a little boy, climbing trees higher than it was safe, riding his bike on the streets in New York in all that traffic. Imagine trolleys, automobiles, horses pulling all manner of carts and wagons filled with all kinds of food, barrels of beer, and merchandise. And little Harry weaving in and out. If there was danger involved, he was right there." Doris Buckley laughed. "There were days when I wondered if he'd make it to fifteen. Prayed a lot for that child, I did."

"Well, it looks like your prayers were answered." Olivia turned back toward the door. "I'll get this set up for Detective Blackwell and let you get on with your work. Thank you, Mrs. Buckley. I'm looking forward to your *boeuf bourguignon.*"

Opening the door to Cabin A, Olivia turned on a lamp to foil the gray day and checked the fire. It looked as though Rider had beaten her to it. The flames crackled, radiating waves of warmth and making the cabin blissfully comfortable.

Leaving her outer garments and boots by the door, Olivia gathered her supplies and padded to the second bedroom in her stocking feet, grateful for the thick rugs covering the wooden floors. She chose the largest section of wall uninterrupted by a window or door and used a yardstick she'd found in the kitchenette as a straightedge to cut two sizable pieces of the butcher's paper. Steven was several inches

CHAPTER TEN

taller than Olivia, so she pulled a chair over and stood on it to tape the papers up high. *Good*, she thought. *Now, should I do what Will does and get it started? Why not?*

Glad that Mrs. Buckley had armed her with a variety of writing implements, but wishing markers were among them, Olivia grabbed a piece of chalk and wrote THE CRIME + EVIDENCE on the top sheet of paper, then added:

GIL RACINE - poisoned with KCN while playing the piano
- evidence: Prussian blue stain on keys
When - Thursday, December 13, at approx. 9:30 pm

She wrote FAMILY, FRIENDS, and STAFF on the lower piece and listed the names of everyone present and their relationship to Gil.

Unsure what else Steven would want on this makeshift murder board, Olivia left it at that. He could finish the way he wanted. Wondering how his phone calls were going, she decided to return to the lodge. It wouldn't be long until lunch, and she wanted to talk with Irene.

As Olivia passed the empty stretch of property between Cabin A and the garage, she felt a pull, as though someone had grabbed the side of her jacket. *What the...?*

Thinking maybe somebody had nudged her from behind and she had misidentified the direction, Olivia turned around.

No one was there.

She stood still, trying to figure out what had happened. Then she heard an unexpected sound. *What's that?* She closed her eyes and cocked her ears. It sounded like music, but it wasn't coming from the lodge or any of the cabins. It seemed to emanate from the empty space alongside Cabin A. Olivia concentrated harder. With her eyes shut and ears straining, she suddenly felt dizzy and grabbed onto one of the logs forming the corner of the cabin to steady herself.

She listened hard and was able to make out the words *Chinatown* and *Riverside.* Her eyes flew open. *Billy Joel?* It sounded like "New York State of Mind." *What in heaven's name is going on?*

Before she could finish the thought, the dizziness hit again. She threw her other hand onto the log and gripped tighter. Was she playing the song in her head, or had she actually heard it?

No, this sounded real.

Feeling steadier, Olivia pushed back from the cabin wall and examined the empty area between the garage and Cabin A more carefully. Now, the scene looked exactly like it did when time folded over in her and Steven's house.

When time folded over at home, Olivia would be in her bedroom near the door in 2014. Steven would be standing in the hallway on the other side of the doorway in 1934. From Olivia's point of view, the pale painted walls in her hallway would fade away and be replaced by the navy-and-white wallpaper in Steven's house. From his point of view, what had been his mother's Art Deco bedroom would slowly disappear, and Olivia's clean, modern bedroom would come into focus. It was the same every time.

Olivia gasped. Sophie's metallic beige SUV sat shimmering a short distance away. The vision of this 21st-century vehicle in the middle of a forest in 1934 shocked Olivia so much that she couldn't move. She didn't dare approach it.

Was this another portal between her time and Steven's? It sure looked like it. What if it allowed her to cross over into her time but barred her from coming back?

Steven and Olivia always had to touch—they usually held hands—to travel to the other person's time. But when they wanted to return to their own year, they only had to walk over the threshold of her

CHAPTER TEN

bedroom door. Did all portals work the same?

Olivia stepped back. She couldn't take the chance that she'd miscalculate where the threshold was and accidentally step out of 1934, then not be able to return. Steven would have no idea where she had gone.

The music played on. She heard Billy Joel singing about taking a Greyhound bus.

What was Sophie doing here, anyway? As soon as the question arose, Olivia knew the answer. Sophie was worried about her. Like always. She bet Sophie was checking to make sure Olivia had not been pulled back to 2014 in the past twenty-four hours. That would be just like her.

As she came up with the answer, the vision of Sophie's 21st-century vehicle faded away along with Billy Joel. *Oh, my God! I have to find Steven.*

Olivia cautiously backed onto the path and ran to the front door of the Great Camp.

Chapter Eleven

Friday, December 14, 1934

Knightsbridge, New York

Sergeant Will Taylor picked up the receiver and asked the operator to connect him with The Shubert Theatre in New York City. Mrs. Racine sure hobnobbed with some impressive people. Will enjoyed the theater but rarely had the chance to attend. The job took much of his time.

"Shubert Theatre. How may I direct your call?"

"I'm a police officer investigating a death. I'd like to speak with the theater owner, please."

"Mr. Shubert's out of town. He's gone home to Syracuse for Hanukkah and for opening night at the Syracuse theater."

"Oh!" Will exclaimed. "I'm not far from there. Would you mind giving me a number where I can reach him?"

"Of course, he's at his other house. It's GR7-5920."

Will thanked her and wished her Happy Holidays.

After a second operator connected him, Will listened as the telephone rang five times. He was about to hang up when a man's voice answered. He sounded out of breath. "Hello, Shubert residence."

CHAPTER ELEVEN

"This is Sergeant Will Taylor with the Knightsbridge police. I'm looking for Mr. Shubert."

"This is Lee Shubert. How can I help you?"

"I understand that Margery Racine sits on your board of directors."

"It's not as formal as that, but yes, Margery is a special patron of all the Shubert theaters. Is she alright?"

"Yes, she's fine, but her husband was killed last night."

"That's terrible. But why are you calling me?"

"I should explain...Mr. Racine was murdered."

"Murdered! How dreadful," exclaimed Shubert.

Will went on. "In the case of a murder, we need to find out as much as we can about the victim's family members, close friends, and people they worked with."

"I see. How is Margery holding up?"

"As you'd expect. She's putting on a brave face," said Will.

"That's Margery, all right. Listen, Sergeant, you caught me walking out the door. How long would it take you to drive here? I know it's an imposition, but Knightsbridge isn't too far. It's just that I need to be at our Syracuse theater all day and into the evening as well. Final details for a show opening tonight. Would you mind coming here? I'll treat you to lunch, and you can ask me all your questions."

"I wouldn't mind at all, Mr. Shubert. Give me the address, and I'll see you in an hour and a half."

Great Camp Onontaga, Adirondack Mountains

Margery Racine had taken a second cup of coffee to her bedroom and was seated in her favorite chair by the window, looking out on the snow-filled landscape, watching birds flitting from branch to branch. *Now what?* she thought. *If we were in the city, I'd call the funeral home and start making arrangements. I suppose I should make a list of things to do, so when we get home I'll have everything organized. Maybe I should call the important people from here.* A fox ran across her field of vision, distracting her. Beautiful auburn coat, with its tail pointed down. *I wonder how long we'll be stuck here. Did I do the right thing last night asking Steven to investigate? I wonder if Lewis is back yet. I need to talk with him.*

Margery finished her coffee, crossed the hall, and knocked on Lewis's door.

"Just a minute," he called.

The door was flung open a moment later.

"Margery!" Lewis stood aside as she walked in, then closed the door behind her. Margery turned and stepped into his embrace. Leaning in, she rested her head on his chest. Neither said a word for a long minute. Finally, he broke the silence.

"My dear, how are you this morning? I didn't want to get into a conversation in front of everyone at breakfast. I hope you understood," he said.

"Of course. I can read your looks by now." She stroked his cheek. "Oh, Lewis, I can't seem to think straight. What should I do? Should I start calling people? I don't have anything to tell them other than Gil's dead. When do you think we'll be able to go home?"

"Let's take one thing at a time." He took her hand and led her to a small settee in front of a wide window overlooking the front of the Great Camp, where the driveway had disappeared under several feet of snow. "Now, you've asked Steven to look into the poisoning. That's a good first step. I listened to the weather report earlier. They say the snow's going to ease up in a day or two. So, we have to wait it out. Maybe making some lists would be a good idea. It'll give you something to do. I know you always like to feel that you're accomplishing something. How about a list of people to call? And one for the kind of service you'd like. The police are going to want to take

CHAPTER ELEVEN

charge of Gil's body once we get out of here. Even when we get back to the city, you won't be able to have the funeral right away. They'll likely order an autopsy."

"I didn't think of that. Yes, yes, you're right. I'll start some lists. And you know, Lewis," she said, sitting a little taller, "I have guests this weekend. What kind of hostess would I be if I ignored them? I'll see if I can organize some tasteful activities."

"That's my girl." He gave her hand a squeeze. "Let me know how I can help. You know I'm always here for you."

She smiled and touched his cheek again. "You've been here for me for as long as I can remember. I can't imagine my life without you."

"Me, too. Now, let's both put on a brave face and see about entertaining our guests."

Olivia found Steven hanging up the receiver in Gil's study. She closed the door so they could talk in private.

"How did your calls go?" she asked.

"Samuels gave me some background on several people. Greenpoint wasn't there, away on business until Monday. I might be able to skip him. Depends on what we learn about Julian and his novel." Steven told her what Thomas Samuels had said.

"Is not getting your novel published a strong enough motive for murder?" Olivia asked.

"I think that everyone in this family is strong-willed and used to getting what they want. Not getting a book published might not be a big deal to you or me, but it could mean everything to Julian. We'll see." Steven pocketed his notebook and came around to the other side of the desk. "Did you find some paper?"

"Yup, got your murder board all set up and ready to go." Olivia grinned, then her face fell.

"What's the matter? What just happened?"

"I need to tell you something. Can we go back to our cabin?"

"Of course, come on. Jeez, Olivia, you're scaring me."

She reached up and kissed his cheek. "It's okay, but I had a weird experience."

"Uh-oh. I don't like the sound of that."

Steven closed the door to their cabin and led Olivia to the cozy chairs near the fire. He pulled his chair close to hers so their knees touched and he could hold her hands.

"What happened?" he asked.

Olivia told him about hearing the music and seeing Sophie's car. "I checked the license plate to be sure. It *was* Sophie's. She's got a vanity plate that reads *#1 Café*. Besides, even if it had been someone else's, it was a 2011 SUV. They don't exist in 1934."

"And it looked the same as the two versions of our house when we meet at the door—how one fades away, and the other one comes into view?" Steven said.

"Yes, exactly the same."

"So, you think you found another portal? Holy mackerel." Steven blew out his cheeks and ran his fingers through his hair. He rose from the chair, walked back and forth across the room twice, then sat down again.

Olivia noticed that when he was concentrating, his shoulders tilted forward, and his hands moved as though he was sorting things out, putting them into categories or piles.

"Let's think about this, Steven. We can't possibly be the only people in the world who've discovered how to travel through time. The odds are against it. And if other people can do it, it makes sense that there must be portals all over the place. The only real surprise is that we haven't discovered one before now."

"I agree. But, now that we know it's there, you need to be *very* careful

CHAPTER ELEVEN

to avoid it this weekend. Let's assume it works like the one in our house. You could walk through the portal into your time, but you'd need me to bring you back here to 1934. And if you did go through it, everyone here would think you disappeared—or worse, that you killed Gil and ran away. I would have to know you'd gone through the portal, and I'd have to go to that exact spot to bring you back—with no one watching. And again, assuming it works the same, I could probably walk between the cabin and the garage, and nothing would happen." He scrunched up his face. "Does that make sense?"

"Yes. Listen, we can't afford to get distracted from the case. Let's talk more about it tonight. For now, I want to show you your murder board."

They entered the extra bedroom, which Olivia had started thinking of as HQ. She flipped a switch, and the room was awash with light. She put out her hand, showing him the papers on the wall. "So, what do you think, Detective Blackwell?"

"Hey, this is swell! Thank you. It's exactly what I need. We'll have to secure the cabin now. I want us to feel free to write everything we need here, and we can't risk someone reading it. Would you stay here while I locate Rider and get a key for the lock? Now that I think of it, I should have asked for one before."

"Of course, we should keep the curtains drawn, too. We don't want anyone looking in and seeing this. I'll make us some coffee. We can share what we've learned so far when you get back. And we need a key for the darkroom, too," she called after him.

Steven returned in less than ten minutes. "I secured Cabin D and made sure there weren't any extra keys. These are the only two for our cabin. Rider reminded me we'll have to be responsible for our fires since he won't be able to get in."

"No problem. Remember I told you my parents used to take me on camping trips when I was a kid? I'm a whiz at building a fire. I don't

81

mind taking the responsibility for it. You've got the investigation on your mind."

"A division of duties, huh? I always knew we'd be a good team."

They took their coffee into their HQ, and Steven updated the murder board.

"Do you know how long the potassium cyanide would stay potent on the piano keys?" asked Olivia.

"No idea. I'll see if Lewis knows." Steven made a note in his book.

"We need to figure out who had a chance to put it there," Olivia said.

"Yeah, but we know it had to have been from some point on Wednesday between the time Gil, Margery, Aunt Emily, and Jack arrived and when we all sat down for supper Thursday night." Steven looked at the board. "You know, you did a really good job…what's that expression you use?"

"Winging it?"

He laughed. "Yeah, that's the one. So, let's call our window of opportunity from noon Wednesday to seven Thursday evening. No, make that six. We need time for the liquid to evaporate."

"Okay. Who do we think has the personality to take the chance of getting caught?" Olivia asked.

"More important than that, who would be daring enough to risk inhaling the poison or getting some of the powder on their hands?" Steven said. "Whoever it is, he or she was highly motivated to risk their own life in order to kill Gil Racine."

"You're right. I say Victor is out."

"Why?"

"When we met last night, he was appalled that I had a job. He told me how he spends his day—which, by the way, is doing nothing—before he ventures out of his apartment mid-afternoon to go to his club for drinks with his friends. He sounds like the laziest person on the planet."

CHAPTER ELEVEN

"That doesn't say much for his character. But it could be an act," said Steven.

"Although we know he wants to marry Irene, and Gil wasn't going to give his approval. Maybe it's Irene's money that he wants."

"Money makes people do all kinds of things. Victor stays on the list."

"What did Aunt Emily say when you went into the corner this morning? It looked like she was eager to talk," Olivia said.

"Not as much as I hoped. She wasn't about to accuse any of her relatives, but she did seem to have a soft spot for Gil. She wants us to get to the bottom of this. I also got the impression she's never warmed to Margery."

"Really? What did she say?"

"It was more like what she didn't say. She told me Margery did all the right things to support Gil, like hosting dinners for business associates and attending galas, but that she spends most of her time volunteering." Steven listed four organizations where Margery served on the murder board.

"She keeps busy. I imagine she never saw Gil much with the long hours he worked, and it seems like she wouldn't be the sort of person to get a paying job," Olivia said.

"No, people like Margery and Irene Racine aren't expected to work. When I asked Aunt Emily about Lewis, she made a face and mumbled something. I asked what she'd said, but she clammed up. And it wasn't the right moment to quiz her on a possible relationship between Lewis and Margery. I'll talk with her again."

Steven told Olivia what he'd learned from Samuels about Margery and Lewis spending time together at public events.

"That goes along with what we heard and saw last night, Steven. But who knows? Maybe they're just good friends."

"Do you think you could get her to talk, Olivia?"

"I'll give it a shot. Do we think Margery has the nerve to get the poison and spread it on the keys?"

"She'd certainly know about Harry's darkroom supplies. And she could have gotten up in the middle of the night to mix it in a glass of water. She probably had the most opportunity," Steven said.

"I think under that polite exterior, Margery Racine has a steel core," observed Olivia. "I say she's a top contender. We heard Lewis say, 'don't have to wait.' That sounds like an affair that's been going on for a long time. With Gil dead, she gets a lot of money, and she doesn't have to put up with a husband she doesn't love. She keeps her wealthy status and gets the guy she wants. It beats a messy divorce. I like her as a suspect."

Steven laughed. "Whoa, hold your horses there, Broncho Billy. Not so fast."

"Broncho Billy? Who the heck is that?"

"My childhood cowboy hero. A little respect, if you don't mind."

"Good grief!"

"Getting back to Margery, I happen to agree with your reasoning," Steven said. "Margery's high on our list. Using your reporter skills, what do you think about Lewis? He's been nothing but cooperative. How do you read him?"

Olivia said, "As a doctor, he'd know all about poison. For all we know, he brought some with him. And being a doctor requires a certain kind of courage. He wasn't here overnight, but he could have sneaked downstairs when everybody was changing for dinner and put the poison on the piano. It wouldn't have taken long. He's probably my number one suspect at this point."

"Once again, my unofficial partner, I like the way you're thinking. Will had better watch out."

"You'd never replace Will as your partner. You like him too much, and he does an...," she whispered the 21st-century slang, "...awesome

CHAPTER ELEVEN

job."

If anyone had been eavesdropping, they only would have heard Steven laughing.

Chapter Twelve

Syracuse, New York

Sergeant Will Taylor was pleased to be making good time on the road to Syracuse. The farther west he drove, the less it snowed, though it looked like the clouds had settled in to stay. Will was happy to have this time alone to think and particularly glad Syracuse was his destination. He had a confidential and highly sensitive matter to take care of in that city.

Will's problem was Olivia. Something wasn't right about her and, no matter the angle from which he approached it, he could not put his finger on what was bothering him.

Will liked Olivia. She seemed like a good person. She was friendly, smart, and well-educated. He believed her when she'd said she had a degree in journalism and had worked for *The Syracuse Journal*, although he had a hard time reconciling her supposed research agency. Could she really make a living doing research for writers and professors? Didn't that sort of person go to the library and look up their own material? And what about the overseas trips she seemed to have taken? They must have cost money. Had she traveled before the Depression hit? Who had the money to go to Europe nowadays? Olivia didn't appear wealthy. And what about all the time she spent at

CHAPTER TWELVE

Steven's? How could she work when she was in Knightsbridge?

Then, there was the question that bothered Will almost more than all of them: how did she get to Knightsbridge? Nobody ever seemed to notice her arrive or leave. He had never heard anyone mention that they'd seen her drive through town. No one had ever said, "Oh, I was on the bus from Syracuse with Miss Watson," or "We took the same train as Detective Blackwell's friend Olivia."

When he'd first met Olivia back in the spring, Will was oblivious to anything about her. He simply didn't care. Steven said she was a friend of his family, and he seemed to like her, so that was good enough for Will. But as the months went by, he noticed little things.

There was that instance in April when he'd witnessed an unbelievable display of physical...well, he didn't even know what to call it. Steven said what Olivia had done was a sport called kickboxing. Will had never heard of it.

And there was that night when he and Trudy had gone out to dinner with Olivia and Steven. Somehow, they'd gotten into a conversation about the Great War. Although he and Steven had been too young to fight, they remembered what everyone had called *doing their bit* for the war effort. Both boys had helped collect scrap metal and rags. Trudy had commented on how afraid she'd been when her father left for France. Olivia had said nothing. Not one word. And Olivia was never short of words. Will had had the impression she didn't know what to say. He thought that was odd.

Then, to top it off, the other day, when they probably thought no one was around, Will overheard Olivia use an unfamiliar expression. It had surprised him so much that, for the moment, he couldn't remember what it was. But it had sounded like German.

Will was no fool. He knew from the news reports that trouble threatened Europe. He believed it stemmed from that Austrian who was now called the *Führer* of Germany. Above the law and not accountable to the German constitution, Hitler was nothing less than a dictator.

Will cast his mind back to the conversation he'd overheard. The more he thought about it, the clearer the words became.

Will was sure Olivia had said something in German.

What if she was a spy?

Great Camp Onontaga, Adirondack Mountains

Harry sat huddled on the front steps of the Great Camp, smoking. It had stopped snowing. The air was fresh, and the cold felt good on his face. Margery always had the fires banked too high, making him wish he could strip off some of his clothes. That would shake that controlled look off her face. He laughed to himself.

Harry heard the door open then close behind him, followed by footsteps on the wooden boards that made up the porch and the squeak of that one loose board. He felt someone sit down next to him before he looked to see who it was.

Aunt Emily was bundled up in her fur coat, wool cloche pulled down over her ears, and leather gloves with rabbit fur lining that went halfway up to her elbows—he knew because he used to tease her about them.

"Want some company?" she said.

"Sure. Want a cigarette?"

"Why not? Thanks." She took the Lucky Strike, recalling the ad she'd seen in her magazine the other day. "Nature in the raw is seldom mild." Predictable that Harry would choose this brand. She inhaled deeply as he struck a match and held it to the tip.

Tipping her head back and blowing out a lungful of smoke, Aunt Emily asked, "Want to tell me what's bothering you? And don't say it's

CHAPTER TWELVE

Gil's death. I know you didn't like him much."

Harry looked at her from under the wild bangs covering his brow, then brushed them off his face. "I don't know."

"Sure you do. You know I won't tell anyone. Your secrets have always been safe with me."

"Yeah, I know." His mouth twisted into a grotesque shape, and he shook his head.

"Looks like this one's a doozy," she said. "Go ahead. It'll make you feel better to get it off your chest."

"I killed a guy in South America a few weeks ago."

"That trip in the Amazon?"

"Yeah."

"Tell me." Her topaz eyes bore into his, compelling him to confess everything, as he always did.

"We were going down the river. Me, Al, the guide, and a porter. The guide backed up into a box of provisions and knocked them overboard. It was our last full box. And we still had several days to go." He looked up at her. "I lost my temper and pushed him. He fell into the river."

"Oh, dear. What was it? Piranhas?"

"Crocodiles. Two thirteen-foot-long caimans."

"My God, that poor man."

"Al and I grabbed poles and tried to get him out, but the crocs were too damn fast. He didn't have a chance."

Aunt Emily exhaled deeply. "I see. Well, I can't blame you for being upset. I assume you would have starved without the food and, in that heat, you needed the water. Did you notify the authorities, or is that a dumb question?"

"No one around for miles. We decided to cut the trip short. We managed to get the boat turned around, then made our way back to Manaus. We told the harbor master he tripped and fell in, that we tried to save him but couldn't. Said it was an accident. We paid the porter to keep his mouth shut. Al and I swore we'd never tell anyone the whole truth."

Aunt Emily put her arm around his shoulders and gave a squeeze. "Listen to me, Harry. Nobody gets out of this life without making mistakes. Big ones, small ones. We all make 'em. Put it out of your mind. Brooding won't solve anything. And it won't bring him back. It was an accident. Forget about it."

She stood up, threw her cigarette into the snow where it glowed, and went out, then she walked back into the lodge, leaving him alone with his memories.

Chapter Thirteen

Syracuse, New York

Will pulled the police department's Ford up to the curb alongside the Shubert Theater. As instructed by Lee Shubert, he entered through the stage door and gave his name to the man sitting on a tall stool behind a makeshift desk that was no more than a piece of wood attached to the wall with a bracket. Will showed his badge and ID.

The man checked a list. "Mr. Shubert's in the theater watching the rehearsal. Probably sitting in the last row." He jabbed his thumb in the direction. "Down the hall to the end. Turn left and go through the door on the right."

Will followed the man's directions and emerged from the back hallway into an aisle on one side of the theater. Looking toward the rear, he spotted a man who appeared to be taking notes as he sat in the lush burgundy-colored velvet seats.

The man must have heard the door because he looked up and waved Will over.

"We're almost ready for a lunch break. Ten minutes," Shubert whispered.

Will enjoyed every one of those ten minutes and, when the lights came on and they stood to leave, said, "I forgot how much I love watching plays."

"I see that glimmer in your eye, Sergeant. You're as besotted as I am."

As soon as they were seated in the Japanese Tea Room at the back of Schrafft's, Will knew he was going to bring Trudy here for lunch on her birthday. The crisp white linens and crystal would impress her and let her know how much he cared.

Lee—as Shubert had instructed Will to address him—said that Will was his guest and he should order anything he wanted from the menu. When the waitress arrived, Will asked for onion soup and a hot roast beef sandwich.

"So," Shubert began as he placed his napkin on his lap, "what can I tell you?"

"Anything you know about Margery Racine or her husband," Will said.

"I never met Gil Racine, and I only know Margery superficially. We've collaborated on various projects. She's organized, passionate about the theater, easy to work with. She's a good leader. People like her and seem to want to do what she asks of them. Whenever I've seen her at a performance, Dr. Salisbury has been with her."

"What can you tell me about that relationship?" Will asked.

"Only that they seem friendly and quite comfortable together."

"Would you say they might be romantically involved?"

"The thought crossed my mind once or twice, but I really have no idea. I've never seen anything to indicate a romance."

"Would it be accurate to say they have a very close relationship?" Will asked.

"Yes, but a lot of relationships are close, and they're not romantic. And they don't lead to murder," Shubert said.

CHAPTER THIRTEEN

Will felt the theater owner's defenses rise. To lower them, he said, "Yes, that's certainly true. I doubt there's any Shakespearean drama going on here."

Shubert relaxed and smiled. "I hope not! The only other thing I can tell you, Sergeant, is that Margery is a strong woman. Whatever the outcome, she'll get through this. She'll be alright in the end."

The waitress brought their lunch, and both men settled in to enjoy the food and conversation. Will asked numerous questions about how Lee had gotten started in the competitive theater business. Shubert wanted to know what it was like being a police officer.

After coffee and dessert, Will sighed. "That was a swell meal, Lee. Thank you."

"You're most welcome, but I'm afraid I haven't helped your investigation much."

"Never underestimate the value of background information. Sometimes, it's the smallest detail that cracks a case."

"Well, I hope your trip wasn't for nothing," said Shubert.

"Not at all. It was a pleasure meeting you and watching the rehearsal. I also have a couple of errands to do on another investigation while I'm here."

The men shook hands and went their separate ways at the curb, Shubert heading back to the theater and Will driving to the offices of *The Syracuse Journal* at Herald Place.

Will was surprised to discover the snow hadn't been cleared as well in this part of town, and he had to drive an extra block before finding a parking spot in the slush along the curb. After locking the police sedan, he strode down the sidewalk to the large multi-story newspaper building.

"Hello. I'm Sergeant Will Taylor with the Knightsbridge Police. Is Susan Taylor working today?" he asked the woman behind a counter in the lobby.

"Taylor?" The receptionist raised her brows.

Will laughed. "She's my cousin."

"Ah. Yes, Sue's here. Wait a moment, please."

The woman picked up the telephone receiver, dialed several numbers, and said, "Susan, you have a visitor. It's your cousin Will." Hanging up, she indicated several chairs near the front windows. "You can have a seat, Sergeant. She'll be down in a minute."

Will surveyed the lobby, saw a stack of newspapers on a small table, and picked one up. Glancing at the day's news, he learned that a jury had found a bank robber guilty, and the man would be sentenced before Christmas, an ocean liner from Bremen was late because of storms in the Atlantic, and the TVA intended to build three more power plants. He paged ahead to the ads. He still needed to buy Christmas gifts for Trudy and his mother, and he had no idea what to get.

An attractive, dark-haired woman about Will's age came through a swinging door to his left. She held out her arms, and they hugged.

"Hey, I missed you at our celebration this year. What was so important that you couldn't come to our annual birthday party?" Susan asked.

Will grimaced. "Work. You know that's the only thing that would keep me away. It's not every day two cousins are born on the same day." He rubbed her arm. "Happy twenty-ninth, by the way."

She punched him in the arm. "You too. So, what are you doing here?"

"Can we go someplace private?"

"Sure." Susan led him back through the doors and into a closet-sized room holding half a dozen filing cabinets. "What's up?"

"I'm not working on an investigation. This is personal. For me," Will said.

"Okay, what is it? You're not in trouble, are you?"

CHAPTER THIRTEEN

"No, of course not."

"I didn't think you would be, but...."

"There's a woman who's been spending a lot of time in Knightsbridge. She's gotten close to Steven," Will said.

"Mmm. Your sexy partner."

"Jeez, Susan. Are we really in the same family?" Will shook his head. "Anyway, I think there's something not quite right about her, so I'm doing a little investigating on my own."

"Fair enough. What do you want from me?" his cousin asked.

"She said she worked here a while back. Can you check?"

"Sure, I can get you the low down." She pulled a small notebook and the short stub of a pencil from a pocket in her dress. "What's her name?"

"Olivia Watson."

Great Camp Onontaga, Adirondack Mountains

With their first official briefing in the rearview mirror, Steven and Olivia left their HQ and returned to the main lodge.

Olivia spied Jack in an overstuffed chair by the fire, reading.

Raising his head from the book, he asked, "Are you looking for something, Olivia?"

"Your niece. Have you seen Irene?"

"Somebody said she's still in her room. Hasn't come out yet today."

"Do you know which one is hers?"

"The Eastern White Pine. Second door to the left at the top of the stairs."

Olivia knocked softly. "Irene? It's Olivia."

The door opened, revealing a disheveled, red-eyed Irene Racine. "What do you want?"

"I won't say 'to see if you're okay' because how could you be? But, I thought maybe you felt like talking with somebody. I can get you a cup of tea, and you could tell me about your father if you think that might help."

A weak smile crept onto Irene's face. "That's genuinely decent of you. Yes, that'd be swell."

"I'll be right back."

Olivia flew down to the kitchen, hoping by the time she returned Irene wouldn't have changed her mind.

"Mrs. Buckley," she panted, catching the cook by surprise, "can you get me a small pot of tea and some toast? I want to take it up to Irene."

"Bless you! That's such a thoughtful idea. I always keep a kettle of boiling water on the stove. It'll only take a minute."

Doris Buckley busied herself making tea, gathering cups and saucers, a pitcher of cream, and a sugar bowl. She piled everything on a tray, added a small plate of buttered toast and jam, and handed it to Olivia, who pushed open the swinging door with a thrust of her hip and carefully climbed the staircase.

When Irene opened her bedroom door, Olivia was glad to see that Gil Racine's daughter had used the time to throw water on her face and brush her hair, not only making herself presentable, but Olivia knew those small actions would help Irene's mood and contribute to her feeling more like her normal self.

Irene held the door as Olivia slid in, crossed to the windows, and set her burden on a small table flanked by two comfortable-looking chairs upholstered in black-and-white toile.

Once settled, Olivia said, "First, let me tell you how truly sorry I am for your loss. I adore my father and can't imagine what you must be going through."

Tears oozed out of Irene's bloodshot eyes, and she dabbed them with a cotton handkerchief.

CHAPTER THIRTEEN

"Thank you. Do you know that, except for Victor, no one has even said that to me yet? I'm always invisible in this family. Until I want something they object to, of course."

"And you want Victor, don't you?"

Irene smiled a ghost of a smile. "You could tell, couldn't you? Well, of course, you could, you're a woman. I saw how you looked at Steven. You understand." She shrugged and took a sip of the hot tea, into which she had stirred three spoons of sugar, mumbling something about how adding some whiskey would help. She sighed. "What does it matter anymore? Victor asked me to marry him, but my father refused to give us his blessing. He called Victor a grifter and said he was after my money. As though he couldn't be in love with me, for God's sake."

"What do you think will happen now that your father's gone?" Olivia asked.

"I have no idea. One of my uncles will probably inherit the businesses. Maybe Uncle Jack because he's the oldest now. My mother will carry on like she always has."

"Which is what?"

"Her volunteer work. You'd think the theater and museum people were her kids for all the attention she pays to Julian and me," Irene said.

"Will you need someone's permission to marry Victor now?"

"I don't know."

"I hope you won't let the recent disagreement between you and your father cloud the wonderful memories you have of him," said Olivia.

"You sound like you're speaking from experience."

"Actually, I've been lucky so far. My parents supported me in the things I've wanted to do, but I have friends where that wasn't the case. I know someone who refused to speak with her father for several months until her mother sat them both down and said, 'Work it out!'"

"Did they?" asked Irene.

"Yes, because at the end of the day, they loved each other. They found a compromise."

"I'm glad I wasn't in that position. My father listened to me. It's just that...." Irene made a face and shook her head. "I know he was trying to protect me. But he didn't know Victor like I do. I was going to talk to Daddy one more time this weekend. I had a plan that I think he would have accepted. It was, like you said, a compromise." She chuckled. "Julian always calls me Daddy's little girl. And I think it was true. I know my father loved me. That helps a lot right now."

"What was your plan, Irene?"

"I was going to tell him I'd stop fighting him if he would give us a year to prove Victor really loved me. After one year, if he could see that Victor's love for me was real and he still wanted to marry me, Daddy would give us his blessing. My father's life was all about negotiations. I think he would have appreciated my idea of negotiating. I truly believe it would have worked. Now, I probably have to start all over with someone else who'll be in control of my life. I really hate it, you know?"

There was a knock on the door. Irene went to open it.

"My darling," Victor McAllister said, pulling Irene into his arms. "I overslept this morning. When I got up and arrived at the main lodge, you were still in your room. I wanted to come right away, but your mother said to let you sleep. Were you able to get any rest last night? How do you feel?"

Olivia was no expert in romantic relationships, after all, her ex-fiancé had cheated on her right under her nose, but she recognized real emotion and genuine caring in someone's voice. She was sure Victor McAllister was in love with Irene. Did that make him more or less of a suspect?

Olivia stood and walked to the door. "I'll leave you two alone. I

CHAPTER THIRTEEN

hope we see you at lunch, Irene."

Irene Racine grasped Olivia's hand. "Thank you. I mean it." She looked into Olivia's eyes and gave her a feeble smile.

Olivia noticed a strength and determination in Irene that had been missing. It reminded her of Margery's resolve last night.

At that moment, Olivia felt certain that Irene did not poison Gil Racine. About Victor, she wasn't sure. Love can be as powerful a motive as hate. Love of money even more so. And there was a lot of money at stake here.

Lunch was a casual affair. Rider had set out a buffet—a tureen of hot chicken soup and noodles, crusty breads, and a cheese and fruit platter. Everyone wandered in around one o'clock. At first, only the sound of clinking cutlery broke the silence. Then, Julian Racine said what they were all thinking.

"So, Steven, have you figured out who killed my father?"

"Julian!" Margery exclaimed.

"We're all wondering, Mother. Nobody wants to say it, that's all."

"I understand how difficult this is, Julian. I do," said Steven. "We're gathering information. That's all I can tell you right now."

Margery sat taller in her seat and touched her glass with her spoon, making a ringing noise. "Listen, everyone, we all know how difficult and sad this is. But there's nothing we can do until the roads are cleared, and we can go home. I spoke with Lewis this morning, and we agreed we should try to stay busy. I'm still your hostess, and you are still my guests. We have games and cards that will help pass the time. There are a couple of jigsaw puzzles, which will surely take hours to complete. You might want to go ice skating if someone can clear the snow off a small area on the lake. Or maybe cross-country skiing or snowshoeing. If anyone has other ideas, I'm willing to try. If you'd prefer to spend quiet time reading, we have plenty of novels to pick from." She held out a hand toward the bookcases that framed the front windows. "We'll have to make the best of it." Her voice caught, and Olivia thought she was going to lose her composure. But she took a sip of water, then cleared her throat. "Mrs. Buckley is making a wonderful dinner for tonight. Let's do something energetic this afternoon to work up an appetite. We're in for a treat."

Lewis reached over and squeezed her arm. "Well said, Margery." He contemplated the people around the table, one of whom was likely a killer, then continued. "Olivia and I went snowshoeing this morning. The path is perfect for it. If anyone's interested, I'll go again."

"Margery, would it be alright if I looked at your photo albums?" Olivia asked. "I keep albums, too, and when I was little, my mother let me help with hers. It was something special that we did together."

"Of course. That's a wonderful idea. Maybe I'll look at them with you. It would be nice to reminisce a bit."

As they were finishing lunch, Jack asked, "Steven, want to help me get some snow off the lake? We'll clear a small spot so people can go skating."

"I'd like to talk with Julian first. Would you mind giving me fifteen, twenty minutes?" Steven asked.

"Sure. Let me know when you're ready."

Steven approached Gil Racine's son. "Julian, how about a short stroll to walk off some of our lunch?"

Julian shrugged. "Why not? That's the only thing I enjoy doing up here."

They headed out along the path Steven had taken yesterday on the sleigh ride.

Was that only yesterday?

Julian lit a cigarette the minute they stepped off the porch. He seemed lost in his thoughts, and Steven didn't want to disturb him,

CHAPTER THIRTEEN

so they walked quietly for some time. The crunch of their boots on the snow, a woodpecker hammering at a tree, and the wind rushing through the pines were the only sounds Steven heard.

After several minutes, he said, "Tell me about your relationship with your father."

"What relationship?" Julian sneered.

"Were you close?"

"Kind of hard to be close with someone who's never around."

"Lewis said although your dad worked a lot, he made a special effort for you and your sister's birthdays and on Christmas. Is that true?" Steven asked.

"Two days a year don't make up for the other three-hundred-and-sixty-three, though, do they?"

"I'm sorry about that, Julian. Kids deserve to spend time with their father." Steven let the silence take over again. Then, he asked, "Your father must have been excited about your novel, though, wasn't he? It's a wonderful accomplishment to write a book. He must have been proud of you."

"I have no idea what he thought. I don't even know if he read it."

"What's it about?"

Julian leaned away from Steven, narrowing his eyes. "Do you really want to know?"

"Yes."

"It's about a young boy who's ignored by his father. Their gardener takes the boy under his wing and teaches him how to make topiary. He works hard to perfect his skills, and by the time he's a young man, he's acclaimed throughout Europe. He wins an international competition. The father doesn't attend the ceremony, doesn't even send a telegram congratulating his son."

"So, how does it end?" Steven asked.

"The young man stabs his father with his topiary scissors."

Steven stopped walking and stared at Julian.

"Don't worry, Detective, I killed a character in my book. I didn't kill my father."

After fifteen years on the force, suspects rarely shocked Steven, but Julian Racine had done just that. It took him a few seconds to formulate his next question. "What happened when you asked your father to publish your book?"

"He told me to give the manuscript to Ed Greenpoint at Racine Literary. That was about six months ago. Last week, Ed called me and said they wouldn't be publishing my novel."

"Did he say why not?"

"Something about it not being the kind of writing the company wants to be known for. What the hell does that mean, anyway? His own son. And he couldn't do that one thing for me. Bastard."

"I'm sorry. That must have hurt."

Julian scowled. "How am I supposed to approach another publisher now when everyone knows my own father's company rejected me? I'm finished before I even started."

Syracuse, New York

"Nothing?" Will said, his mouth agape. "How far back did you look?"

"Fifteen years," said Susan. "I checked the personnel files and the folders we keep on our volunteers. I also looked where we store information on sources. She's not there, Will. You're sure she said *The Syracuse Journal*?"

"Yes, of course. I'm a cop, remember? I don't make that kind of mistake." He shook his head and frowned. "I don't understand. Why would she lie about something like that?"

"Do you have any other leads on this girl?"

CHAPTER THIRTEEN

"Yeah, she said she graduated from journalism school at Syracuse University. That's where I'm going next. Do you have any contacts there?"

"Not in student records, no. Gee whiz, good luck," said Susan. "Let me know what happens with this, okay?"

"Will do. And thanks anyway, for looking. I appreciate it." Will gave his cousin a hug. "Tell your mom and dad hi for me. I'll be over to visit one of these days."

"What are you doing for Christmas?" Susan asked.

"Going up to Ottawa to spend it with my mother's side of the family. At least, if the weather cooperates. And if I don't get a case that can't wait."

As Will drove up the hill that was Adams Street, he debated where he should start—the newly independent School of Journalism or the Registrar. He went with journalism. A secretary might remember Olivia. Or maybe one of her professors, if any were around. Will turned right on Crouse Avenue and continued climbing into the heart of the university campus. He found an empty spot at the curb and entered a building.

A middle-aged woman sat at a desk in the outer office. Clearly struck by the holiday spirit, she wore a green plaid skirt, white blouse, and red sweater. She'd pinned a gold wreath to the shoulder of her cardigan.

"Good afternoon. May I help you?" She smiled up at Will.

Will pulled the small leather folder from his pocket and identified himself, showing her his badge and ID. "I'm looking for the records of a journalism student who graduated about twelve years ago. I'm not sure of the date. Her name is Olivia Watson. Do you keep student records here?"

"We have some, though not the official transcripts. The Registrar has those. But, let me see. If she was a student in our department, I should have something in the files."

"Would you mind checking graduating students during the years 1922 through 1927, to be sure?" Will asked.

"Not at all. I have everything cross-referenced. I'll check her name first." The secretary stepped to a large file cabinet against the wall. "What's the name again?"

Will told her.

"Hmm, Watson…W…W A…Nope. No Olivia Watson in the general lists. Let's check the graduating classes." She moved to an adjacent cabinet.

Will saw the labels were numbered in years rather than lettered like the first cabinet.

After going through several file folders and shuffling through numerous pages, the secretary turned to Will and said, "I'm sorry, Sergeant. I don't see anyone named Olivia Watson ever graduating from our department. Are you sure you don't want English? Or maybe Business? We were part of the Business College until earlier this year, you know."

"No, that's alright. Thank you, ma'am. I appreciate your time."

After checking the Business College and the Registrar and getting the same results, Will sat in the police sedan, waiting for the engine to warm up, wondering what to make of what he had learned this afternoon. Olivia had lied—to everyone. But most importantly, as far as Will was concerned, she had lied to Steven.

Who was Olivia Watson, and what was she doing in Knightsbridge?

Chapter Fourteen

Great Camp Onontaga, Adirondack Mountains

Steven returned to the lodge after his walk with Julian. "I'm ready when you are, Jack."

"I'll get the snow-blowing machine."

Steven watched from the front porch as Jack drove up in one of the strangest vehicles he had ever seen. The front resembled the front end of a truck, but there was a tall cylinder attached to the side behind the driver's door and angled away from the vehicle. On a flatbed in the back sat what looked like a pile of tools under a canvas tarp—the handle of something stuck out—and a large metal box that appeared to house the driving power of the mechanism hanging off the side. As the machine moved forward, the snow was drawn into the bottom of the tube, then was propelled out of the opening in the top. It reminded Steven of a harvester he'd seen on a friend's farm, although that machine had pushed through a sea of crops and had blown grain out of the chute instead of snow.

"That's aces," Steven said, getting in on the passenger side. "Why are we snowed in if you have this?"

"It's only good for small areas and short lengths of time. The drive from the main road to Onontaga is a good three miles long. It would take days to clear enough for a car to get through. The motor wouldn't survive."

Blowing a shower of snow as they went, Jack and Steven carved a path around the left side of the Great Camp, across the lawn in the back, and down to the edge of Raquette Lake.

"Are you sure the lake's frozen?" Steven wasn't used to driving onto a body of water, although he knew a lot of fellas back home who couldn't wait for winter so they could go ice fishing.

"Yeah, I'm sure. Gil always asks Mr. Murphy when he brings the horses over. He's the farmer who takes care of them when we're not here. Murphy said it's been frozen for several weeks now. It's easily a foot thick, so we're safe. If you look, you might be able to make out the ice fishermen's markers."

Steven pointed. "Yup, there's one."

Jack squinted. "And look to the left. There's more."

"That's not safe. How can anyone tell where the holes are under all this snow?"

"They limit the diameter of the opening to twelve inches, and the fishermen put the marker about two inches behind the far side of each hole," Jack explained. "Imagine taking a straight line from the shore to the marker. When you see the marker, you know that there's an opening a foot wide in front of it. It's standard. I've never heard of anyone falling in. Besides, given the size, the most that would happen is that your leg slips in. Someone would help you out, and you'd hurry home to get dry. But, we're not going anywhere near them. Don't worry."

As Jack expertly cleared a small skating rink on the frozen lake, they chatted.

"Are you an ice fisherman, Jack?" Steven asked.

"Not anymore, although I used to enjoy it. When he was little, I took Julian out a few times. He seemed to like it. But then, I suppose

CHAPTER FOURTEEN

it's quite an adventure for a kid to drive out into the middle of a lake in a truck!" Jack laughed. "Those were fun times. I wonder if he remembers."

"Tell me what it's like living on a ship, Jack, being out in the middle of an ocean for weeks at a time with hundreds of men and not a girl in sight." Steven chuckled, having heard of Jack's fondness for women.

"It's not for everybody. But I like it. There's a sense of freedom with the wide expanse of the ocean and nothing but sky all around. Although, I have to admit there are times when you feel trapped. Some of the boots struggle with claustrophobia."

"Boots?"

"The new guys fresh out of boot camp."

"Ah," Steven said.

"Anyway, we go ashore often enough, so not having girls on board isn't too bad. I've enjoyed seeing some of the world. I like the Far East. There are some beautiful cities." He turned the machine and headed down the long side of the soon-to-be skating rink.

"What do you do all day on the ship?" Steven couldn't imagine being confined in one space, even if it was the size of a fleet carrier.

"As commander, I oversee everything, but each of my officers and every sailor on board has his duties. We have daily routines. Time goes by pretty good." Jack shot a glance at Steven. "So…Olivia…she's some dame."

Steven didn't know what to say to that.

"How long have you two been stepping out?" Jack asked.

"A while."

"She from Knightsbridge?"

"No, Syracuse."

"What's she doing in Knightsbridge?"

"Working part-time at *The Gazette*," Steven said.

"Secretary?"

"No, reporter."

"Well…." Jack raised his brows and shot Steven a look.

"Not to change the conversation or anything," said Steven, "but you know I've got to ask, what do you think happened last night? You know everyone here, and I don't. Who could have hated your brother enough to do such a horrible thing?"

Jack's hands left the wheel of the snow-blowing vehicle for a moment. He shrugged, turning his palms up. "Steven, I have no idea. My brother wasn't widely loved, but nobody hated him that much. I mean, sure, we all had our problems with him at one time or another—I know I did. But, no matter what it was, we always worked it out in the end. To go to such lengths…." He whistled, and the sound reverberated around the vehicle's cabin like a metal whip, "To do what the killer must have had to do…and how would you know how to handle such a dangerous chemical?" He paused as he steered the vehicle around a corner. "Of course, Harry works with it when he's developing photographs, but I can't imagine why he'd want to hurt Gil. Gil's helped him out with money from time to time and out of a couple of scrapes a few years back. If anything, I'd think he'd be grateful."

Jack went on. "And Lewis has been Gil's closest friend since they were in their twenties. Like I said last night, there was no great passion between Gil and Margery, at least on Margery's part, but they seemed alright. She wasn't happy with my brother working so much—evidently, the newspaper business requires lots of long hours—but I can't imagine her taking such drastic steps as this. And if it had been Margery, why didn't she do it when they were in the city? It would've been a lot easier." Jack cleared his throat. "Steven, are you sure it's one of us? Maybe somebody snuck in and put that stuff on the piano. A business rival who followed him up here, maybe. And are you positive Gil was poisoned from touching the keys?"

CHAPTER FOURTEEN

"Yes, he was definitely poisoned by the residue on the piano keys," Steven said. "And an outsider doesn't make sense because of the storm. Why would someone risk their life to trek up here in the wilderness during a blizzard when they could poison him in New York City? No, it has to be one of the people at the Great Camp."

Jack frowned. "I can't believe someone in my family would do this. You should look at Victor. Gil was dead set against him marrying Irene. Thought he was no good."

"It's a possibility. But how would he know about potassium cyanide? As far as I can tell, he's never had a job or any experience where he would have learned about it."

"He worked in a pharmacy during the Great War."

"What?" Steven was stunned. Why hadn't he and Olivia found that out? "How do you know that? Are you sure?"

"Irene mentioned it once." Jack shrugged. "Sorry, I thought you knew." He guided the machine along the side of the emerging skating rink. "Hey, what about the staff? Maybe Rider had a beef with my brother. Or Mrs. Buckley. Don't they say poison is a woman's weapon?"

"We talk with everyone, Jack. I'll be speaking with the staff," Steven said. "When was the last time Gil played the piano before last night?"

"Wednesday after dinner. He wanted to practice before everyone arrived."

"Then the poison must have been put there between late Wednesday evening and before we sat down for supper on Thursday." Steven's mind was working through the possibilities, automatically numbering them as if he were writing notes: 1. late Wednesday evening after Gil, Margery, Jack, Aunt Emily, and the staff retired; 2. during the night while they slept; 3. before breakfast Thursday morning; 4. before Thursday's dinner, when everyone was in their respective cabins or rooms, changing into their party clothes, getting ready for the festivities.

Steven needed to get back to the murder board, to Olivia, and to their quiet place where he could organize his thoughts and write all of this down.

"There we are," Jack said with a note of satisfaction in his voice. "Almost done. Now, I'll get the push broom and sweep off those last few inches, so it's nice and smooth in case somebody wants to skate later."

"Jack, do you mind if I leave you? I need to make some phone calls."

"Sure, go ahead. I won't be far behind."

Steven jumped out of the cab and headed back to the Great Camp.

Syracuse, New York

After Will returned to the police vehicle, he consulted his watch. Not two o'clock yet. He'd told the fellas they'd get together for a briefing at five-thirty. Plenty of time to investigate one more thing before returning to Knightsbridge.

He pulled away from the curb and headed down the hill on Harrison Street toward the center of town. He was tempted to visit Lieutenant Fred Schultz, their colleague at the Syracuse Police Department. That would be the most efficient means of finding an address or telephone number for Olivia, if she had one. But if they found no listing for an Olivia Watson in the Syracuse area, what would he tell Fred? Surely, being Steven's friend, Fred would mention it the next time he and Steven got together for a meal or when they spoke on the phone regarding a case. Will decided the prudent course of action was to check with the telephone company.

Will Taylor was not an emotional man. He'd been surprised at his reaction when he learned Olivia had not graduated from Syracuse University with a degree in journalism, nor had she ever worked at *The*

CHAPTER FOURTEEN

Syracuse Journal. Instead of feeling triumphant that his investigation had so far confirmed his suspicions, he felt sad.

Will liked Olivia. He'd been happy for Steven when his friendship with Olivia had grown into something more. Lately, he noticed Steven was happier when she was around.

He hated himself for investigating her, but he had no choice. Steven would be the perfect target for someone whose mission was to discover what the United States knew or was planning with regard to Hitler and his machinations. Steven's father was none other than Admiral Robert Blackwell, a highly decorated officer with an important position in the Department of the Navy. If Olivia was gathering information and sending it to Germany, Steven needed to know, and Olivia belonged in prison.

Will's stomach churned—going behind Steven's back made him physically ill. Pulling up to the curb in front of the Central New York Telephone and Telegraph Company on Montgomery Street, he braced himself for what he was about to find.

At first glance, the building appeared to be a plain beige box, but gazing above the doors and windows, Will saw elegant Art Deco scrollwork and beautiful artistic reliefs. Pulling open the front door, he wondered how often people appreciated these details.

A receptionist directed Will to a suite on the top floor where a large, well-appointed office overlooked the city of Syracuse. *What a swell sight!*

"Hello. I'm Sergeant Will Taylor with the Knightsbridge Police. I'd like to ask your manager a couple of questions," he told the secretary.

"I'll see if he's available. You can wait there if you'd like," she said, indicating a row of chairs pushed against the wall of the small foyer.

Will walked to the almost floor-to-ceiling windows and gazed out at Syracuse. Across the street, the YMCA was a carbon copy of Knightsbridge's gym. Looking north, he identified St. Paul's church and the Art Deco State Tower building, which resembled the new Empire State Building in New York City.

A tall, husky man strode toward Will, his hand outstretched. "Good afternoon, Sergeant. I'm Howard Byron. Come back to my office. We'll see if I can help you."

Entering the beautifully furnished office, Will could see Byron was a businessman proud of his accomplishments—framed certificates and commendations filled the wall behind his desk.

Will settled in a comfortable upholstered chair and explained. "Let me say first that the person I'm inquiring about has not been accused of a crime. Her name has come up in an investigation, that's all. It's background information."

"Understood," said Byron, leaning back in his leather chair, steepling his fingers. "Go on."

"I'm looking for an address or telephone number for a young woman. Both, if possible. I'm interested in any time during the past ten years."

"I see. And her father's name?"

"Ah, no. She lives alone as far as I know," said Will.

"A modern woman, huh? Alright, what's her name?"

"Olivia Watson. And I don't think she's married, so the listing would be under *Olivia* Watson."

"Well, if she lives or has lived anywhere in the Syracuse area and she's had a telephone, she'll be listed in our directory." Byron stood and indicated a shelf in the middle of a rich mahogany bookcase. "See here, Sergeant? This is every single directory the company has ever published."

Byron removed an armful of thin booklets. "Here we go. 1924 through this past year. There's an empty office next door. You can work in there. Come on. I'll show you how we organize our directories."

Chapter Fifteen

Great Camp Onontaga, Adirondack Mountains

When Steven entered the main lodge, warmth from the fires blazing in both hearths swept over him. He stood by the door, rubbing his hands together, not wanting to remove his jacket until the chill left his bones. Scanning the room, he saw Olivia on one of the couches in the living room, paging through a book that rested in her lap. Margery Racine sat next to her. He watched Margery point to something and laugh. Steven remembered Olivia had asked their hostess if she could look at the family photo albums after lunch. He bet that's what they were doing. Leave it to Olivia. If she couldn't uncover the Racine family secrets from Margery, nobody could.

Steven hung his outdoor clothes on the hall tree, untied the laces on his below-zero snow boots, and exchanged them for the shoes he'd left on the rug. The boots were Canadian-made and had cost more than he normally spent, but they couldn't be beat on days when he was forced to spend time outside, investigating a case during the winter. As Steven walked to the sideboard where a silver urn of coffee was available all day long, he called hello.

"You're back," Olivia said, looking up. "How did it go?"

"They've got a swell machine that blows the snow out of the way. Let me say that if you want to go ice skating later, there's a rink waiting for you."

"That sounds like fun. Where's Jack?"

"I left him putting on the finishing touches. I wanted to make a couple of phone calls before it's too late."

Coffee in hand, Steven wove his way around several overstuffed chairs. He skirted the enormous glittering tree and stopped at a square, leather-topped table where Aunt Emily and Irene were playing cards. Glad that Gil Racine's family was making an effort at keeping their spirits up in an extraordinarily difficult situation, Steven asked, "Who's winning?"

"Irene always cheats, so it's not fair," said Aunt Emily.

"I do not," Irene declared. "Aunt Emily's the cheater. She's trying to mislead you."

The two women laughed, and Emily slapped down a card. "So there!"

"In case you're tempted to corrupt this friendly game, remember I'm a policeman," he kidded.

They laughed again.

Steven smiled. This was obviously a beloved routine.

Margery called him over. When he sat down, she whispered, "Have you found out anything?"

"Not yet. But we're making progress."

She clasped her hands to her chest, and Steven saw her eyes welling up. "We'll get to the bottom of it. Don't worry. It takes time. Margery, would you excuse me? I need to speak with Olivia."

Margery wiped her eyes and sat straighter. "Of course, we'll continue later if you want to, Olivia."

"I'd like that."

CHAPTER FIFTEEN

Once in Gil's study, Steven said, "I want to see if I can catch my father before he leaves the office for the day."

"Oh, good idea. I take it you're going to ask him for information about Jack, right?" Olivia asked.

"Yes, I should have thought of it sooner. He would have had all day to look up Jack's Navy records." Steven consulted the gold-filled watch he always wore, a gift from his parents when he'd made detective. "Not quite three-thirty. Dad never leaves until six, even on a Friday. There's still time for him to search. And I want to talk with you, too. We need to share what we both learned in the past few hours."

Steven picked up the telephone. "Operator, I'd like the Department of the Navy in Washington, D.C., please."

While he was being connected, Olivia whispered, "Do you think your father's going to discover something?"

"I don't know. When Jack and I were out on the lake, something didn't seem right. I can't put my finger on it, but I had the feeling he was lying. I don't know if it had to do with people here or if it was something in his own life. Would you talk with him? See what you make of him."

"Of course. By the way, you won't believe what I found...."

Steven held up a finger. "Yes, this is Detective Sergeant Steven Blackwell of the Knightsbridge Police Department in New York State. May I speak to my father, Admiral Robert Blackwell?...Oh, Grace, is that you? I didn't recognize your voice...Oh, darn!...Do you know when he'll be back?...Tomorrow morning, huh? Working overtime?... Yes, it must be...Oh, that's an idea. Yes, I need everything you can find about a Commander Jack Racine R A C I N E...That's right....No, I'll call back. I'm not home. I'm in the Adirondack Mountains at a friend's...Wait a minute, I just thought of something. In case you don't hear from me tomorrow morning, have my father call the station. My partner, Will Taylor, will be able to get the information to me…But, Grace, it's extremely important. It has to do with a murder investigation…Alright, thanks…You, too, have a very Merry Christmas…Bye."

Steven hung up and said to Olivia, "My father's up on The Hill in meetings for the rest of the afternoon. Grace'll pull files and tell him what's going on tomorrow morning. I'll call back after breakfast. Let's go to the cabin and update our murder board. We can talk more freely there."

Skating as he pushed the broom across the lake's smooth surface, Jack Racine was clearing the last dusting of snow from the rink, but he wasn't enjoying it anymore. He was annoyed that Steven had asked about his life in the Navy, although he should have known the question would come up. After all, Steven had no idea what had happened. It was an innocent enough question, but it had angered him. He'd done his best to block out the whole terrible incident, and he didn't want to think about it now. Unfortunately, it was *all* he could think about.

Jack loved shore leave on the tropical islands in the Pacific. Each island was more beautiful, more lush than the last. However, tonight he found himself in noisy, crowded Manila. The evening was hot and steamy, his body slick with sweat. The white uniform clung to him—damp marks under his arms ruined the look. As Jack was walking out of a bar after having downed a few too many, another drunken sailor stumbled out behind him. The man crashed into Jack, propelling him into the busy road. Jack narrowly missed being crushed by a speeding car. Jack spun around and leapt back onto the sidewalk. He pulled back his left arm and punched the man in the face.

The sailor's head jerked backward like whiplash in a car crash, gray-gold eyes rolling up out of sight. His body elevated, then fell flat on the concrete. Jack winced as the man's skull hit the sidewalk with a thump, the man's colored irises sliding back in place.

CHAPTER FIFTEEN

Time seemed to stop.
Jack gazed down at the young man's face. Empty eyes stared back.

Steven inserted the key and ushered Olivia inside Cabin A. They dropped their coats on a chair and entered the spare bedroom. Olivia clicked a switch, and the ceiling light illuminated their makeshift murder board.

"Olivia, what did you start to say before?" Steven asked. "Did you learn something from Margery?"

Olivia grinned like the Cheshire cat. "You know how we thought she was having an affair with Lewis?"

"Yeah?"

"He's her cousin!"

"What? How did that come out?"

Olivia had been enjoying looking at what she considered vintage photographs in Margery's beautiful, leather-bound albums. The first one she'd grabbed covered Irene's and Julian's childhoods. Each of the black pages was captioned in white ink—Julian's Baptism, Irene's First Communion, Christmas 1908. The tiny black-and-white, deckle-edged pictures measured two by three inches and were framed in a thin band of white. Although they were interesting, Olivia learned nothing new.

The second album held photos of Margery's childhood and teenage years. Olivia turned a page. Someone had written: Picnic at the Lake 1898.

"Oh, what a lovely day that was. We were celebrating my sixteenth birthday," Margery said.

Olivia leaned in and squinted at a group of teenagers posed, standing near a tree. They appeared older than 21st-century teens and looked as though they were going to a nice restaurant for dinner rather than to a picnic. The girls wore dresses, the boys pants and shirts—no jeans, no t-shirts one hundred years ago. Looking beyond the clothing, though, Olivia could see *adolescent awkwardness: many of the boys adopting what they had surely thought were manly poses, many of the girls appearing shy. One face looked familiar.*

She pointed to the boy. "Who is that? He reminds me of someone."

Margery laughed. "That's Lewis."

"Oh, I thought he and Gil didn't meet until they were in their twenties."

"That's true. But Lewis is my cousin. They met because of me."

"I wonder why she didn't mention he was her cousin," Steven said.

"Gil introduced him to us, remember? He said Lewis was his best friend. That was *their* relationship. Maybe we would have known if Margery had introduced him."

"That's a good point. Well, anyway, it explains a lot, doesn't it?"

"Exactly. We assumed they were having an affair, but we didn't see them kiss. And Samuels said he never saw them holding hands or doing anything to indicate a romance. If Lewis doesn't know many society people in New York, it makes sense that he'd hang around with his cousin at social events," Olivia said.

"But it doesn't change the fact that, according to Jack, Margery didn't love Gil. Her motive *still* could have been getting out of the marriage. She *still* had the most opportunity to spread the poison on the piano keys. None of those things have changed," Steven said.

"That's true, and if Lewis loves her like family, he *still* could have helped her. Maybe he feels protective of her."

Steven frowned. "So, we're no further along with those two."

As Olivia was crossing out *Affair* on their murder board, she stopped. "Hang on a minute. Do you remember exactly what Lewis said last night when we caught them at her bedroom door?"

Steven cast his mind back to the dark shadowy hallway, to Lewis holding Margery in a tight embrace, then Lewis leaning back and saying…"Something like 'don't have to wait,' right?"

CHAPTER FIFTEEN

"Wait for what? Wait to tell Gil's business associates, his vice-presidents, or managers he's dead? Wait to plan the funeral? We should find out, although that'll be tricky," Olivia said.

"I'll think of something. What's important right now is that although their relationship may have changed from our point of view, their possible motives are still valid."

"I think we can eliminate Irene as a suspect, and maybe Victor. The woman I talked with this morning was different from the haughty, entitled rich girl we met yesterday. She let her guard down. She told me she was going to suggest a compromise to her father." Olivia explained Irene's plan. "Irene adored her father. I can't see her hurting him, even to marry the man she loves. And I saw how Victor treated her when he came to her room. His feelings for her are real."

"I'll agree to cross out Irene," said Steven. "But whether Victor loves her or her money, he's a strong suspect."

Olivia shook her head. "I don't think it was him. I saw a gentle man caring for the woman he loves. Is he really that good of an actor? I don't think so. I believe he would have gone along with her compromise. And I'll tell you another thing—Victor *has* to know how much Irene loved her father. If he had hurt Gil, he had to have known his actions would have destroyed his relationship with her. He might have gotten rid of Gil standing in the way, but he would have ultimately lost Irene. She would have found out that he'd killed her father, and she wouldn't have been able to live with that."

"I disagree. Victor McAllister is arrogant enough to believe he wouldn't get caught. He may be a lazy man who only wants to socialize with his pals, but he needs money to do that. I bet Irene stands to inherit a bundle. Love and money make an extremely strong motive when combined together. They can push a person to do things they wouldn't ordinarily do. Maybe Victor doesn't want to wait a year."

Jack Racine was nearly finished clearing the ice skating rink, and he still couldn't get Steven's questions out of his mind. He sure as hell had no intention of telling anyone what his life was like nowadays. It was nobody's business. Besides, the Racine family honor would suffer. They'd all be humiliated—if not for him, for themselves.

Jack blamed his present situation on that damned left hook of his.

The Racine family was a class—or two or three—above boxing. They left that so-called sport to the riffraff. To the poor people. To the uneducated. To the Irish immigrants. The Racines played tennis and rode horseback.

When Jack first enlisted in the United States Navy, his commanding officer had encouraged the men to take up a sport they could do while out at sea. He said it would help keep them fit and pass the time. No tennis, no horses on board ship. So Jack, against his better judgment and natural inclination, let himself get talked into boxing. Surprisingly, he was good at it. Even more surprising, he liked it. Jack discovered the energy it provided made him clear-headed, made him feel more alive than ever before. He was also aware that boxing released his anger and pent-up frustration.

Jack had a temper—to put it mildly. It had gotten him into trouble more than a few times when he was a kid. His father had always taken care of things, though. Usually, that meant a substantial donation to his school or a city program for children, maybe some swings in a park or a fountain for cooling off during the hot summer months.

Jack took to boxing like nobody's business. When he wasn't on duty, his fellow sailors found him in the gym practicing, hitting the punching bag, focusing on his footwork, and lifting weights. Soon, he reached the point where his coach had to caution him.

"Jack," he warned, "you've got a deadly left hook. And I mean that literally—deadly. You have to pay attention to it in the future. Anytime you're in a match. Anytime you're fooling around with the fellas.

CHAPTER FIFTEEN

Anytime you get mad and want to take a swing at somebody. You've got to keep in mind that you could seriously hurt someone. Maybe even kill them."

For years, things sailed along fine. Once, Jack had the opportunity to train with the Bureau of Investigation in the hopes of eliminating a spate of petty crime aboard ship. He took to police training like a natural and wondered if he'd missed the opportunity to do the job that was meant for him. Jack thought he'd like being a cop. But he had signed up with the U.S. Navy for the duration, so he reported back to his ship when his course on policing techniques ended. Over the months following his police training, Jack impressed his commanding officers. The plague of petty theft and card-game brawls decreased thanks to the skills Jack had acquired.

As the years passed, Jack continued to be promoted and steadily moved up in rank.

Then, on that fateful night last year in the Philippines, everything changed.

Chapter Sixteen

Syracuse, New York

Will searched through three years of telephone directories, making sure he checked all the outlying areas—Liverpool, Dewitt, Baldwinsville—and had not found Olivia's name.

The door opened and Byron's secretary entered with a steaming cup of coffee, small pitcher of milk, and sugar bowl on a tray. "I thought you could use a cup."

"That's very thoughtful of you. Thank you...I'm sorry, I don't know your name."

"It's Velma, Velma Michaels."

"Thank you, Miss Michaels."

"How are you coming along?" Velma glanced at the small pile of phone books in the middle of the table.

"It's slow because I have to page through all the suburbs."

"I've finished my work today," said Velma. "Would you like some help?"

"That'd be swell. Grab a seat." Will pushed three booklets across the table. "The name I'm looking for is Watson, Olivia Watson."

"And you don't know which part of town she lived in?"

CHAPTER SIXTEEN

Will shook his head.

For the next twenty minutes, the only sound was the rustling of pages as the policeman and secretary worked their way through the remainder of the directories. By three-thirty, all the telephone books had been pushed to the center of the table, and lay in a messy pile.

Velma looked at Will and made a face. "Is it good or bad that we didn't find her, Sergeant?"

Great Camp Onontaga, Adirondack Mountains

Steven finished updating Olivia on what Jack had told him. "He made it look like Victor was hiding his knowledge of poison. Jack doesn't want the killer to be one of the family. He'd much prefer it was Victor or an anonymous person who just happened to pass by."

"A stranger wandering around in the mountains in the middle of a blizzard?" Olivia said. "I don't think so."

"I told him that in so many words." Steven grabbed the chalk and boxed off an area on the improvised murder board. He wrote *Window of Opportunity Wednesday 9:00 p.m. - Thursday 6:00 p.m.* "Jack said Gil practiced playing Christmas carols after supper Wednesday night. So someone could have put the poison on the piano when everybody was sleeping or early in the morning before breakfast. People were in and out all day Thursday, so that's unlikely. The only other time the room would have been empty was when we went to our rooms and cabins to get ready for dinner, say between 5:00 and 6:00. The liquid holding the poison had to evaporate before we all returned, but I think the fires at both ends of the room would have made short work of that."

"I'd say when we were getting ready for dinner is most likely because it was the shortest amount of time the poison would have sat there. Leaving it on the keys all day Thursday would have been a bigger risk," said Olivia.

"Right. Too many chances of somebody accidentally brushing against it or of Gil sitting down at what the killer would have thought of as the wrong time," said Steven.

"Yeah. The killer probably knew about the do-not-touch rule. I bet he thought the chances of someone other than Gil touching the keys were zero to none."

"I agree. But, if the poison was put there on Wednesday night, it would have to have been Margery, Aunt Emily, or Jack. Maybe I'm wrong, but I can't see Aunt Emily killing her nephew. Why would she? And I don't see a motive for Jack at this point, although maybe he inherits everything."

"Why wouldn't Margery inherit? She's the widow," Olivia asked.

"She'll most likely get enough money to live on and the right to stay in the house in New York, but a man would leave his businesses to another man in the family. There's probably someone who will act as trustee for Margery."

Olivia scowled.

"Don't blame me. I didn't make the rules," Steven said, holding up his hand.

"Okay, fine," Olivia said, throwing him a dirty look. "We'll move past that for now…So, what if Jack's sick of life at sea? He's been in the Navy a long time. It must wear on you sooner or later. Maybe Jack wants to take over his brother's business. He might think it's easier or more interesting than what he's doing now."

"I still need to ask Lewis about the life of the poison. I'll do that now. Maybe it will change our thinking."

"Steven, what do you think about making a timeline of where everybody was during our window of opportunity?"

"Yeah, we do that at the station. But I want to find out what Lewis says about the poison first. It might change the way we're looking at it. Let's go back to the lodge. You can try to get more out of Jack while

CHAPTER SIXTEEN

I talk with Lewis."

In Cabin C, Victor McAllister lay on the couch smoking, sipping a brandy, and daydreaming. A fire warmed the room, making him drowsy. He closed his eyes and let his mind drift back to the night he met Irene.

It was the spring of 1930 at Leta Morris's debutante ball. He'd donned his tux, revved up his black Vauxhall 20/60—speeds up to seventy miles per hour!—and tooled over to Park Avenue to pick up his pal Gary Thack-Kemper. They hadn't been in the ballroom fifteen minutes when Victor saw her.

"Who's that?" he asked Gary, surreptitiously pointing. "The girl talking with Ellen Tuck French."

"That's Irene Racine. Her father owns The City Chronicle *and Racine Literary Press. She's only just started coming to these affairs. Word has it Racine keeps her on a tight leash. Nobody's good enough for his little girl."*

Victor pursed his lips and nodded slowly. "Not much to look at, but what the hell. I like a challenge. Any brothers and sisters?"

"What do you care about her siblings?"

"Figuring out who'll inherit when it's time for her old man to pop off."

"Inherit? You're thinking ahead." Gary took a drink of his Dom Pérignon.

"Needs must, old chap."

"She has a younger brother. I forget his name."

Victor stopped a passing waiter, set his half-full glass on the tray, and grabbed two flutes of champagne. As he approached Irene Racine and her friend, an older woman joined them. She said something Victor couldn't make out, then took Ellen Tuck French by the elbow and steered her toward John Jacob Aster, leaving Irene Racine alone. Perfect timing.

"Hello," Victor said, handing Irene the champagne. "I'm Victor McAllister. I don't think we've met."

Irene looked up at him and smiled. Victor nearly gasped at her eyes. They were such a deep brown that in the shadows of the ballroom, they looked black. He couldn't stop the image of being sucked into an abyss that flew through his mind.

"Irene Racine." *She held out her gloved hand.*

Never looking away from her gaze, Victor bent and kissed the air above her fingers.

They stayed together the entire evening. Monday morning, Victor sent a dozen red roses. On Tuesday, he sent a messenger with his calling card and a note. The messenger returned to Victor's apartment with an affirmative—Miss Racine would see him at four o'clock.

By autumn, Victor knew Irene had fallen in love with him. He did his best to act appropriately, though never committing himself. When he took up with another girl, he made sure it was out of town, in a place none of their set frequented, so word wouldn't get back to Irene.

But, somewhere along the way, at some point during the past four years, everything changed. One day, Victor realized he had actually grown fond of Irene. And, one night last summer, it hit him like a freight train. He had fallen in love with Irene Racine.

Now, Gil Racine was dead. And nothing stood in his way anymore.

In the main lodge, Olivia made a beeline for Jack, who stood at the bar cart pouring a drink. Hearing the oak floorboards creak, he looked up.

"Hello, Olivia. Can I fix you something?"

"Sure, how about a gin and tonic?"

"You got it."

"I hear we've got a swell ice skating rink thanks to you, Jack."

"Yup, if anyone feels like going out, it's all shipshape. Although it's getting dark, so maybe tomorrow would make more sense."

"I agree." Olivia chuckled. "I like that Navy expression you used.

CHAPTER SIXTEEN

Haven't heard that in a long time."

"Do you spend time with a lot of sailors, then?" Jack asked.

Olivia laughed. "No, that's not what I meant. My grandfather was in the Navy. He always sprinkled his conversations with sailors' jargon. You reminded me of him."

Jack handed Olivia her drink. "Why don't we sit by the fire?"

They commandeered the club chairs in the empty dining area. Olivia pulled hers closer to the fire and turned it so she faced Jack.

"Where will you go next, Jack? On your new assignment?"

The simple question caused Jack to freeze and sent his mind fleeing.

Unfortunately for Jack, his executive officer happened to be walking by the Philippine bar at the moment when Jack hit the sailor and had witnessed everything. The man had no choice but to report it. Jack was charged with involuntary manslaughter and given a dishonorable discharge from the Navy. He never knew why he hadn't been thrown in jail, but had never been more grateful for anything in his life. He'd felt bad about what happened to the young man and wondered who he was and how his family was coping, but as time passed, he no longer thought about him. He had enough challenges in his own life now.

When the ship docked in California, Jack decided to stay on the West Coast, as far away from his family as possible. If his brother Gil ever found out, there would be hell to pay. For the past year and a half, Jack Racine, former commander of a Navy vessel and pampered son of New York City royalty, had worked as a stevedore on the docks, first in San Francisco then, as the Depression worsened and traffic slowed, across the bay in Oakland. Given the economic climate of the country, Jack knew he was lucky to have a job. He lived as best as he could, but it was a lousy apartment in a rough neighborhood. Ironically, his boxing skills came in handy after all.

"Your next assignment, Jack?" Olivia repeated her question, hoping for a clue to the odd look on his face. Asking again seemed to shake him out of his reverie.

He took a swig of his drink. "I'm not sure. There's talk of Pearl Harbor. Have you heard of it?"

Olivia gulped. "Yes, I've seen pictures of Hawaii. It looks beautiful. Lots of bright colors and palm trees."

"That's what I heard, too. I've been thinking about retiring when this tour of duty's over. I've put in enough years for my pension. Maybe if I like Pearl Harbor, I'll stay there, live in Hawaii for good. I've had enough snow and cold weather. Sunshine three hundred days a year sounds pretty good to me."

Whenever Olivia found herself in a conversation like this, her heart skipped a beat. Jack's idea of moving to Pearl Harbor was innocent from his point of view. After all, how could he know what was coming?

This was one of the more difficult things 21st-century Olivia Watson had to contend with when she time-traveled to Steven's 1934. There was nothing she could say or do, no hints she could drop without giving it all away. In a few short years, the world would be at war. And Pearl Harbor would forever be linked with President Roosevelt's pronouncement: *December 7, 1941, a day which will live in infamy.* Over two thousand American service personnel killed, more than one thousand wounded. Would Jack be one of them? Olivia had to swallow the discomfort and fear and simply listen, and Olivia Watson wasn't good at *not* saying something.

She tried to sound normal. "What will you do when you leave the Navy?"

"I don't know. Something outdoors. Maybe construction work. I like the idea of Roosevelt's Civilian Conservation Corps. I wonder if they have that over there. Probably not, since Hawaii's not a state, but we have the base there, so maybe. Wouldn't it be swell to work in a

CHAPTER SIXTEEN

forest all day long?"

Olivia laughed. "You've got a whole forest right here, if that's what you want to do. Move to Onontaga." She took a sip of her drink and changed the subject. "What was it like when you got back to your ship after training with the Bureau of Investigation? Did the men treat you differently?"

Jack's eyes grew larger and he grinned. "In all the years since, I don't think anyone's asked me that question. Is this what Steven means about your journalistic skills?" He chuckled. "Well, alright, *Miss Watson*. I'll play along." He took another drink of his Scotch, the amber color sparkling in the firelight. "At first, the fellas didn't know what to make of it. They had no idea what I'd learned or how things might change. They soon found out different. We were trained to stand our ground when confronting a suspect. I had a lot of petty theft to deal with and sometimes that led to brawls. All I can say is I followed orders and did my job. After a month or so, the thieving stopped. I did some boxing, so I've got some strength in these arms." He held up his arm like a bodybuilder, formed a fist, and flexed, although Olivia couldn't see anything beneath the thick woolen sweater.

"Boxing is one of those difficult sports, though, isn't it? I mean, you have to be careful how hard you hit and where it lands," Olivia observed. "I've heard of people whose brains are permanently damaged. Or worse."

Jack's face grew dark. The fleeting moment only lasted a few seconds, but in that time, the transformation frightened Olivia, causing her throat to go dry.

What has he done? she wondered.

Written with a wood-burning tool, the sign above the door read *Black Spruce*. Steven knocked, and Lewis opened the door a crack.

"Oh, Steven, it's you. Come in."

The drapes were drawn. Steven noticed Lewis's tussled hair, then an indentation in the mattress and pillow.

"Apologies for disturbing your nap," Steven said.

"That's alright. I had a good rest. Didn't get much sleep last night, though. I imagine no one did. What can I do for you?"

"I'm trying to pin down the time when Gil's killer..."

Lewis winced.

"...had the opportunity to deposit the poison on the piano keys. Do you know how long potassium cyanide would remain viable after it was mixed in water, then the water evaporated?"

"As long as there was residue left to be transferred, I should think." Lewis returned to the bed and sat on the edge. He rubbed a hand over his face, then pulled his fingers through his hair—gray liberally mixed with brown—making it stand on end. "Do you have any idea yet who it was?" Steven thought the doctor had aged in the past twenty-four hours.

"No. It takes time."

Lewis reached for a pack of Chesterfields. He clicked his lighter and inhaled. "I wish I could help you, Steven, but I'm out of my depth here. I *know* these people. They're like family. Well, actually Margery *is* family."

"Olivia mentioned that you're cousins?"

"That's right. Distant cousins, although I've known her since she was born. We grew up together. She doesn't have any brothers or sisters—well, there was a brother who died in infancy and a sister who died during the influenza pandemic in '18. I'm a couple years older. I've always felt protective of her, like an older brother."

"How's she coping?" Steven asked.

The shadow of a smile touched his lips. Lewis said, "Margery needs to be busy. All the time. She's not happy unless she's organizing something, or starting a new project, or entertaining a houseful of

CHAPTER SIXTEEN

guests."

Steven found it interesting that Lewis spoke of Margery's personality rather than her emotions at a time like this.

"Jack hinted that Gil and Margery didn't have what you'd call a passionate marriage, that perhaps they didn't love each other."

"They had an arranged marriage, like many people did back then. Gil genuinely cared for her, and I think she grew fond of him over the years. She always supported him in his work, entertaining business associates and so forth. And he never objected to all her committees."

"Do you know if either of them strayed outside the marriage?" Steven hadn't been sure how to phrase this, but evidently, he'd succeeded because Lewis answered without hesitation.

"I doubt it. Gil was simply too busy and, frankly, too tired at night to have the energy. He worked long hours and didn't get home until ten or eleven some nights. And as I said, I believe he loved her. And Margery...." He shook his head. "That would be out of character for her."

Steven left Lewis sitting on his bed, smoking, and went down into Gil Racine's study to place a call to his partner in Knightsbridge.

At his desk in the CID room, Will picked up on the first ring.

"Steven, how are you making out up there?"

Steven updated Will. "I hope my father will have something to add tomorrow when I talk to him. By the way, if I can't get a connection here because of the storm, he may try to get in touch with you."

"Sure, that's fine. We don't have much, but here goes. We confirmed that Margery Racine is busy most days with her volunteer work; she seems devoted to the organizations you mentioned. I met with Lee Shubert today for lunch." Will explained the circumstances preventing Shubert from talking on the phone and that Syracuse was the theater owner's hometown. "He told me Lewis Salisbury always accompanies

Mrs. Racine to the theater, and they go at least twice a month. He never witnessed anything to indicate a romantic relationship, but he said they appeared very close. *Very.*"

"Interesting, but we found out they're cousins." Steven explained what he and Olivia had learned. "What else?"

"Lewis Salisbury has a private practice in Manhattan. He's not wealthy, but he's well-off. Pete tracked down some information on Emily Racine. She's the sister to the Racine brothers' father, Claude. She's a spinster, never married. She's wealthy, inherited a bundle from *their* dad, lives in Brooklyn. Pete said she doesn't flaunt her wealth, but she lives near the Brooklyn Academy of Music, which she helps support with generous donations." Will cleared his throat, then continued.

"Nothing on Gil Racine's two kids or on Victor McAllister. Jimmy came up empty on Jack Racine—nothing beyond what you told him this morning. But Harry Racine seems to be quite the traveler. And an excellent photographer. His photographs have appeared in *Life* and *National Geographic*. It's no easy feat to get your work accepted in those magazines. Harry also belongs to The Adventurers' Club in New York. According to a manager or concierge, he's traveled all over the world, mostly in dangerous or exotic places. He stops in for drinks and dinner once in a while when he's in town. He's quiet. Sits alone but, when approached, he gets along with the other members. The concierge hadn't heard of any problems. Or at least he didn't share any. You know how those places are, Steven. They protect their own."

"Thanks, Will. That's a lot considering you had to do everything long distance, and it's been less than a day," Steven said.

"Yeah, but where does it get us?" his partner asked.

As Will hung up the receiver, his thoughts went to the other investigation—his secret, unofficial one into Olivia. Frowning, he shook his head. How was he going to tell his partner and best friend

CHAPTER SIXTEEN

that Olivia Watson was a fraud…or worse, a spy?

Chapter Seventeen

Great Camp Onontaga, Adirondack Mountains

They walked companionably in the moonlight, the snow clouds having blown away. The air, though cold, smelled fresh and clean. Icy wind scoured their throats. They heard the snort of a deer, and once, a gray fox, with his flat smiling face, ran across the path in front of them. But they were alone in the night, silence surrounding them, the snow having muffled any sound. They reached the lake.

"Let's go check the tip-ups while we're out here."

"You know, you were right. It is a nice night for a walk. I'd rather stay off the lake, though. What if somebody was harvesting ice and didn't mark the spot? We could fall in. Let's go over to the trail in the woods. It'll be easier. Not as much snow under the trees," said Julian.

"Aw, come on. I remember how much you loved ice fishing when you were a kid."

"Seems like a long time ago." Julian flicked the end of his cigarette with a finger, sending a spiral of sparks off to the side. He sighed. "Yeah, okay."

They walked out onto the ice for several hundred yards. Julian's companion went around to the far side of what was evidently a fishing

CHAPTER SEVENTEEN

hole next to a flagged marker and peered down into a black abyss. "What was I thinking? It's too dark. I thought maybe the moon, but… come here and look. Tell me if you see anything."

Pulling his glove from a pocket where he'd shoved it while smoking, Julian Racine walked across the ice to where the opening should have been. Without warning, he plunged straight down into the frigid lake, arms shooting above his head like an arrow, glove flying. He disappeared, then bobbed up, flailing, screaming.

"Help me. Give me your hand."

He managed to squeeze one arm and shoulder up out of the hole, but the opening was too small for him to maneuver the other one out and onto the surface of the ice. The bulk of his body remained submerged. Julian's heavy water-logged jacket weighed him down, and the freezing water was already affecting his ability to move.

Julian's killer pulled the metal marker out of the ice, where it had been shifted earlier that day, and thrust the pointed end into the collar of Julian's jacket. The killer intended to hold Julian's head under the water, but the tip punctured Julian's jacket, and the razor-sharp edges bit into his neck. Julian screamed again as he was pushed back under the water. The killer kept the pressure on while watching the bubbles from Julian's breathing decrease and the ripples in the water still. It didn't take long. Julian's head popped back up, but his lifeless eyes saw nothing.

The killer used the pole to smooth out the snow where they'd trod, then reinserted the marker into the ice where it originally stood. Under a calm moonlit sky, Julian Racine's killer returned to the Great Camp and quietly slipped inside while everyone slept.

Chapter Eighteen

Saturday, December 15, 1934

Great Camp Onontaga, Adirondack Mountains

Steven and Olivia awoke to another gray day. Hearing the howl of the wind, Olivia jumped out of bed and peeked around the curtains. Heavy clouds shredded the sky as they raced above the forest. It wouldn't be long before it snowed again.

She grabbed some fresh clothes and went to take a hot shower. Standing in the steam-filled bathroom, she let her mind drift as water pelted her back. Who could have killed Gil Racine? The people here this weekend were his family and friends, for heaven's sake. What grievance could have pushed someone to murder? Who hated him that much?

In the short time they'd spent with Gil, he'd seemed like a nice man. Olivia had enjoyed his sense of humor and intelligence and had delighted in his childlike passion for Christmas. She admired his work ethic, although he'd probably worked too much. Steven had thought highly of Gil, and Steven was an excellent judge of character. Because of their shared love of art and Gil's admiration for Evangeline's paintings, Steven and his mother had maintained a close

CHAPTER EIGHTEEN

relationship with Gil Racine.

Naturally, Gil would have acted differently when it came to business; after all, no one achieved his level of wealth and success in the corporate world without making enemies. But how could he have enemies among the people here this weekend? His wife? Olivia couldn't picture elegant, put-together Margery sprinkling cyanide on the piano keys in the middle of the night. His adoring daughter? The anguish in Irene's voice when Gil toppled off the piano bench had cut through the atmosphere in the room like a razor through flesh. That hadn't been faked.

Although Steven disagreed, Olivia thought Victor was too smart to have committed the murder, knowing it would risk and likely destroy his relationship with Irene if she found out—and people *always* find out.

Gil's younger brother Harry seemed happy traveling the world. Moving back to the States on a permanent basis would mean living in his apartment in the Racine mansion in noisy, crowded New York City, forgoing the excitement and danger his current lifestyle offered, and on which he seemed to thrive. According to Mrs. Buckley, the cook, Harry had always loved taking risks.

Hmmm. Taking risks. Olivia remembered the conversation she and Steven had had yesterday. The killer took tremendous risks when he poisoned Gil Racine. Maybe Harry had the personality most aligned with murder.

And what about Jack? Nearly ten years working as a reporter had honed Olivia's skills of observation and her understanding of people. Jack was a man with a secret—at least one—and she was certain it had something to do with boxing. There had been no mistaking the shadow that crossed his face or the dark look that lingered in his eyes. Olivia made a mental note to find out what had happened—but to tread very carefully at the same time, just in case.

Finally, there was Julian and his unpublished novel. Olivia hadn't formed an opinion of Gil's son yet. Had he inherited his father's ruthlessness? How far would he go to get his novel published?

Olivia decided Julian would be her target this morning. It would be easy talking with him about writing—she'd been doing it for years. As she dressed, she realized she was looking forward to her conversation with Julian Racine.

When they entered the main lodge shortly after eight, Steven saw most of the family and the Great Camp's guests already at the table eating breakfast.

"Good morning, everyone," he and Olivia said at the same time. They looked at each other and smiled.

Steven headed straight for the buffet, where he filled his plate with eggs, sausages, home fries, and toast.

"All I want right now is coffee," said Olivia.

They selected two seats toward one end, Olivia next to Margery at the head of the table and Steven on her other side next to Harry.

After several minutes of silence, while Olivia sipped her coffee and Steven ate, Steven turned to Harry and said, "I'm interested in the photographs you take on those exotic adventures of yours, Harry. Do you keep them in albums?"

"I do have some albums, and some are in boxes. Since the war ended, I sell most of my photographs to magazines."

"I think I heard that. Impressive! How does it work?"

"It started because of the war." Harry swallowed hard. Steven and Olivia waited while he composed himself. "I enlisted in the Army and, after basic training, I was attached to a unit as a photographer. When I was working near the front line in Northern France, I met a Brit. Later, he introduced me to Howard Carter." He smiled. "Do you want the long version or the short version?"

CHAPTER EIGHTEEN

"Howard Carter, the archaeologist?" Olivia exclaimed. "Oh, my goodness! Are you about to say what I think you're going to say?" She leaned forward, peeking around Steven. "The long version, Harry, please. Wait. Steven, switch seats with me. I don't want to miss a word of this."

Harry laughed while Olivia changed places with Steven.

"All set, Olivia?" Harry's eyes sparkled. "Okay, long version...so Howard had recently renewed his agreement with Lord Carnarvon. One of his photographers became ill and he needed to replace him. I was in the right place at the right time."

Olivia gasped. "Were you there when they opened the tomb?"

Steven interrupted. "I'm sorry to sound like I don't keep up with current events because I do. But these names don't ring a bell."

Harry shrugged, as if to say many people didn't recognize the now-famous names. "Do you want to tell him, Olivia, or shall I?"

Olivia took a deep breath. "Egypt. 1922. King Tutankhamun. Valley of the Kings. King Tut's tomb!" Her face glowed. "Oh, Harry, tell us everything. I've always been fascinated by ancient Egypt."

For the next half hour, Harry had Olivia on the edge of her seat with his story of the discovery of King Tut's tomb and his role in recording the event in photographs. If there was one place she could time travel to, it would be the Valley of the Kings on November 4, 1922. Olivia asked question after question. "Do you have any of those pictures here at Onontaga, Harry? I'd love to see them."

"I've kept a box in my cabin. I can show you later."

Although she was bursting to shout out *Awesome!* Olivia said, "That'd be swell."

Irene entered the dining area, approached Margery, and kissed her mother on the cheek.

Margery squeezed her daughter's hand. "Are you sleeping alright, sweetheart?"

Irene made a face. "I got a few hours." She headed to the sideboard, poured herself a cup of coffee, then filled half a bowl with oatmeal and sprinkled some raisins on top. She chose the seat across from Harry, next to her great-aunt. "How are you doing today, Aunt Emily?" She rubbed her aunt's arm. "I know Dad was special to you. Are you okay?"

"Not much makes a dent at my age, dear. Tragic though this is, it's a fact that we all have to go some time. It was your father's time. That's all. I'll mourn him when I get back to the city." She patted Irene's hand.

Victor entered and went straight to Irene. "Did you sleep?"

"Some." She poured whole milk into her bowl, added several spoons of sugar, and began to eat.

For some time, the only sounds were the clinking of silverware and the wind rattling the windows.

"Is Julian up yet, Mother?" Irene asked.

"Not yet. I'll go wake him if he's not down by the time we're finished. He can't sleep all morning, even though it is the weekend. We have guests, after all. I'd like him to organize a skating outing today."

"I'd like to go ice skating," Olivia said. "Especially after all the effort Jack put into clearing a spot for us."

"That's right," Steven exclaimed. "I'll go with you."

"Sounds good to me, too," said Lewis. "I always like getting fresh air. Although," he grimaced, "that wind sounds like a freight train!" He pushed back his chair. "Margery, I'm finished. I'll go wake Julian."

"Thank you, Lewis."

As Lewis mounted the stairs to the bedrooms above, Rider entered with a large pot of coffee, which he added to the urn. He checked the various breakfast items under their silver domes, then left.

Lewis re-entered the room. "He's not there. Must have gone out

CHAPTER EIGHTEEN

early." He peered out the front windows onto the porch. "He's not outside smoking. Maybe he went for a walk."

"Julian? Go out in this wind? He likes walking, but even he wouldn't go out in this. Besides, it's too cold," Irene exclaimed. "He might be in the kitchen with Mrs. Buckley. Sometimes, she makes something special for him."

Rider returned with a rack of hot toast.

"Rider, is Julian in the kitchen?" Margery asked.

"No, ma'am. I haven't seen him this morning."

Steven's cop instincts roared into full alert. He set down his fork and went to the front entrance. Opening the heavy door, he leaned out and looked left, right, and down the stairs. Fresh, untouched snow. Not a footprint in sight. If he had left the Great Camp this morning, Julian hadn't gone out this way. Although, Steven reminded himself, the force of the wind could have covered Julian's tracks.

He crossed the room to the back hallway, entered the kitchen, then opened the back door and scanned the ground. As far as he could see, the freshly fallen snow had not been disturbed by human footprints. Steven swallowed hard. *No, please, not another one. Especially Julian. How will Margery survive, losing both her husband and her son in two days' time?*

Doris Buckley, curious about what Steven was doing, left the stove where she'd been stirring a pot of something that smelled delicious. "Can I help you, sir?"

"Have you seen Julian this morning, Mrs. Buckley?" Steven asked.

"No, he usually sleeps a bit late, sir."

By the time Steven returned to the dining area, Margery Racine was pacing the large room, mumbling, "Where could he be? Where could he have gone? This isn't like Julian. Maybe one of the cabins? But why?" She looked up when Steven came in.

Steven thought she looked ready to break down. "We need to

organize a search party. I don't see any footprints near the front door or the back. I'm going to run up to his room for a minute. Margery, which room is Julian's?"

"Balsam Fir. Second on your left."

Steven noticed she was trembling. Lewis went to her and put his arm around her shoulders. He whispered something Steven couldn't hear.

"Everybody, go get your heaviest outer clothes. Divide up into teams of two. I'll coordinate a search when I come back," he said.

Steven ran up the staircase, taking two steps at a time, then opened the door to the empty bedroom. The sheets, blanket, and quilt were pulled all the way up to the top of Julian's bed. Two pillows stood against the headboard. Steven slid his hand under the covers. If Julian had slept here last night, there was no warmth left on the mattress now. He looked in the closet and found several items of clothing hanging on the bar. A small suitcase sat on the shelf above. Steven checked the dresser. Folded woolen sweaters filled one drawer; underwear and socks, another.

Is there any way he could have left without leaving tracks in the snow? As soon as the question entered his mind, Steven answered it. *No.*

Back in the great room, Steven surveyed the group of silent people, all bundled up except Margery Racine, who sat by the fire wringing her hands as though any minute she was going to jump out of her skin, and Aunt Emily, who was attempting to console her late-nephew's wife. Rider had joined the group, muffled in a long scarf, bulky jacket, and knit hat. "I want to help, Detective."

"Thank you, Rider. By the way, is there an attic or cellar that I don't know about?"

"No, sir, neither."

"Is there someplace I should look?" Steven persisted.

"No, Detective, not here in the lodge. Of course, you know there's

CHAPTER EIGHTEEN

the garage and the cabins we're not using, but why would Mister Julian go to any of those places? And didn't I hear you say there aren't any footprints outside?" said Rider.

Steven turned back to the volunteers. Everyone had paired up and was waiting side-by-side in three distinct groups—Rider and Lewis, Irene and Victor, Jack and Harry. He and Olivia would make the fourth search party. Steven laid a large piece of paper on the table. He sketched and labeled Onontaga and the circular drive in front, the lake behind the Great Camp, and, to the right, the garage, six cabins, and a small stable strung out along the lane. There, at the entrance to the forest, he sketched the path they'd taken on their sleigh ride Thursday.

"Jack and Harry, you fellas are probably the most familiar with the property. Look at my map and tell me what makes sense for four separate groups."

Jack indicated the area with which Steven was familiar. "People don't always stay on the path. If Julian went for a walk, he might have strayed off the trail and gotten disoriented in the forest. I'd say look for a sign that he went into the woods."

"We'll take that," Lewis said.

Olivia noticed Irene frowning and shaking her head. Julian's sister still didn't believe her brother went out for a stroll in the wind and frigid temperature.

"Hand me your pencil, Steven," said Harry, and he drew a second path, which started out parallel to the first one, then veered off to the far right. "This trail goes about a mile. It's worth checking."

"I know that area. Victor and I'll go there," said Irene.

"What about along the shore and around part of the lake?" Olivia asked.

"We could establish a middle point, then Olivia and I take one half, and Harry and Jack take the other side," Steven suggested.

"That's almost a hundred miles if you follow the shoreline," Jack exclaimed. "There's no way we can cover the whole thing."

"Hey, Jack, remember the bench Gil had made for the lookout?" Harry said. "Maybe Julian went over there."

"That's an idea," Jack said.

"Show me where you mean, Harry," said Steven.

As his brother pointed out the spot, Jack continued, "Harry, the two of us could go there, then make our way through the woods." He looked at Steven. "There's a trail that will take us out to the access road about a half- or three-quarters of a mile down. It's the drive we all took to get here. It leads right to the front door."

"Yeah, piece of cake. We used to trek through there as kids all the time. I remember the way," Harry said.

"Alright, how about if Olivia and I walk around the other side of the lake for about forty minutes, then turn back?" Steven suggested. "At least we'll have covered a portion of it."

"We can keep an eye *on* the lake as well, Steven. Although I don't know why Julian would go out on the ice," Olivia said. "Does everybody know how to snowshoe?"

"Been doing it since we were boys, huh, Harry?" Jack said.

"This will be my first time, but I'll do it. Irene can show me how," said Victor.

Jack slapped him on the back. "Good for you. That's the spirit."

"Okay, we have our plan. Is somebody in each pair wearing a watch?" Steven asked.

A hand in each group went up.

"Good. I've got one, too," Steven said. "It's nearly nine-thirty. Let's meet back here at eleven."

"That should be enough time," Harry said. "It'll be slow going in some spots."

"What are we going to do when we find him? What if he's hurt and

CHAPTER EIGHTEEN

can't walk back with us?" said Irene, her voice filled with worry.

"Rider, do you keep any kind of emergency whistles here?" Steven asked.

"I can make a shrill whistle you'll be able to hear for miles," Victor said.

"So can I," said Jack.

"I'll go in the kitchen and grab a couple of pots and heavy metal spoons," said Rider. "We can make a racket with those. And I'll get some coffee, too. We'll need it."

Rider returned with four backpacks, two with a pot and metal spoon, each carrying a Thermos with hot coffee.

"Everybody ready?" said Jack, reaching toward the entry. He turned the knob, and a gust of wind grabbed the door, slamming it against the wall. Replies to Jack's question were buried in the crash and the screaming wind.

Chapter Nineteen

"Steven, I have a bad feeling about this," Olivia said after they'd struck out along the shore.

"Me, too. I can't come up with any reasonable explanation of where Julian might have gone, or more importantly, *how* he could have left without leaving at least some footprints. The wind might have blown away most, but there should be some sign of him leaving."

"We've been talking as though he went out this morning, but if he went for a walk last night—and I'm with Irene on this, I think it was too cold—the snow that fell overnight would have covered his footprints. Do you think there's a chance he left this morning and used the snow blower to cover the path he took?"

Steven stopped dead in his tracks. "But why? Are you saying Julian may have killed his father?"

"I don't know. Maybe. Maybe the fact that Gil rejected his manuscript was all it took, and he snapped."

"That can't be why Gil was killed. Over a book? No, I don't believe it. Besides, someone would have heard the snow-blowing machine, wouldn't they? That thing makes a lot of noise." He frowned. "Although, we probably would've thought it was Rider or Jack clearing another area. Olivia, are you saying he left the lodge, took the snow-blowing machine, filled in his footsteps—or at least blew snow all over the area to cover his footprints—and then…went where?"

CHAPTER NINETEEN

"I don't know. Maybe he thought he had a better chance of escaping before you worked it out," Olivia said. "Did anyone look to see if it was in the garage or wherever they keep it?"

"No, I didn't think of it. Damn! I guess we'll have to wait to check until we get back." He shot her a look. "I could use one of your cell phones now." He stepped over a fallen tree branch. "But, coming back to Julian...I could see Jack or Harry making a run for it. Even Lewis. They're all physical, athletic men. They'd have the strength to endure a trek to freedom after cutting a path in the snow. I can picture any of the three of them grabbing that machine and tearing out of here, then making their way to a town or train station. But Julian seems soft. I know they've said he enjoys walking, but that's not the same as escaping from the middle of the forest during a blizzard after you've killed someone. When I think of him, I picture him in a library reading or in a study writing. He doesn't appear to have much stamina. And what would he do after he cleared a path? He'd have to come back here and get his car. No, Olivia, I can't see any of that happening."

"Those are all good points."

They trudged on through the deep snow, the icy air tearing at their throats.

"So if he didn't run away, and he didn't get stuck walking in the snowstorm, do you think that whoever killed Gil murdered Julian, too?" Olivia shivered in her heavy clothing. "God, Steven, what kind of person are we looking for?"

"If that's what happened, we're looking for somebody who's desperate. And that's the scariest thing about this. Because desperate people do desperate things. Rash, dangerous things."

"I'm going to hope we find him injured, Steven. Maybe Irene's wrong, and he did go for a walk. He got lost, then tripped over a log and fell and sprained his ankle or something. Maybe the wind destroyed his footprints, or the snowfall covered them. I don't want to think of that young guy, with his whole life and potentially a successful writing career ahead of him, lying out here dead. Maybe I'm not ready to be your unofficial partner after all, Detective Blackwell."

"Irene, can you slow down, please?" Victor struggled through the deep snow. "You know I've never done this before."

"Lift your feet higher. That should help. And, no, I can't slow down, Victor. My brother's out here someplace. He could be bleeding. Or hurt. Or God knows what."

"I've only ever heard you complain about Julian, Irene. What's the rush?"

Irene stopped dead and maneuvered her snowshoes around so she faced him. "What's the rush? Are you kidding me? Tell me you didn't have anything to do with this." She nailed him with a stare.

"Are you crazy? Of course, I didn't. Jeez, Irene, don't you know me by now?"

"Sometimes, I'm not so sure." She glared, then turned and set off again.

Victor reached out and grabbed her arm. "Hey," he said softly. "Stop a minute." He took a step closer but could not draw her into the hug he desired because of the large snowshoes. "Hey," he whispered. "You've been like a wind-up doll ever since Steven said we should come out here and search."

"Victor, if I stop moving, I'll fall apart."

He looked into her eyes and saw fear. She was trembling. "We'll find him, Irene. He can't have gone far. We'll find him, and then he'll tell us why he left and what he's up to. You know Julian can be a bit of a spoiled child. Don't worry. He'll be alright."

"I can't lose Julian, Victor. Not after Daddy. I can't. We *have* to find him."

CHAPTER NINETEEN

Lewis and Rider had been walking for half an hour. They agreed early on that the best way to cover the area was to stay on the path together for a short distance, then they would take turns entering the forest on each side of the trail and search that section. While one of them searched, the other would stay on the trail, acting as a beacon for their partner to return to the main path. They didn't want to lose sight of each other and make the situation worse, needing to be rescued. Hopefully, Julian had tripped and fallen, then couldn't get up, or had been attacked by an animal and was somehow hanging on. So far, they had discovered nothing.

"Hey," Lewis shouted. "Rider, look over there. It looks like a man in dark clothes."

Rider squinted and followed the direction of the doctor's finger. "Yes! That's definitely something there."

They hurried as fast as their snowshoes allowed, glad they were expert at the sport. Lewis arrived at the sighting first.

A large branch had fallen and, from a distance, the partially snow-covered limb had created the illusion of a man in a brown jacket and pants.

Both men sagged, breathing hard from their rush to know if it was Julian.

"What do you think has happened to Mr. Julian, Dr. Salisbury?" Rider asked.

Lewis closed his eyes and shook his head. "I don't know, Rider, but I don't think it's going to be good. My God, what's happening to us this weekend? I don't understand any of this. First, Gil's murdered. Now, his son is missing."

"Tell me the truth, Jack. What do you think is going on?"

Brothers Jack and Harry Racine had made good time covering a fair distance along the western shore and had stopped to catch their breath. Jack brushed the snow off the Adirondack bench, made with branches from local trees, and they sat.

"The truth, little brother, is I have no idea. Gil could be a bastard in business, we both know that, but there aren't any business rivals up here." Jack scowled. "Unless they've camped out someplace here in the woods, which is ridiculous and I sincerely doubt. And what about Julian? Even he isn't that crazy about walking to go out in this weather. It's too damn cold. And he's so skinny, he'd have to fight this wind to stay on his feet or it'd blow him away. None of this makes any sense."

Harry interrupted. "We don't know that anything's happened to Julian yet."

"That's true. But where the hell is he?"

Harry shrugged. "I don't even have a guess. Tell me what you think about Victor. Gil wasn't going to let Irene marry him. That relationship's been going on for nearly four years now. How long can the guy wait?"

"When he's waiting for a lot of money, probably a long time," Jack said.

"Do you think he loves her?"

"How should I know? I haven't had a dame for longer than one night since I joined up. You don't think about those things when you're picturing life in the Navy, do you?"

"Don't ask me. I'm never around long enough to start anything. None of the girls I've met wanted to hang around waiting while I took off for the Arctic or the Sahara Desert. Can't say I blame them. I'm not a very good catch. Can't stay still long enough," said Harry.

"Who do *you* think killed Gil?" Jack asked.

"Not a clue. If they hadn't figured out that business about the poison, I would have sworn he had a heart attack. Damn, Jack. It's got to be one of us!"

CHAPTER NINETEEN

After they'd left Onontaga, Jack and Harry agreed that since they were experienced and the snow cover wasn't too deep under the tree canopy, they'd overshoot their target, then double back before entering the forest. Moving fast, they estimated they'd be able to cover close to four or five miles by the time they returned to the lodge. They knew Julian wasn't athletic. It was unlikely he had gone farther than that, but they wanted to be sure. They rose to walk the next half-mile along the frozen lake before turning back and joining the forest trail.

Steven and Olivia had walked nearly forty minutes when they spied a large tree limb that had fallen, making it the perfect bench seat.

"Steven, can we stop and catch our breath? This deep snow is a lot harder to navigate than I thought it would be. I'm in good shape, and I figured my daily runs would've prepared me for this, but it's a completely different challenge."

"At least you exercise every day. Look at me. I spend most of my time tracking down suspects and doing paperwork. This is a good reminder to get to the YMCA a few times a week and do something to keep fit."

He brushed the snow off the log, and they sat. Olivia reached into the backpack that Steven carried and extracted the Thermos of hot coffee. She poured some into the small cup, took a sip, then handed it to Steven.

"Do you think we'll find Julian alive?" Olivia asked. "It won't take long in these frigid temperatures for hypothermia to set in. He could easily freeze to death. Nobody mentioned anything about a shelter somewhere on the grounds. An old treehouse they used when they were kids. A cabin for hunters. A blind for duck hunting. Something!"

"There are lean-tos scattered throughout the forest, all over the mountains here."

"What are those?"

"Small three-sided cabins built out of rough logs. They provide shelter to hikers during unexpected snow squalls. Sometimes, surprise snowstorms hit even in September. But, to answer your question," he shook his head sadly, "no, I don't think we're going to find him alive. It would be a miracle. I'm just hoping we find him at all. He might have been injured, and if he was bleeding, the scent would attract animals. There are wolves, bobcats, lynx, coyotes. Any of them or a pack could have made off with him."

Olivia shuddered. "Oh, God! Don't even say that. I can't imagine what this is going to be like for Margery and Irene. How do you keep going after something like this?"

Steven nodded, but said nothing.

Olivia took a deep breath and looked up at the sky. "It looks like the wind might blow some clouds away. We could see some sun. That'd be a nice change."

"Something to offer a bit of cheer. Although that's going to be thin on the ground. I should be used to this after fifteen years on the force, but this one hits close to home. The Racines were committed to supporting my mother's work, and Gil was a friend."

Olivia took off her mittens and held his face with her bare hands. "How many times have you told me the thing to do is focus and work the scene? That's what we do now. And, hey," she said with excitement in her voice, "you'll be talking with your father in a little while, and maybe Will, too. That should cheer you up. Hopefully, your father'll give you a reason to cross Jack off the list. That will get us closer."

Steven took a last drink of coffee and passed the cup to her. "Let's get this done."

They turned and headed back the way they came.

"Steven, do you think we should walk out on the lake on the way back?" Olivia asked. "I don't know why Julian would wander out onto the ice, but I keep thinking of all these ice-fishing holes. What if he

CHAPTER NINETEEN

got disoriented and accidentally walked onto the lake? What if some of those markers with the little flags on top got blown over, and he couldn't tell where the openings were?"

"The holes the fishermen make are only about a foot in diameter at the most. Even someone as skinny as Julian couldn't fall in."

"That's good to know," Olivia said.

"I do think your idea of snowshoeing out onto the lake is a good one, though. If Julian could come to harm on shore, the same can be said for on the ice. Let's go. But be very careful. We've got to look ahead to where we're going. We'll go slow."

Steven and Olivia inched their way onto the frozen lake. The wind, with nothing to break its assault, stung their faces and settled into their bones.

"Just so you know, when we get back, I'm going to stand in a hot shower for an hour," Olivia exclaimed.

"Ha! I'm coming in with you."

Twenty minutes later, across the expanse of ice, a portion of Great Camp Onontaga came into view as the shoreline curved. Huffing and puffing, Steven and Olivia stopped to survey what lay ahead. Thus far, they'd encountered no ice-fishing spots.

"You know what the problem is today?" Olivia asked.

"What's that?"

"The quality of the light."

"What do you mean?"

"Even with an occasional glimpse of the sun—which is more like a memory than the real thing, it's so weak—I can't tell the difference between a mound of snow or a flat surface. Somehow, all this white is creating an optical illusion. It looks like everything is on the same plane."

"Oh, I see what you mean. You're right."

They began moving again.

"Hey," Steven shouted. "There's a fisherman's flag and, tell me if I'm wrong, but isn't there something at the base of it?"

"Oh, God. I hope it's him, and he's still alive."

They reached the fishing site in no time. There at the base of the metal pole lay part of a man—his head lolling to the side, one shoulder and arm lying on the ice, and the rest of his body submerged in the water. It looked like Julian Racine had fallen in the hole, had got one arm out, and tried to extricate himself, but was unable.

"I feel like crying, but I don't want my tears to freeze," Olivia said.

Steven leaned over. "Look, his jacket's torn."

He reached out and opened the collar. Olivia gasped. A bloody gash on the side of Julian's neck told part of the story.

"Somebody stabbed this poor guy!" She pulled off a mitten and wiped her brimming eyes. "Steven, we sang Christmas carols with a killer. We had breakfast this morning with a monster. How could anyone do something as horrible as this, then act like nothing happened? What kind of person are we dealing with?"

"It was brutal. Look how big the circumference of this fishing hole is. Somebody enlarged it on purpose." Steven looked up at her, eyes burning with anger. "This was calculated. We've got a second murder."

Olivia dragged her arm up to the backpack on Steven's shoulders and pulled out the pan and metal spoon.

"Cover your ears," she said.

She banged the spoon back and forth inside several times. The harsh sound echoed across the frozen lake and faded into the forest on shore. A moment later, they heard banging from one pair, then a couple of shrill whistles. All the members of the search party had been informed.

"Olivia, would you go to the lodge and get the sled we used Thursday night? We need something to bring him back. And also a broom. I want to clear this area to see if the killer left anything behind. I'll wait

CHAPTER NINETEEN

here."

"Yes, but I'll take pictures first in case some of the others arrive before I return. You want a pristine scene, right?"

Steven smiled a ghost of a smile. "Like I said. Will better watch out." He extracted his notebook and pencil and, for the second time in less than forty-eight hours, sketched a crime scene.

Irene and Victor had reached the stable on their way back when they heard the noise. The snow in the lane fronting the cabins had been trampled, making it easier to navigate.

"Oh, my God," Irene whispered. She tore off her snowshoes and ran down the drive, around the far side of the lodge, and down to the lake, following the open path Jack had made the day before, guided by the sound of the banging pot.

Victor, glad to be done with the constraining snowshoes, did the same, then hurried after her.

Lewis and Rider had arrived back at the Great Camp ten minutes earlier. Rider went to his room to change and continue his duties as butler. The camp was redolent with the yeasty scent of rolls that Mrs. Buckley had made for a late morning coffee break. Lewis sat on one of the sofas, warming himself by the fireplace. Both heard the signal and saw a flash as Irene and Victor ran by the windows. They exchanged grim looks and went for their outer gear.

Jack and Harry were exiting the woods, about to join the long driveway to the Great Camp, when Jack threw out his arm, stopping his brother mid-step. "I think I heard something."

Both men stood still and listened. The echo of metal on metal filled the air, piercing the quiet around them. They winced at the harsh sounds, then looked at each other, not knowing whether to be glad or fearful.

"Let's go." Harry pushed past his brother.

Irene was the first to arrive at the scene. Her face crumbled, and her cries filled the air as she flung herself at her brother.

Steven made a grab for her so she wouldn't push the body farther down into the black depths of the water. "Irene, no." He pulled her up and dragged her away. "There's nothing we can do. He's gone. But, listen, he's perched on the edge of that hole. If you were to push even a little, we might lose him under the ice."

Steven handed her to Victor, who pulled her in tight as she wept.

Lewis and Rider arrived with Olivia, Rider carrying the broom and pulling the sled for her. Lewis carried his medical bag.

"Be careful around the edge of the hole, Lewis," Steven cautioned. "Whoever did this enlarged the opening so Julian would fall through. We don't know how much damage was done to the walls. You might trigger a crack. We could lose Julian's body, and you could fall in as well."

"I don't need to examine him submerged, Steven. Let's pull the poor boy out."

Victor let go of Irene and stepped over to help. The three men carefully maneuvered Julian Racine's body until, inch by inch, they extracted him from the frigid water and laid him down on the lake's icy surface. His body was frozen solid from the chest down.

"Alright, fellas, are you ready?" Steven asked.

All three tilted Julian onto his side, Olivia tucked the sled under his back, and they rolled him onto its surface. Steven pulled the sled off to the side, out of the way. Olivia handed him the broom, and he cleared the snow from the area. Nothing. If there had been any clues, the wind and snow had stolen them.

With the body of Julian Racine covered under a blanket, Steven pulled the sled up the sloping back lawn, around the side of the lodge,

CHAPTER NINETEEN

and across to the front door, the others following in his wake like a funeral cortege. They reached the porch as Jack and Harry approached from the road.

"No!" Harry cried, removing his snowshoes and running to the sled.

"What the hell is going on with our family?" Jack said, looking like he'd aged years.

The drapes framing the windows moved, and Margery Racine flew out of the door, screaming, her hair streaming behind her. Lewis caught her.

"He's gone, sweetheart. There's nothing we can do."

Margery fell to her knees next to the sled. She gently brushed the snow from Julian's face and kissed his cheek. Choking on sobs, she shook and mumbled something Steven couldn't understand.

Lewis pulled her to her feet. "Come on. Let's get you back inside. We'll get something to warm you up. Look at you out here in below-zero weather with no coat or boots. You'll catch pneumonia." Lewis half carried, half dragged a sobbing Margery Racine back into the lodge.

Lewis settled her on a couch next to a blazing fire, piled two heavy woolen blankets on her then went to get a snifter of brandy. Returning, he took her cold hands in his warm ones and rubbed them vigorously to get the blood flowing. When he felt the warmth return, he took her feet and began massaging them, pressing a thumb on her arches, squeezing her frozen toes.

A shattered Margery Racine looked at Lewis through tear-filled lashes. "What's happening to us? Who's doing this? When is it going to stop?"

Lewis had no answers for the woman he had loved his entire life.

Chapter Twenty

Saturday, December 15, 1934

Knightsbridge, New York

Sergeant Will Taylor sat at his battered wooden desk in the CID room, leaning forward, his muscular arms perched on strong thighs, reading and memorizing the morning *Gazette* that lay open on the clean, organized surface. Although it could be a burden, there'd been occasions when Will was thankful for his prodigious memory. Over the years, bits of information and relationships among people involved in a case had resurfaced in his mind when he needed them to solve a crime.

As Will closed the paper, folding it back to its original condition, he thought about the list of people Steven had given him. Something about one of the names niggled at the back of his mind, but he couldn't put his finger on it. He pushed back his chair and stepped to the murder board. *Margery Racine and her two children Irene and Julian, Victor McAllister, Dr. Lewis Salisbury, Emily Racine, and Gil's two brothers Jack and Harry. Who was it?* Will knew he'd read something about one of these people. He scanned the board, willing the information to untangle itself from the maze of minutia his brain had recorded.

CHAPTER TWENTY

There it was! Several weeks ago, Will had read a tiny article in *The New York Times* about a Canadian man killed in the Amazon jungle. Because of his passion for the rain forest, the man had emigrated to Brazil and had been working as a river guide to finance his scientific research. Every two weeks, his family back in Toronto received a letter in which he shared his discoveries and exciting adventures and, most importantly, assured them he was safe. After a period without a single letter, the family contacted the authorities in Manaus, Brazil, and an investigation ensued. The authorities reported the man had been attacked and killed by a crocodile during an expedition on the river. The newspaper article had listed the other members of the research team: a second scientist, a local man who'd served as their porter, and a photographer identified as Harry Racine. Harry Racine, who was in the boat when the scientist was killed. Harry Racine, who traveled to locations where lethal poisons were plentiful and easily available. The same Harry Racine who was now a suspect in a murder investigation in Upstate New York.

Will was curious about the details of the incident and wondered how the man had gone overboard.

Steven would want this information right away.

He returned to his desk and dialed 0. When the operator came on, he instructed her to put through a call to the number he provided.

The telephone in Gil Racine's study at Great Camp Onontaga rang and rang. Will finally gave up, promising himself he'd try again in an hour.

Since the Knightsbridge Police Department had no ongoing cases and, in a rare expression of holiday spirit, the chief had given most of the men an unexpected day off. Jimmy Bou was home studying for his detective exam. Will pictured Ralph and Pete making jokes and laughing with their children as they enjoyed a fun winter activity—building snowmen, sledding, or riding toboggans down a nearby hill—while their wives caught up with their Christmas shopping. Will found himself listening for the lumbering sounds of Chief Thompson moving through the hallway, coughing from the many Camel cigarettes he smoked every day.

Will regarded the empty chair behind the desk facing his and realized he missed the activity of the station and the comradery of his fellow officers. Most of all, he missed his partner of nearly a year, Detective Sergeant Steven Blackwell. Will yearned to discuss his suspicions about Olivia and the information he'd discovered with Steven. Or, lack of information to be more accurate. He sighed. What was he going to do about Olivia?

Will had never obsessed about anything until now. But once the suspicion had tiptoed in, it had settled in to stay. And he couldn't shake the feeling, now backed with circumstantial evidence, that, at the very least, Olivia had lied to everyone for the past year.

Frowning, he decided his next move was to find out which high school she had attended, then contact them for her records. In order to do that, he'd have to trick her into revealing the part of Syracuse where she'd grown up. How would he accomplish that without her suspecting what he was doing? Olivia was smart. If he wasn't careful, she'd see right through him.

All the same, if Olivia Watson was lying to everyone about her past, the question remained: *Why?*

Will could not shake the suspicion that she might be a German spy. After all, Mata Hari had been a dancer, and no one had suspected her. It wasn't out of the realm of possibility that an enemy nation had recruited a smart, skilled reporter like Olivia.

The phone rang, releasing him from his dark thoughts, its shrill sound echoing through the tomb-like station. He picked up the heavy receiver and identified himself.

"Hello, Sergeant. It's Robert Blackwell, Steven's father."

CHAPTER TWENTY

"How are you, Admiral?"

"Fine, fine. Listen, Steven was going to call this morning, but I haven't heard from him. You're in the loop in his investigation, right?"

"Yes, sir. Completely."

"I thought so. What I discovered is so explosive that I wanted to tell him right away. The trouble is no one's answering the telephone up at the Great Camp. I'd like to give you the information, so if you speak with him before I do, he'll know as soon as possible."

"Alright. Go ahead, sir."

As Admiral Robert Blackwell shared what he'd learned about Commander Jack Racine, Will's brows rose higher and higher up his sizable forehead until they disappeared behind the dark hair falling onto his face. After clarifying one item, Will thanked him and promised he'd do everything possible to reach Steven.

Will gazed down at his notebook, absorbing the shocking information Steven's father had disclosed. He never ceased to be amazed at the lies people told.

Great Camp Onontaga, Adirondack Mountains

In the driveway at the lodge's entrance, Steven instructed Irene to go inside and ask Lewis to come back out. "I really need your help right now, Irene. I know it's hard and I wouldn't ask you if it wasn't necessary. Can you stay with your mother until Lewis finishes examining your brother? I need him out here, and it can't wait."

"Of course," Victor answered for her. "I can help."

Steven could see Irene summoning strength to calm down and regain a measure of control. She wasn't quite there yet. Her jaw trembled as she wiped away the tears. Victor put his arm around her and led her stumbling up the stairs and into the lodge.

A moment later, Lewis rejoined the group. He took his medical bag from Jack, who had held onto it. "What do you think, Steven? Shall we put him with his father?" Lewis asked.

"I don't think we have a lot of choices."

With Steven pulling the sled, followed by Olivia, Lewis, Jack, and Harry, they made their way to Cabin E. Steven keyed the lock and opened the door. The men, each lifting a shoulder or a leg, carried Julian Racine into the cabin.

Like the others, this cottage had one bedroom with a double bed and a second one with two singles. They brought Julian into the room where his father lay on one of the twin beds.

"Jack and Harry, I'm going to ask you fellas to go back to the lodge while we take care of a few things here," Steven said.

"Sure, Steven."

"Of course."

After the door had closed behind them, Steven asked Lewis to remove Julian's upper clothing so Olivia could take photographs.

"I didn't say anything out on the lake, Lewis, because I didn't want Irene to see this." Steven indicated the gash along the side of Julian's neck.

"That looks deep," Lewis said, peering down at the wound.

"I see a lot in my line of work, but this was vicious. Not only did someone lure him out onto the lake and get him to walk into that hole in the ice—because I have no doubt that's what happened—but the killer pushed a weapon into this boy's neck," Steven said.

"But why, Steven?" asked Olivia. "Julian would have frozen to death anyway."

"I think he pushed him under the water and drowned him. The killer made sure he was dead before he left the scene."

"Look at where the wound is, Steven," said Lewis. "An inch or two over, and it would have severed the carotid artery. Julian would have bled out in seconds."

CHAPTER TWENTY

"What do you think caused it?" Olivia asked.

"I'd say it was something like an arrow. The end would have been pointed, three-dimensional—not flat like a knife—and razor-sharp, almost certainly metal."

"Like the end of the ice-fishing markers," Steven said.

Lewis looked up at him. "Yes, exactly like that. The sides of the tip would have to be long and smooth. Although it's deep, you can see that the wound is clean. There aren't any jagged edges. There isn't any tearing from when the killer pulled it out again."

"What about a spear?" Olivia asked. "Harry said he was on Baffin Island not long ago. Don't they hunt with spears there? I've read about walruses in the Arctic. I imagine spear hunting would be popular. It's quiet but lethal."

"I don't want to think where this is leading," Lewis said. "I've known Harry since he was a boy. He's wild, yes, but why on earth would he want to kill his nephew? It doesn't make sense."

"That's what we need to find out," said Steven. "Is there anything else you can tell us, Lewis?"

Lewis took each of Julian's hands in his. "The nails on his right hand are broken. The tips of the fingers look shredded. I wonder if he tried to claw his way out onto the ice after he got that one arm out of the hole."

"Or if he was trying to get a grip on the underside of the ice," Olivia said. "I'm picturing someone walking along, then suddenly there's nothing underfoot. The frozen lake is gone. There's a gaping hole in the ice. What's the most natural movement a body would make?"

"His hands flew up in the air," Steven said.

"Exactly. I bet he shot down into the lake like a bullet. Maybe his glove flew off. Or he'd already taken it off to hold a cigarette or wipe his eye. My eyes water in the winter, especially if there's a wind."

"You paint a compelling picture, Olivia," said Lewis. "I'm inclined to agree with you. Let's see if there's anything else." He unbuttoned the rest of Julian's shirt, peeling it off the frozen torso. "No other wounds in front. Help me turn him over, Steven."

It was awkward, but they succeeded in placing Julian face down on the bed. Lewis checked his back. "No, there's nothing here aside from an old scar. Without the benefit of an official autopsy, I'd say he plunged into the hole, tried to get out, used one hand to get a grip on the ice—whether it was above or below the surface—and then his killer stabbed him in the neck with an unknown weapon. Like Steven said, maybe the killer was trying to keep Julian's head under the water. They'll know when we can get an autopsy."

"Let's cover him and lock the cabin again. I'm going back out on the ice to get that marker before the killer takes it from the scene," said Steven. "Just in case."

"I'll go back to the lodge with Lewis," Olivia said.

"I have a feeling Margery and Irene are going to need something to calm them down. I have some tranquilizers in my bag. I think they'll be more able to cope after they've had a good rest," Lewis said.

Olivia and Lewis entered the Great Camp to near-complete silence. The flames in both fireplaces crackled—in one, a log shifted, and sparks flew. Grief filled every corner of the room. Sorrow clawed the air like an animal in a cage.

Margery and Irene sat in the living room—Margery on one sofa, Irene across from her—flanking the hearth like stone statues. Their eyes, red and swollen, appeared empty. Purple blotches covered Margery's face. A trail of black mascara ran down Irene's cheeks. Neither woman spoke. Victor perched on a footstool facing Irene, holding her hands and leaning forward as if to give her strength. Jack and Harry idled by the mantle, glasses of whiskey in hand. Aunt Emily suffered alone in one of the chairs facing the fire.

CHAPTER TWENTY

Throwing his jacket on the hall tree, Lewis hurried across the room to Margery and knelt in front of her. He took her hands in his. "Margery?"

She gave him a blank look.

"I don't understand what Julian was doing out there on the lake," said Harry.

"And how could he have fallen in?" Jack remarked. "Those ice-fishing holes are never big enough to cause an accident like that."

"Julian didn't accidentally fall in, Jack," Lewis said.

Jack, Harry, and Victor glared at him.

"What do you mean?" Harry said roughly.

"Julian was killed. Someone did it on purpose."

The stunned silence dragged on until finally, Jack said, "You're saying someone murdered Julian as well. You're sure about this?"

Lewis's face resembled an old man's—the ruts and furrows carved forever. "Yes, I'm sorry, but there's no doubt." He took Margery's arm. "My dear, let me help you to bed. I have some medicine that'll help you sleep. It'll take the edge off this nightmare."

Margery Racine slumped as though there was nothing inside to hold her upright. Tears continued to flow, washing her ravaged face.

"Lewis." Her throat was raw. The word uttered as though it had been dragged over a rock-filled road. "My Julian. Why?"

Lewis gently pulled her to her feet and, with an arm around her back, led her to the staircase.

Olivia ran over to the foot of the stairs. "Margery, wait, please."

Margery directed a vacant look at her.

"Please, when was the last time you saw Julian?"

"Can't this wait?" Lewis asked irritably.

"No, after your tranquilizer, she'll be even more confused, Lewis. We need to make a timeline now."

"When did you last see Julian, Margery?" Olivia repeated.

"Um...Julian...." She looked off into the distance, as if trying to conjure him up. "Uh...hot chocolate. I took him cocoa last night."

"When was this, Margery? Please, think," Olivia pleaded.

Irene's voice came from several feet away. "It was shortly after ten. Julian said he was tired and was going up early. I remember being jealous that you hadn't asked me if I wanted some, too, Mother." A violent sob escaped her. "Now, I'd crawl on my hands and knees to bring him as many cups of cocoa as he wanted." Irene buried her face in Victor's shoulder, and he slid closer.

"Thank you, Irene," said Olivia. "Thanks, Lewis, go ahead. I'll let Steven know Margery's in her room. How long will the sedative last?"

"Given the state she's in, probably six or seven hours. She'll sleep until dinnertime."

"Doc," Victor said, "Irene could use a sedative as well. I'll help her upstairs and into bed if you'll stop by and give her something before you come back down here."

"Yes, thank you, Victor."

Olivia wasn't sure what to do, so she went to the sideboard in the dining area and poured a cup of coffee, then joined Jack and Harry at the fireplace at that end of the room.

"Some family we've got, huh, Olivia?" Harry said, slugging back an amber-colored liquid.

"What a horrifying way to die," Olivia whispered. "I could probably come up with reasons why someone hated a powerful, successful man like Gil enough to kill him, but Julian? He barely had a chance at life. What could he have possibly done to make someone hate him enough to murder him? And in such a gruesome way?"

"I didn't know my nephew as well as I would have liked, but I loved the kid. I used to take him fishing when he was young. Whenever I was home on leave," Jack said. Olivia was surprised to hear the crack in his voice. "I was already in the Navy when he was born. I saw him

CHAPTER TWENTY

when I could—usually at Christmas, sometimes during his summer vacation. I tried to spend time with him. I know he was upset when Gil wouldn't publish his novel. But that doesn't explain why someone would kill *him*."

"I'm in the same boat as Jack," Harry told Olivia. "I was eighteen when Julian was born." The shadow of a smile brightened his solemn face. "I remember that day as clear as anything. I got home late from school because we had football practice after classes. When I walked into the kitchen—I remember smelling an apple pie baking in the oven, and I was excited because it was my favorite. I remember thinking I was going to have two pieces for supper—Mom said, 'You're an uncle again. Your brother and Margery had a baby boy this afternoon.' By the time Julian was old enough to talk to, I'd started learning how to use a camera and develop photographs. After I enlisted in the Army, I was never around much. I'm sad to say I didn't really know him at all."

"We can't always have the families and relationships we'd like or that we think we should have. I don't know anyone who has the ideal family," Olivia said.

Harry reached over and squeezed her hand. He mouthed *thank you*.

Olivia turned toward the entry at the sound of the front door closing behind Steven. She noticed he didn't have the fishing-hole marker and hoped he'd left it in their cabin. She thought it unlikely the killer had had a chance to retrieve it during the short time they'd left the scene unattended. Besides, everyone had been in this room. *Hadn't they?*

Steven approached the threesome, leaned toward the fire, and rubbed his hands together. "It's snowing again. And the temperature's dropping."

Jack and Harry groaned. Olivia studied his face, looking for clues.

"I need to make a phone call. Olivia, want to come with me?" Steven asked.

"Sure. Would you like a cup of coffee?"

"Thanks. That'd be swell."

Olivia closed the door to Gil's study and set the coffee on the desk. Steven was asking the operator to connect him with the Department of the Navy in Washington, D.C.

"Where's the marker?" Olivia whispered as they waited for the call to go through.

"I hid it under the bed in our spare bedroom."

"Was there any blood on it?"

"No, but the killer could have wiped it off. *If* it was the weapon he used. We don't know that yet."

"By the way," said Olivia, "I hate to say this, but it's already after noon, and we never talked with the staff yesterday."

"Aargh, you're right! We *have* to get that done today." Steven pursed his lips as he listened to the telephone ringing in his father's Washington, D.C. office. "Grace should have picked up by now." He looked at his watch. "Maybe they're out to lunch." He set the receiver back in its cradle. "I'll try again in an hour."

"While we were waiting, it made sense to start a timeline of where everybody was last night. Who saw Julian, where, and at what time? I only got as far as Margery," Olivia said. "She took a cup of hot chocolate to him in his room shortly after ten. Irene confirmed it. I was about to ask Jack and Harry when you came in. I got them talking about their relationships with their nephew. Harry's sad that he never got to know Julian very well because he's never here. Jack seems more upset about Julian's death than Harry is. I think it was the first time I saw any real emotion in him. Jack took Julian fishing when Julian was a kid. He didn't specifically say ice fishing, but even so...."

Tired from the morning's ordeal, Steven dropped into Gil's leather chair and took a sip of his coffee. "This is good, thanks. And thank you

CHAPTER TWENTY

for everything you've been doing. So, Jack took Julian fishing, huh? Maybe there's something in that, although Jack's too smart to drop an important piece of information like that. But, you never know. It could be a ploy."

"Steven, it's been bugging me how the killer got Julian to go out on the lake with him. Do you think this happened last night or this morning?" Olivia asked.

"Last night. He was frozen solid. He couldn't have been out there only a few hours."

"Okay, then how the heck did somebody get him out there in the freezing cold *and* in the dark? It would have taken a lot of persuading. Julian wasn't stupid."

She dragged a spare wooden chair next to him. Steven took out his notebook and began a timeline for the previous night.

The telephone rang, startling them. Steven grabbed the receiver. "Hello. Great Camp Onontaga. Detective Steven Blackwell speaking."

"Steven, it's Will."

"Will! Am I glad to hear from you! We've had a second murder."

"Oh, no! Who? What happened?"

Leaning in close to Steven, Olivia heard Will's reaction. She motioned to Steven to hold the receiver so she could hear the conversation. He accommodated her and told Will Olivia was with him, listening in.

"It was Julian Racine, Gil's son," Steven said. "It looks like the killer enlarged an ice-fishing hole on the lake and lured Julian to the spot in such a way that he fell in. Somehow, Julian got one arm and shoulder out and up onto the ice, but the killer pushed him under the water and evidently held him there until he stopped breathing. There's a deep gash on Julian's neck from something with a pointed metal tip."

"The violence is increasing, Steven. Poisoning someone is easy when you don't have to see the victim's eyes or touch him or when you don't even have to be in the same room. This new murder was hands-on and vicious. I wonder if it had been planned for a long time or in the few days you've all been there. You say he enlarged the opening in the ice, so of course, that was deliberate. That could have been done days ago or hours before. Although, now that I think about it, the ice must be a foot thick by now. Your killer would have needed heavy tools to cut through that, and it probably took a fair amount of time. I bet it wasn't quiet either."

"We're thinking along the same lines, partner," Steven said.

"Listen, Steven, I spoke with your father earlier."

"Swell! Did he find out anything?"

"He sure did. You'd better brace yourself for this," said Will.

"Uh-oh."

"Yeah, your father told me that...."

Steven and Olivia heard an odd sound and then dead air.

"Hello? Will?" Steven said. He clicked the button in the cradle several times, hoping to re-establish the connection. "Will?"

The lights flickered twice. They blinked again, but stayed on.

Steven tried to call Will back. He held the receiver to his ear, listening for a dial tone. The phone was dead.

Chapter Twenty-One

Knightsbridge, New York

"Steven? Steven?" Will toggled the button on the cradle of the phone. Nothing. He set the receiver down, then picked it up again. When he heard a dial tone, he called the operator back. "Hello, Operator. I got cut off. Will you try this number again, please?"

A moment passed. "I'm sorry, sir. The line seems to be dead. I believe they're having a snowstorm in that location. The lines are probably down."

Will thanked her and sat at his desk. Now what? He could *not* leave Steven alone in the mountains—isolated, trapped with a killer. He had to do something.

Will grabbed the phone and dialed Chief Andy Thompson's home telephone number. At the sound of his boss's booming but raspy voice, Will explained the situation and shared the latest news.

"Chief, can I borrow one of the department cars?"

"Of course, you can, Taylor. Get up there and rescue your partner. You're not thinking of going alone, are you? I know you've spent a lot of time outdoors in all kinds of weather, what with your hunting, tracking, and camping. But this is a serious storm. And I don't think we've seen the end of it yet."

"No, sir. I'll be fine, and I'm hoping Jimmy Bou will come with me."

"I'm sure he will. Do you need anything, Will? Can I give you a couple of dollars? You never know if you'll need to stay someplace overnight. Some of those hotels in touristy places like the Adirondacks cost two bucks a night!"

"Thanks, Chief. That's okay."

"Alright, call me when you can. Let me know as soon as Steven and Miss Watson are out of danger, and you fellas are on your way home."

Will pushed and held down the button in the cradle, then released it and listened with the receiver at his ear. When he heard a new dial tone, he dialed Jimmy Bourgogne's number.

"Hello," a cheery voice answered the call. "KB-39. Bourgogne family."

"Jimmy, it's Will."

"Will! What's up? Did something happen? Do we have a case?"

Will told him about Admiral Blackwell's call, Steven's news about the second murder, and being cut off from the call at the Great Camp. "Jimmy, I'm going up there. Steven's looking for a sociopath—a crazy killer—and he and Olivia are trapped in that camp with whoever it is. Who knows who will be next?"

"Oh, my gosh, Will! I'm coming, too."

"Good! I thought you'd say that. I talked to the chief. We're taking one of the department cars. They're nice and heavy. It'll be able to plow through a lot of this accumulation. But, Jimmy, at some point, we'll probably have to abandon the car and hike the rest of the way. Wear heavy clothes and bring your snowshoes."

"We could be out in the elements for a few days, Will. Maybe we should pack some sandwiches, a Thermos of coffee, and some water. What do you think?"

"Yes, those are good ideas. I'm bringing my sleeping bag and tent as well. I'd rather have them and not need them than get stuck without them."

"Yeah, it's better to be prepared. I'll bring my sleeping bag, too. And I'll bring a small lantern and matches," said Jimmy.

"Swell. I'm going home to change my clothes and pack everything up." Will looked at the clock on the wall in the CID room. "It's nearly quarter to one. I'll be at your house no later than one-thirty. If we can get on the road before two, we might be able to get there while it's still light out."

"Yeah, I'd rather not have to snowshoe in the dark in a place I've never been before. I'll bring my compass too, Will."

"Good thinking."

Great Camp Onontaga, Adirondack Mountains

"Dead," Steven said with a hitch in his voice, setting the receiver in the cradle.

"What do you mean, *dead*?" Olivia's eyes grew large. "Are you telling me we're trapped up here in the middle of nowhere with a killer on the loose and no phone service?" She leaned in close and took his hands in hers. She whispered, "Let's go through the portal to my time, and I'll call Liz or Sophie to pick us up. Remember, I left a cell phone with emergency gear in a bag. Everything is in what would be Cabin B now." Olivia inhaled. "Steven, I'm truly sorry for this family—and I know Gil was your friend—but are we really going to risk our lives? It's been two days and we have no idea who the killer is. It's different when you're hunting down a murderer at home. For some reason, I never feel you're threatened. But up here, we're *living* with the killer." She took a deep breath and went on.

"And at home, you have Will and Jimmy Bou and the guys on your team. You have the chief. And you can come home at night. I feel safe with you in our house—even when there's a killer on the loose. But this is different. I'm *scared*." Her voice broke on the last word.

Steven stood, pulled her up out of her chair, and wrapped his arms around her. He buried his face in her hair and kept his voice low in case anyone was listening on the other side of the door. "I know you're scared. I think you should go back to your time. I can tell everyone you're feeling sick, that you're resting in our cabin. I'll keep the door locked and pretend to bring you food. It won't be the best explanation, but I don't care. I want you safe. That's all that matters to me."

"Absolutely not. I'd never leave you. We're in this together."

"That's my girl." Steven hugged her tighter, closing his eyes and sending a silent prayer that she'd remain unharmed. Then he let go, gently steered her back into the chair, and sat in front of her, their knees touching, holding hands. "Alright, listen, we make a plan, and we stick to it. The first thing is that you never, ever, under any circumstances, go anywhere on your own. We won't make it obvious, but I want us to stay together every minute."

"Don't worry. I'm sticking to you like glue."

"Good." Steven pushed his fingers through his hair. He looked tired, somewhat frayed at the edges. Olivia realized that the events of the weekend were taking a greater toll on him than she had understood.

He went on. "I can't imagine what it feels like to lose a child. Margery is probably out as a source of information. She's a wreck. I don't know if she'll be able to leave her bed in the next few days. Maybe you can get Harry to show you the Egypt pictures you were talking about, and you can find out what it was like for the three brothers growing up."

"I can do that."

"Let's assume it's one killer."

"Please! Let's not have two lunatics up here running around knocking off members of the Racine family." Olivia clapped her hands to her mouth and looked aghast. "Oh, Steven. I am so sorry. That was a stupid thing to say. I'm really sorry."

CHAPTER TWENTY-ONE

"It's okay. Don't worry. Yes, Gil was a friend and loyal patron of my mother's. But in reality, I don't know most of the people here that well, and a couple of them I've met for the first time this weekend.

"My priorities are keeping you safe until we can get out of here and figuring out who's done this. So...our plan...when we try to get information from someone, we do it together. Or, if it's somebody you want to talk to alone, you take that person into a corner in the main room where I can keep my eyes on you."

"I agree. Let's go over our list of suspects again and try to narrow it down more. I say Margery and Irene are off the list. There's no way Margery would have killed her son, especially so brutally. Even if she wanted her husband dead, she'd never kill Julian."

"Right. And the same goes for Irene," Steven said. "She's in shock. She didn't do this either."

"Irene is barely holding it together. And I'm going to extend our reprieve to Lewis and Victor," said Olivia. "I believe Lewis loves Margery, and Victor is in love with Irene. I don't think they'd risk their relationships by doing something as horrific as these two murders."

"Alright, I'll agree on both counts. Despite what I said about Victor being arrogant and assuming he'd never get caught, I don't think Julian would go out on the ice with Victor. Still assuming it's one killer, I'm going to eliminate Aunt Emily. She doesn't have the physical strength to alter the size of the fishing hole or to push the metal pole or whatever it was into a struggling young man's neck with enough force to hold him under the water. She's out."

"Absolutely, to say nothing of the fact that I don't see *why* she'd do it."

"Okay, so that leaves Jack and Harry," Steven said.

"What about Rider? You were going to talk with him," Olivia said.

"Damn! I was going to interview him yesterday and I ran out of time. I *have* to get to him today." Steven paused and thought for a moment.

"We'll come back to Rider in a minute. First...look at the money in this family, Olivia. Who stands to gain from these murders?"

"If Julian hadn't been killed, I'd say maybe Jack or Harry wanted something their older brother had—one or both of the companies, money, the house, or Onontaga. Maybe all of it. Or Julian wanted his inheritance sooner rather than later. But I can't see what motive connects both Gil and Julian," she said.

"The reason for Gil's murder could still be inheriting those things. Maybe Julian stood in the way. With Julian out of the picture, the remaining family members get more," said Steven.

"What if the motive for killing Julian is as simple as him witnessing Gil's killer put the poison on the piano keys?"

"Could be. If that's the case, the poison was put on the keys before supper Thursday because Julian didn't arrive until that afternoon."

"I imagine Rider and the maid were in and out of the dining area getting things ready. Maybe they saw someone near the piano," Olivia said. "I could question her."

"Remember our plan, Olivia. We stay together. Let's question Rider first, then we'll talk with Corinne."

"Okay, what do you want to do about Jack and Harry?"

"We'll stick with our idea of you getting information from Harry over the photographs. Stay in the main room, but go into a corner so he'll feel comfortable talking," said Steven.

"I can do that. You'll talk with Jack?"

"I'll approach him as though I'm looking for help."

"Your comment about me not being alone should apply to you as well, Steven. I don't like the thought of you going anywhere with him alone. Just in case."

"Alright, although I'm going back to our cabin to get my gun."

Olivia's eyes popped, and she swallowed hard. "You brought a gun to a Christmas party?"

CHAPTER TWENTY-ONE

"Blame it on my job. It never occurs to me to go anywhere without it. And my handcuffs. You never know."

"Yeah, like now." Olivia grimaced. "Okay, we've got our plan for the afternoon. Guess I'll go with you to the cabin."

"Sticking like glue, remember?" Steven seized the telephone receiver, brought it to his ear, then shook his head. "Nope. Still dead."

Knightsbridge, New York

When Will Taylor pulled up in front of Jimmy Bou's family home, he saw the curtains in the front window fall back. Jimmy had been keeping a lookout.

The young officer threw open the door. "Only quarter after one, Will. Good timing. We'll get there before dark." He hoisted a backpack onto his shoulders, grabbed the edge of the front door, and called out, "Mom, I'm going now. Will's here."

Mrs. Bourgogne hustled to the door, wiping her hands on a kitchen towel. She tightened the scarf around her son's neck. "You be careful, now. We need you back here in one piece. Don't take any chances."

"Mom, this is my job. I know what I'm doing." He leaned down and kissed her plump cheek. "But don't worry. Nothing's going to make me miss my detective exam next week." He turned away from her and picked up his snowshoes and poles, which were leaning against the house. His pack, with a sleeping bag rolled up and secured and lantern hanging off the bottom, bumped his back as he took each step down to the sidewalk he'd shoveled an hour ago.

Mrs. Bourgogne clung to the door frame, her face etched with worry. She stood motionless until Will had pulled away from the curb and only then waved at the back of the large black Ford as it cut deep channels in the snow-filled street. She watched until the car carrying her son was a dot in the distance, then disappeared.

Great Camp Onontaga, Adirondack Mountains

When Steven and Olivia returned to the main lodge after retrieving his gun, they saw Lewis, Aunt Emily, and Victor eating lunch, though not seated together. Lewis and Aunt Emily were at the two opposite ends of the table, where Margery and Gil had sat that first night; Victor sat in the middle of one side. *How curious,* Olivia thought.

All three looked drained. Aunt Emily appeared to have aged ten years. Her once sparkling eyes were dull, her cheery face sagged, and her previously erect back slumped. Olivia feared for the woman's health. After all, she was well into her eighties, maybe approaching ninety. How much shock could her system tolerate? Olivia chose the seat next to the octogenarian.

"May I sit with you, Miss Racine?"

Glassy eyes turned to Olivia. "Oh, certainly, my dear."

Close up, Olivia noticed that Aunt Emily's hand trembled as she lifted a spoon to her lips. A drop of minestrone soup trickled down her chin. She placed the spoon in her bowl and dabbed her chin and mouth with a linen napkin. She exhaled, then sat unmoving.

Olivia leaned toward her. "I'm so sorry. I wish there was something I could do for you."

When Emily Racine turned to reply, Olivia caught her breath. In a matter of seconds, the old woman had transformed. The corners of her mouth turned down, her eyes glared like molten rock, and she sat a little taller. "Just find the bastard who did this to my family," she growled.

"We will. Steven is good at his job."

Aunt Emily gave a curt nod and returned to her lunch.

Some distance away, Steven was talking with Lewis. *This is interesting,* he thought. Over the past two days, Lewis had taken Gil's place. Backing up Margery when she had suggested they work up an

CHAPTER TWENTY-ONE

appetite yesterday. Taking Gil's seat. Steven wondered what other duties and privileges Lewis had in mind.

"I left her sleeping soundly," Lewis was saying. "Rest is the best thing for her right now. I only wish I could wave a magic wand and make it all go away. This is like a bad dream."

Victor pushed back his chair and stood. "I need to check on Irene." He left the room.

Lewis tore a piece of bread from the baguette in front of him and slathered butter on the soft inside.

"Lewis," Steven whispered, "have you had any ideas? Aside from Aunt Emily, you're probably my best resource. What can you tell me about the three brothers growing up? I know Gil was nine or ten years older than Harry—that can be a huge gap when you're a kid. What about Jack?"

A puzzled look crossed Lewis's face. "What do you mean 'what about Jack'?"

"What do you mean, what do I mean? Is there a big gap between Jack and Harry? Were they close as boys?" Steven asked.

"Well, there was the same gap as between Gil and Harry."

Now it was Steven's turn to look puzzled. He stopped eating. "What? I'm sorry, Lewis, but I don't understand."

"You don't know? I thought everybody knew."

"Knew what?"

Lewis laughed. "Gil and Jack were twins."

"But, they don't...."

"Look alike," Lewis interrupted. "I know. They're fraternal twins. Gil was born a few minutes before Jack."

This revelation hit Steven like a wall of water—the implications rushed at him swirling, tumbling, spawning ideas, and forming theories. The repercussions of this startling new information twisted and turned, then settled in a confused tangle. Steven struggled to grasp the glimmer of an idea that flickered by. He needed to weave something logical out of this, but he couldn't quite see the pattern. Yet.

Chapter Twenty-Two

On the Road, Adirondack Mountains

"So far, so good, Will," Jimmy Bou chirped from the passenger side of the plush bench seat. "At least it stopped snowing."

"Yep," said Will. "And we're making good time. To tell you the truth, what I'm most concerned about is the access road. Steven mentioned that the Great Camp sits about three miles from a county road. That's where we might have to get out our snowshoes."

"Where there's a will, there's a way, right? Get it, Will?"

Will groaned at the dumb cop joke and rolled his eyes.

"Talk about where there's a will, there's a way. Want to know the strangest thing I ever saw?" Jimmy asked.

Will smothered a grin. "Sure."

"1922, a month after my eleventh birthday, my grandfather said, 'Jimmy, I got a treat for you. I'm taking you to Syracuse to watch 'em move a hotel to the other side of the street.'"

"That rings a bell."

"Yup, sure enough, a bunch of men—engineers, I suppose—hoisted a four-story building, the Hotel Truax, onto rollers to move it across the street so they could build the new Hotel Syracuse. And do you know what the most unbelievable thing about it was?"

"You mean as if that wasn't enough?" Will chuckled.

"Huh? Oh yeah, right. Well, I'll tell you...they did it with the employees doing their jobs and all the people in their rooms! Can you believe it? The barber was still giving shaves and cutting hair. The lights were on. I don't know how they did it, but it was like magic."

"There's no such thing as magic, Jimmy. There's always an explanation."

Will pulled the heavy car toward the side, plowing through a mound of snow covering what should have been their lane. "Can you read that signpost, Jimmy?"

"I'll get out and look."

Jimmy brushed the snow off the marker, then hopped back in the car. "This is it, Will, our turnoff. It says Camp Onontaga."

"Okay, here we go." Will brought the automobile back onto the road, then turned up the snow-covered access road.

Great Camp Onontaga, Adirondack Mountains

Steven was eager to discuss the ramifications of Gil and Jack being twins with Olivia. As soon as she finished eating, he hustled her into Gil's study for a private talk.

After sharing the bombshell information, Steven said, "What was the actual relationship between Gil and Jack? Were they as friendly as Jack's led me to believe? How jealous was Jack of his older brother?"

"Right, being twins changes everything. We're not talking about Gil being older by years, but by minutes! Gil was born a few minutes before Jack, so he became the first son and inherited everything. Jack was completely left out. A difference of minutes and it all could have been Jack's. I think it would take a lot of hard work, or a generous disposition, *not* to feel resentful. So, what's the plan?" Olivia asked.

"Let's talk to Rider now...."

CHAPTER TWENTY-TWO

"Finally...."

"Right...and see what he has to say about the boys growing up. I'm pretty sure he worked for the family back then."

They caught the butler checking the luncheon buffet.

"Rider," Steven began, "I'd like to speak with you if you can take a moment from your duties."

"Certainly, Detective."

"Can we use your room?"

Rider led Steven and Olivia out of the great room to a door at the end of the back hallway, then ushered them into a small but well-appointed sitting room. A fire crackled in the stone hearth. Nearby, a pair of comfortable-looking wingback chairs upholstered in a well-worn brocade flanked a low chest of drawers, which doubled as a side table. The dark green of the fabric paired with the red shade on the lamp gave the room the year-round cozy feel of Christmas. A book lay open, a satin ribbon marking the place where its reader had paused. Two framed photographs occupied most of the space on the dresser top: a wedding photo of a tall man and striking woman and a young man in uniform.

"Rider," Olivia began, "this is a lovely room! I think I'd want to spend all my time here." She smiled at him, then bent to look at the photographs more closely. "What a beautiful woman."

"Thank you. My wife," he murmured.

Olivia heard something in his voice. "Is she...?"

Rider nodded. "The Spanish flu. 1918."

"Oh, I'm so sorry. Is this your son?"

"Yes, Thomas. He was in France during the war."

"A brave young man. You must be proud." Olivia hoped to lighten the tone after learning of his wife's death. Unfortunately, she sunk in deeper.

Rider closed his eyes. "He was killed."

Olivia shot Steven a glance that said *Help me get out of this.*

"Rider, I'm truly sorry to hear this," said Steven. "We don't mean to intrude on your privacy. If we could ask a couple of questions, we'll let you get on with your work."

"Certainly. Please have a seat." He held out his hand toward the two chairs. "I'll get myself another chair from the bedroom."

The butler returned carrying a wooden chair and settled on the cane seat, crossing his long legs.

"First of all, how are you holding up?" Steven began.

"That's nice of you to ask, Detective. It's been hard, but we must all do our part."

"That's a good attitude. I have the impression you've worked for the Racine family a long time," Steven began, his notebook open on his knee, pencil in hand.

"Yes, I was hired by Mr. Claude Racine when I was ten years old."

Olivia couldn't stop the word from escaping. "Ten!" she exclaimed.

Rider gave a wistful smile. "It wasn't uncommon in those days, Miss. Families like mine often sent their children into service at a young age. I finished my fifth-grade studies, then, in July, I went to work for Mr. Racine, Senior."

"What kind of work did a ten-year-old do?" Olivia was repelled yet fascinated.

"My main job was cleaning all the shoes for the household and their guests, who often stayed with them. Sometimes, I acted as a crossing sweeper when Mrs. Racine went out." At the look on Olivia's face, he explained, "I swept a clean path in the street so Mrs. Racine wouldn't get the bottom of her dress dirty when she crossed to the opposite side."

Olivia felt as though she had followed Alice down the rabbit hole. This was a world she'd never heard of, much less imagined that it existed. Here she was, talking with someone who had lived in it.

CHAPTER TWENTY-TWO

Rider went on. "I was only seven years older than Gil and Jack. Sometimes, when the nanny had to leave for a short time, I was instructed to watch them play, to make sure neither one hurt the other. I suppose it was unusual, but I enjoyed the break from my other duties."

"You mentioned making sure neither child hurt the other. Did that happen often, then? Did one of them hurt the other?" Steven asked.

"Oh, you know how boys are, Detective. Always tumbling, scuffling. Sometimes fighting, but nothing serious. Just being boys."

"I'd like to know more about the relationship between Gil and Jack, Rider. Do you know...did you ever observe anything that would suggest Jack resented the fact that he was the second son?" Steven asked.

"Oh, most definitely! It wasn't a secret that Jack felt cheated by the order of their birth. As he got older and understood better, he was always going on about the 'seven minutes.' He'd say, 'Seven minutes. Seven lousy minutes, and it could have been me.' You see, Gil was born seven minutes before Jack. It made all the difference in their lives."

"Do you think he still feels that way, or was it something he got over as he became a man?"

Rider gazed off in the distance, as if trying to picture long-ago incidents and interactions between the brothers.

"I'd say by the time they reached their teenage years, Jack accepted the circumstances of his birth and what his future was going to be. Mind you, he wasn't happy about it, but he seemed resigned to the reality of his situation. He also saw how his father treated Gil, pulling him away from the carefree childhood they both enjoyed and into the business. By the time they were twelve, Gil had no more freedom. He was expected to work at home with their tutor in the morning, then at the newspaper offices all afternoon, learning the business from the ground up. After their morning studies, Jack had the afternoons free to do whatever he wanted. I think that made it easier for him to accept things."

"Did either of the boys ever confide in you, Rider?" Olivia asked.

The butler recoiled, horrified at the suggestion. "Confide in me? I was a servant, Miss Watson. The children were never encouraged to talk to me in any way other than to ask for something. I sometimes ran down to the kitchen to bring them a drink or a piece of candy. Although I will say that after their father died and I went to work for Mr. Gil—who was in his late twenties by then—he occasionally spoke to me when he needed to get something off his mind."

"Can you give me an example of that, Rider?" Steven asked.

While Rider answered Steven's question, Olivia studied the butler. She put his age at around sixty, maybe early sixties. His light brown hair, liberally sprinkled with gray, was receding, and had already disappeared from the top of his dome-like head. Certainly, he had passed middle age and might be thinking about retirement soon. He was tall and husky, had broad shoulders, and looked strong. *Probably from a lifetime of lifting and carrying on the order of others*, she thought. His eyes were hazel with gold flecks. They looked like they saw everything. *I bet he's good at keeping secrets.* She didn't know where that thought came from. Rider's oval face was clean-shaven. He was meticulously groomed. Olivia couldn't help but wonder what he might have made of himself if the circumstances of *his* birth had been different, or if he'd been born in her time.

"Of course. Mr. Gil worked late most nights. He'd return home perhaps around nine-thirty or ten o'clock, sometimes later. Naturally, I'd ask if he required anything. He usually asked me to pour him a large whisky. Sometimes he'd sigh and look at me almost as if we were friends and say something like, 'I'm so very tired, Rider. You can't imagine the people I have to deal with in this business. All day long,

CHAPTER TWENTY-TWO

day after day.' He might explain further, but most nights, he left it at that."

"I see. So, you were something of a confidant on occasion," Steven said.

"I suppose you could say that, Detective. On occasion."

"Going back to when Gil and Jack were young boys, Rider, did you ever see Jack hurt his brother on purpose?"

Rider exhaled deeply, his hand on his chest, as if pushing the air through so he could breathe. He pursed his lips. "I was afraid you were going to ask me something like that. Yes, once. Although it was more something he *didn't* do, rather than what he did."

Rider shifted his body. He sat taller, squared his shoulders.

"I'd been working for their father, Mr. Claude Racine, for about five years. It was summer, and the family was here at Onontaga for the Fourth of July. They were having lunch on the back patio. Gil and Jack wolfed down their meal, as boys are apt to do." He chuckled fondly. "Then, of course, they wanted to go swimming. Mrs. Racine said they could go down to the lake, but they had to promise they'd look out for each other."

"Can you think of how old they were at the time?" Olivia asked.

"I'd say eight or nine. They were good swimmers and, as you know, the lake isn't far from the house. Their mother could easily check on them from time to time." He raised his brows at Steven as if for permission to continue. Steven waved his hand as though to say *go on*.

"I was standing by the door, ready in case anyone needed anything. Mr. and Mrs. Racine were having a lively discussion, and no one was looking towards the lake. Something caught my eye. I don't know what it was. But I squinted and saw Gil flailing in the water near the end of the dock. He kept going under, then popping up, then going under again. I could see his skinny arm waving each time he came up. Jack was standing on the dock, watching. It was obvious Gil was going to drown if somebody didn't do something. I hurried to the table and interrupted the conversation. I told Mr. Racine that Gil was in trouble. He turned, then ran faster than I've ever seen him move. When Jack saw his father heading toward them, he jumped in and supported his brother's head out of the water. It turned out that Gil had caught his foot in a rope that had a small loop at the end. Unusual accident, really. The odds of his foot going into that loop, then getting stuck must have been enormous. But, it turned out alright. His father quickly disentangled Gil's foot. As soon as he could stand again, Gil's panic subsided, and he came back to the table for chocolate cake and ice cream." Rider laughed. "I suppose things don't leave a lasting impression on children. All's well that ends well in their minds. I never said anything to Mr. Racine about Jack watching his brother and doing nothing to help." Rider sighed as though relating the incident had lifted a weight from his conscience. "Although I do remember how angry Gil was with his brother. He punched him in the arm quite hard when their father wasn't looking."

"Thank you, Rider. I understand the loyalty you must feel toward the family," said Steven. "And I admire you for it. I realize that must have been difficult to recall and especially to share."

"I want to emphasize, Detective, that it was only the one time. And again, like I said, by the time the boys were in their teens, Jack had come to terms with the way it was. I am *not* pointing the finger at him."

"Understood. Understood. I appreciate what you told us. I'm not about to accuse anyone based on one childhood incident, I assure you."

"Is that all, Detective? I really should get back to my work."

"Yes, of course. I'll find you if I have any more questions later," Steven said.

CHAPTER TWENTY-TWO

Steven and Olivia returned to Gil Racine's study. When the door closed behind them, Olivia said, "Wow, that was damning. What do you want to do now?"

"I'd like to get someone's opinion of Rider. For all we know, Jack could have been nasty to him at some point, and now he's getting a bit of revenge."

"Oh, I never thought of that. I'm sure Margery's still out. Lewis says she'll probably sleep until dinnertime. And I saw Irene go up to her room shortly after her mother. I'd imagine she's sleeping as well."

"Let's talk with Aunt Emily," Steven said.

"Yes! The perfect person. I'll get her. She's probably sitting by the fire. That's where she's been most of the weekend."

"Leave the door open so I can see you. I'll try the phone again," Steven said. "With any luck, we'll have a dial tone."

When Olivia entered the great room, she felt as though a leaden cloak had fallen on her shoulders—the grief was palpable.

Jack, Victor, and Lewis were playing an unenthusiastic game of cards, no doubt to pass the time. Harry was sitting alone by the fire, drinking. No one else was in the room.

"Has anyone seen Aunt Emily?" Olivia asked.

"She went upstairs for a nap," said Jack.

"Okay, thanks."

In the study, Steven was standing at the window, looking out on the expanse of snow and thick forest. He turned at the sound of the closing door. "No luck?"

"She's taking a nap."

Steven turned back to the window. The grandfather clock in the corner ticking away the minutes was the only sound.

Olivia knew Steven did his best work when he was able to sit quietly at his desk in the CID room at the Knightsbridge Police Station and analyze the information his team had uncovered. He made notes, sorted things into lists and groups with common themes, wrote masses of questions, marked threads that had to be connected or explained. Then, he'd go to his murder board to write more notes, draw charts, and create diagrams. More than once, Olivia had noticed a Venn diagram on the board, its two circles intersecting to illustrate common ground.

Olivia appreciated and respected the way Steven worked. Not wanting to disturb his thoughts, she tiptoed across the room to a tall, dark wood bookcase full of beautiful leather-bound tomes. She ran her finger over the Morocco spines, where author names and titles were written in gold. She read Nathaniel Hawthorne, Herman Melville, Washington Irving, many of the classics that a well-educated man might be expected to have read. Then Olivia remembered that Gil Racine's education had not been formal, but had consisted of morning sessions with a tutor and what was called "on-the-job training" or "real-life experience" in her time. Maybe Gil had been trying to make up for his lack of a formal education.

A red spine on the bottom shelf caught her eye, and she grinned. *A Study in Scarlet*, by Sir Arthur Conan Doyle, was one of her favorites. She read more titles and saw that Gil Racine had had a plebeian side as well. There were titles by Erle Stanley Gardner, Dashiell Hammett, Dorothy L. Sayers, and Agatha Christie. *Now that's more like it.* Olivia saw a hard-cover book lying open, face down on a small table next to an armchair by the fire. She picked it up—it was the classic *The Postman Always Rings Twice*. Respectfully returning the book to its place, she wondered if Gil Racine had read mysteries to relax after his stressful, demanding days at the newspaper.

Steven's voice caught her attention, and she turned at the sound.

"Olivia, we can question the maid later. I need to sit and think awhile. I want to read the notes we wrote on our murder board, update it, then just look at it."

CHAPTER TWENTY-TWO

"I don't mind curling up in a chair and reading. You can close the door to our HQ..." Steven grinned. "...and pretend you're back in your office."

"Thanks."

On the Road, Adirondack Mountains

Will managed to drive the heavy police sedan about a mile up the access road toward Great Camp Onontaga, thanks to a powerful wind that had blown away enough snow in several areas, preventing them from getting stuck. They reached a point, however, where the accumulated snow covered the running boards, reaching above the bottom of the car doors, and the automobile simply could not continue. Will maneuvered the car to a spot he thought might be the side of the road—it was impossible to tell—and parked.

Will and Jimmy had to put their weight against the doors to open them. After struggling for several minutes, they pushed enough snow away so they could open the doors and squeeze out. Both policemen bundled up, put on their snowshoes, got their poles out of the trunk, and hoisted their gear onto their backs. Will locked the car.

"I'm glad they left plenty of space between the road and the trees, Will," said Jimmy Bou. "It'll be easier for us to stay on track. All we have to do is keep the same distance between us and the edge of the forest. It shouldn't be too hard."

"Famous last words, Jimmy. Let's go."

Great Camp Onontaga, Adirondack Mountains

In his wildest dreams, when he'd first started working for the Racine family, Rider could never have imagined the changing relationships he would have with certain individual members—Claude, who had treated him very well, almost like an adopted son; Gil and Jack, who had sometimes seemed like distant cousins when they were children; and later as Gil's assistant, butler, and majordomo.

Rider believed Gil was trying to help him when he had suggested those investments many years ago. Gil had been enthusiastic when he'd said, "Nothing can go wrong. This is a sure win. It's a guaranteed investment. It'll set you up for life."

And Rider had believed him.

After the Crash in 1929, when Rider had lost almost everything, Gil said something like, "Well, I hope you did your own reading on it. You should never take the word of one man." Then, seeing Rider's face, Gil had offered to raise his salary, but he'd made Rider feel stupid and pitiful. Well, he didn't want or need pity from Gil Racine. But he took the money. In the past five years, Rider had saved his entire salary, making do with what he had, using supplies in the Racine household for his own personal use, things like soap and toothpaste, which he had previously bought himself out of a feeling of pride. He had recovered a lot of what he'd lost, though the feelings rankled, and he still hadn't reached the level of financial stability he'd attained before the Crash.

When Aunt Emily woke, the room was cloaked in semi-darkness. She was confused at first, not being used to afternoon naps. Where was she? What day was it? Was it morning or night?

Then the day's events rushed in at her, and she squeezed her eyes shut as involuntary tears seeped out. Her beloved Julian. Such a sweet boy when he was little. Although she had to admit that he'd been spoiled. Margery's absences seemed to give him permission to run wild. As he grew into his teen years and later his twenties, Emily had not liked the entitled attitude Julian had developed. Not good. Not healthy. Not productive. And that business about his novel. For heaven's sake. She understood it was important to him and knew he'd

CHAPTER TWENTY-TWO

worked on it for quite some time. But really, for a grown man to make such a fuss over a book.

Emily allowed herself the luxury of a good cry, then wiped her eyes and got up. Margery was the one who had the right to cry and feel sorry for herself. Not her. Besides, Racine women weren't supposed to show their private feelings. Stiff upper lip, like the Brits said. Time to pull herself together and go downstairs. Maybe she could help somehow.

As she was making herself presentable to join the family and their guests, Emily had one final thought before she made her way downstairs. *Why in heaven's name would anyone want to kill Julian? What could he have possibly done that would warrant such a terrible death?* She shuddered, trying not to imagine how he had felt in his final moments, struggling to breathe as he flailed in the freezing water, knowing he would lose the fight.

Chapter Twenty-Three

The Adirondack Mountains, New York State

It was slow going for Sergeant Will Taylor and soon-to-be-detective Jimmy Bourgogne. The snow was nearly four feet deep. Will would have preferred hiking in the forest, where the thick tree canopy prevented much of the accumulation, but that would have been foolish. They'd be lost in a matter of minutes. So they trudged along, one foot in front of the other. It didn't take long for the two police officers to find themselves breathing hard and sweating despite the freezing temperatures and their excellent physical shape.

Will estimated they'd gone three-quarters of a mile or so, when he noticed Jimmy wiping his eyes, blinking, and squinting.

"What's the matter, Jimmy? Is something wrong with your eyes?"

"I don't know, Will. I'm seeing spots. The snow is really bright. It sort of hurts."

"Sounds like you might be getting snow blindness. My mother has to be careful in the winter, or she comes down with it, especially if it's sunny."

"That's a shame, but it's not sunny today. Wouldn't you think all these clouds would prevent it?"

"Let's make sure it doesn't get any worse. Stop, I have an idea," Will

CHAPTER TWENTY-THREE

said.

Will removed one of his mittens and swiped a finger in the soot on the kerosene lantern hanging off Jimmy's pack. "Now, hold still," he ordered. "You don't want to get this in your eyes. Close your eyes and don't move."

Jimmy Bou stood stiff as a statue as Will smeared a small amount of soot under each eye.

"There, that should help. You can open your eyes."

Jimmy blinked and looked left and right at the snow-filled forest surrounding them. "Hey, that is better. Thanks, Will."

They plodded along for another half hour. The light was fading; it would be dark soon. Will heard the distant rumble of a train, then its eerie whistle. He'd always loved the sound of a train. It lit up his imagination, and he daydreamed about where he would go if he had the chance.

Suddenly, Will realized that the open road they were following had narrowed. Here the trees loomed higher, blocking the light; they grew thicker, hiding forest trails. An army of pines crept toward him and Jimmy. The forest was coming alive.

"Hey, Will, did we make a wrong move? It feels like the forest is closing in on us," Jimmy said.

"I was thinking the same thing. When we started, there was a much wider space between the edge of the forest and the road. I don't think it gets any worse up ahead, though."

"I hope not. I'm feeling a little claustrophobic."

When Will had stopped walking and turned back to check their surroundings, Jimmy had kept going. Now, still moving, he looked over his shoulder at Will, then gave a shout and went flying. He fell flat on his face in the deep snow, the weight of his body and the heavy pack he carried causing him to sink a foot into the depths.

Will could hear him yelling, Jimmy's voice sounding as if it were coming from the far end of a tunnel. Jimmy struggled to move his arms and position his hands beneath his body so he could lever himself up, but failed. He tried rolling to his side, but the bulky backpack and snowshoes prevented his movement. Will wrenched off his pack, threw it down in the snow, and shouted at Jimmy Bou to stay still. He grabbed the left side of Jimmy's jacket at the shoulder and hip, pulling it up and over so Jimmy was lying on his side with his face free from the crush of snow. Sputtering to get the suffocating snow out of his nose and mouth, Jimmy tore off his mittens and grabbed handfuls from his face. Then, coughing and sneezing, he wiggled onto his back. Will leaned down and unfastened the buckles on Jimmy's pack and helped him free his arms. Jimmy bent his knees and planted his snowshoes flat on the snow, then he reached out and grabbed Will's outstretched hands. After several tries, Will pulled him back on his feet, snowshoes intact.

Jimmy Bou leaned over with his hands on his knees, breathing hard. After a minute, he looked up at Will. "It felt like I was drowning." Moments before, Jimmy's face had been pink from the biting wind and cold. Now, it was the white of bleached linens. He exhaled hard. "That was horrible, Will. I was really scared for a minute."

"What happened?"

"I must have tripped over something, but it happened so fast, I don't know." He turned to look at the path he had taken. A disturbed patch of snow revealed a branch that had broken off. Jimmy reached out and felt a large tree limb hiding under the snowpack. "Jeez. Let's get going…before something else happens."

Will helped Jimmy hoist his backpack onto his shoulders and buckled the straps. Jimmy did the same for Will. Although it was nearly dark, he refreshed the soot under Jimmy's eyes, and they took off again.

"I wish we knew how far we've gone," Jimmy said some time later.

CHAPTER TWENTY-THREE

"What do you think?"

"We should be getting close. Steven said this road was about three miles. We drove a mile in, and we've been making decent progress. Let's keep our eyes peeled for lights up ahead."

Night fell without a warning, and their world went black, as though someone had closed the lid on a box, trapping them inside. Will and Jimmy Bou stopped as one person. Both men, having experienced nighttime hiking and camping, knew it would only take a moment for their eyes to adjust to the darkness. Little by little, black shadows became blurry-edged shapes. Then, those shapes became trees, branches, and needles.

The wind picked up, pushing the clouds away. The moon shone brightly, and thousands of stars glittered, turning the forest into a sea of diamonds as the light touched the snow.

Great Camp Onontaga, Adirondack Mountains

Back in Cabin A, Olivia curled up by the fire with a copy of *The Maltese Falcon* that she'd borrowed from Gil Racine's library. She remembered watching the movie on DVD some years ago and had thoroughly enjoyed it—Peter Lorre was her hands-down favorite—but she'd never read the book. Now, she couldn't resist holding this brand-new first edition in her hands. Liz would lose her mind.

When she traveled into the past, Olivia's best friends, Liz and Sophie, always went with her in her heart and in her thoughts. She hoped someday she and Steven would figure out how to bring them in person. Until then, she brought back 1934 fashion magazines and small gifts from this long-ago time. The only caveat was that they keep these treasures private. No one could ever lay eyes on them, or her and Steven's secret would begin to leak out. That would be a disaster.

At work in their HQ, Steven unrolled two additional lengths of brown butcher paper and taped them on the closet door, one above the other. The wide paper covered the surface from edge to edge and stuck out a bit on both sides.

Determined to piece this puzzle together, Steven started on the bottom paper with what he considered the easier part of his task. He labeled two columns: <u>Eliminated</u> and <u>Unlikely</u>. Under <u>Eliminated</u>, he wrote:

Margery Racine – *would never kill her own son. Grief and distress deemed genuine.*

Irene Racine – *would not kill her beloved father. Immense grief over father believed genuine. Real sorrow over brother.*

Lewis Salisbury – *would not risk his relationship with Margery. She would find out he had killed her child.*

As he wrote, Steven thought, *Killing the son of the woman he loves is out of the question. And I'm sure Lewis loves Margery, cousin or no cousin.*

Victor McAllister – *would not risk losing Irene (and her fortune). He'd know she would discover he killed her father.*

Aunt Emily – *Does not have the strength to hold Julian down under the water/ice or to push the metal pole into his neck and force him under.*

Steven listed two names under <u>Unlikely</u>:

Doris Buckley, cook – *Too busy in the kitchen. No time. Would have been missed by staff. No obvious motive.*

Corinne Kelly, maid – *Busy with her work, watched by Mrs. Buckley. Not strong enough to kill Julian. No apparent motive.*

Now Steven was ready to get at the heart of this case.

He divided the top portion into three sections—one for each suspect—and further split each section in two: Gil's murder and Julian's murder. There, he listed possible motives, means, and opportunities for each murder.

Sensing he was on the verge of a breakthrough, Steven forced

CHAPTER TWENTY-THREE

himself to be calm. He inhaled, held his breath, and counted to ten, then exhaled to a second count of ten. He repeated this until his mind cleared and his thoughts flowed freely, touching on the personality and character of his three suspects, analyzing the relationships between suspects and victims.

When he believed he understood all sides of the case, Steven began to write. When he finished, his makeshift murder board looked like this:

SUSPECT: JACK
<u>GIL'S MURDER</u>
Motive – Resents being born second. Wants family fortune. STRONG MOTIVE
Means – Could have learned how poison works.
Opportunity –YES. Arrived Wed. afternoon.

<u>JULIAN'S MURDER</u>
Motive – Unknown. Did Julian witness him putting poison on piano? Is his inheritance bigger without Julian?
Means – Strong enough to enlarge ice-fishing hole, push Julian into water, keep him under.
Opportunity – YES.
EXCELLENT OPPORTUNITY FOR BOTH MURDERS. He was there!

SUSPECT: HARRY
<u>GIL'S MURDER</u>
Motive – Need more information. Would Harry profit in some way? Did he resent Gil for some reason? Did he align himself with Jack and consider the murder something of a "favor" for Jack? Did Harry help Jack by showing him how to use the poison safely?
Means – Knows how to handle potassium cyanide and how it works. Poison available at all times in his darkroom. **Past experience with potassium cyanide** Is this important? Is someone trying to frame him?
Opportunity –Before supper Thurs. YES. (Was not there Wed. night)

JULIAN'S MURDER
Motive – Unknown. Did Julian see him putting poison on piano?
Does he inherit more if Julian is dead?
Means – Strong enough to handle all aspects of plan and execution.
Opportunity – YES.
SUSPECT: RIDER

GIL'S MURDER
Motive – Possible resentment for lifetime of employment. Maybe not paid enough, not treated well. Was Gil going to replace him? Did he want to retire and could he afford to? Did Gil learn something about his past?
Means – Could learn about poison and how to handle it. Murder weapon always available in Cabin D.
Opportunity – Was there at all times.

JULIAN'S MURDER
Motive – Unknown. Did Julian see him putting poison on piano? Did Julian know something about his past? Did Julian threaten to have him fired for some reason?
Means – Strong enough to accomplish all that was done.
Opportunity – Was there at all times.
NOTE: Rider moves around unnoticed. Staff is invisible to family. Important?

Olivia tapped on the bedroom door. "Can I come in?"

Steven jerked it open. "Of course! I've made some good progress. Thanks for letting me just *think*. Now, tell me what *you* think." He pointed to the closet door.

"Ooh, you really expanded your notes. Let's see." She stood in front of the papers and now and then, she'd say "Oh yeah." or "Good point."

"This is great, Steven. I like the way you laid everything out." She scrunched up her face. "I notice there's no section for physical evidence."

"You're reading my mind. That's the one thing we don't have. It's

CHAPTER TWENTY-THREE

also the one thing we need—a piece of hard evidence in order to accuse someone."

"I've been thinking about something," Olivia said. "Gil wouldn't even publish his son's novel, so why would he trust Julian to run the businesses? I bet Jack does inherit. I like your questions about how Harry might have worked with Jack or helped him in some way."

"The easiest solution is often the right one," Steven said. "Maybe it's as simple as Harry believing Jack should have been the older brother and deserved to inherit everything from their father."

"So, how does Julian's murder fit into this? I think the best reason is he saw whoever put the poison on the piano. Besides, everyone looked devastated when we found him."

"I'm not sure the way anyone looked is important. I've seen people kill someone they loved, then completely fall apart with grief. And it's real, not faked. Even worse, if given the chance and the same circumstances, they'd do it all over again."

"How horrible! There's so much in what you do that I had no idea about." Olivia perched on the edge of the bed.

"Alright, let's examine Jack and Harry. They both seem fairly happy," Steven said. "Jack says he enjoys his life in the Navy. Harry seems to like taking photographs and traveling all over the world. But what if they're both sick of their lives? What if they want to give up what they've been doing and come home?

"If the two of them worked together to eliminate both Gil and Julian, they'd be able to split everything. Jack gets the New York City mansion—Harry could still have his apartment there—and Harry gets Onontaga. They split the money. The business is made up of two companies—the newspaper and the literary press—they each take over one. The more I'm talking about this, the more it makes sense. It answers all our questions. Olivia, we need to look deeper into the two brothers."

"Are you sure about Margery, though? In my time, unless there's a will saying otherwise, she'd inherit everything."

"Not nowadays. Gil would have certainly made provisions for her, like giving her the right to live in the New York City house, to use Onontaga whenever she wanted, and I'm sure he left her enough money to live on for the rest of her life. But, it's more likely he left the businesses to one of the men in the family—Jack, as the next oldest, or Jack and Harry together. I agree with what you said about not trusting Julian."

"I think we've got it. That's the answer. Jack and Harry together." Suddenly, Olivia's eyes grew big, and her hand flew up to her lips, as if to stop herself from speaking. "Oh no, I thought of a stronger motive for Victor killing *both* of them!"

"What? We ruled him out."

"With Gil dead and Julian out of the picture, Irene stands to inherit more. Maybe even twice as much," Olivia said.

"That might be true, but how would he have convinced Julian to go out on the lake in the middle of the night? No, I'm sure Victor's not our killer, Olivia."

Chapter Twenty-Four

It was late afternoon and already growing dark when Steven and Olivia returned to the main lodge. The heavy cloud cover signaled yet more snow, and the temperature was falling. Someone had lit the lights in the great room and on the Christmas tree. Olivia thought the tree looked out of place, given everything that had happened.

Aunt Emily sat alone by the fire as Steven and Olivia approached her.

"Everyone's gone to their rooms," she said. "It was becoming rather difficult to find things to talk about. I took a nap, and I have to say it helped."

"We'll be right back to keep you company. There's something we need to check," Steven said, leading Olivia across the room and down the corridor to the kitchen.

All the lights in the kitchen blazed. The staff bustled about, busy preparing dinner.

"Mrs. Buckley, can you spare Miss Kelly for a moment? We have a question for her. It won't take long."

"Yes, alright. Go on with you, girl."

Steven led the maid to a quiet spot in the corner where they wouldn't be overheard.

"Now, don't be nervous, Miss Kelly. We only want to know what you may have seen or heard. You are not a suspect. Do you understand?"

"Yes, sir."

"We've narrowed down the time when someone could have put the poison that killed Mr. Racine on the piano keys. First of all, did you get out of bed at any time between Wednesday night and Thursday morning?"

"No, sir."

"What time did you go to bed?"

"I finished my evening duties around nine. Then I went to my room."

"Where is your room?"

"If you go out into the hallway to the right," she pointed past the kitchen door, "the staff rooms are down toward the end. Mine is the first one, then Cook's. Rider's at the very end."

"So, you went to your room around nine. I assume you closed the door?"

"Yes, of course."

"Did you hear anyone up after that?"

"Cook was snoring by around ten-thirty. I can hear because there are cracks in the wall. I think Rider was up later, but I couldn't say for sure."

"And you're certain you didn't get up for any reason? A glass of water, or perhaps to use the bathroom?"

"No, I'm sure."

"Alright," Steven continued, "what were your duties Thursday before dinner? Say from mid-afternoon until the meal was served."

"During the afternoon, I helped Mrs. Buckley in the kitchen. When everyone went to their rooms to change—that was around five o'clock—I set the table. It takes about a half hour because Mrs. Racine has me shine all the glasses."

"Was the tablecloth already on the table?" Olivia asked.

"Yes, Rider irons it and puts it on before I start."

CHAPTER TWENTY-FOUR

"I see. Go on."

"After the glasses, I set out the plates and silverware. Then I fold the napkins and set them around."

"Does Rider help in any other way?" Olivia asked.

"He arranges the centerpiece. It's the last thing we do."

"So, you were in the dining area from about five until five-thirty?" Steven asked.

"Yes, about that."

"Did you see anyone near Mr. Racine's piano during that time?"

Kneading her apron while she squinted and scrunched up her face, Corinne Kelly thought, then said, "Mr. Jack came into the living area once, but I don't think he was near the piano. Mr. McAllister forgot his cigarettes. He asked me if I'd seen them. And Mr. Harry came in from his cabin. He said he left something in the lodge. I saw him looking near the piano, but I didn't pay attention. I had my work to do, and I didn't want to be late because Cook needed me in the kitchen after I finished with the table."

"How close to the piano would you say Harry was, Miss Kelly?" Steven asked.

"The only time I looked over, he was picking something up from the little table that's next to the piano bench."

"Did you notice if he had anything in his hands when he came in from outside?"

"I'm sorry, sir. I didn't notice."

"Do you remember if Mr. McAllister or Mr. Harry was wearing gloves?" asked Steven.

"Umm...Mr. McAllister, definitely not. Mr. Harry, I'm not sure. Maybe."

"Alright, Miss Kelly, Corinne, if you think of anything else, please let Miss Watson or me know."

"Yes, sir. I will."

205

Steven turned to the cook. "Mrs. Buckley, do you know where Rider is?" he asked.

"Mr. Jack asked him to shovel the snow along the path in front of the cabins about a half hour ago. I think he's still out there."

When Steven and Olivia returned to the great room, they saw Aunt Emily still sitting on one end of the sofa near the hearth with a wool blanket thrown over her legs and lap; however, in the short time they'd been in the kitchen, everything else had changed. Lewis and Harry conversed by the drinks cart while Lewis mixed a pitcher of cocktails. Jack was near the front door, donning his outer gear. Victor stood by the mantle, smoking.

Steven strode across the room. "Jack, where are you going? It's already dark out."

"I'm sick of sitting here waiting for the next person to be killed. We're all sitting ducks, Steven. Well, probably not you and Olivia, but the rest of us are. We still don't know who's doing this. I'm going to start clearing a path wide enough for us to drive out of here."

"I thought you said the access road was too long for your snow-blowing machine."

"It is. I'm going to see how much I can open up in a half hour. Then I'll let the engine rest and go out for another half hour. The vehicle has headlights. I don't care if it takes me all night. And I don't care if I burn out the motor. I want out of this madhouse." He pulled on his boots. "I should have thought of it earlier," he said in disgust.

Steven wanted to go with him but hesitated to leave Olivia alone. Hoping Jack wasn't planning to escape, Steven decided he'd find time to talk with him later. He was determined to discover what he wanted to know tonight.

As Steven turned to join the others and Jack reached for the knob, there was a powerful pounding on the door. Everyone jumped at

CHAPTER TWENTY-FOUR

the sound. All eyes went toward the entrance. Jack wrenched open the door. A gust of wind blew snow up in the air and into the foyer, swirling around Jack Racine like a cyclone.

Two tall men, laden with backpacks and rolled sleeping bags, stood on the threshold. A thin slice of their faces was visible between scarves and hats.

"Hello, I'm Sergeant Will Taylor of the Knightsbridge Police. This is Officer Jimmy Bourgogne. We're looking for Detective Sergeant Steven Blackwell."

"Is this Great Camp Onontaga?" Jimmy Bou added.

Steven's jaw dropped as he gaped at the new arrivals. "Will! Jimmy! I can't believe it."

Olivia gasped. "Oh, my goodness!"

"Steven!" Will and Jimmy Bou chorused.

"Olivia!" Jimmy Bou exclaimed with a grin.

"What in heaven's name are you doing here?" Steven turned to Jack. "Sergeant Taylor is my partner. Jimmy's an indispensable member of our team."

"Glad to meet you, fellas. Come in, come in." Jack stepped aside, waving them into the warm room. "You must be freezing. How did you get here? Have the roads been cleared?" Jack peered around them, looking for the good news that the road was snow-free.

"No, we abandoned the car about a mile in. We snowshoed the rest of the way," said Will. "Mind if we leave our snowshoes and poles out here? We set them over there in the corner." Will indicated the far end of the porch.

"Of course," Jack said.

When Will and Jimmy Bou entered the lodge, both men sighed.

"This is swell," Jimmy Bou exclaimed. "Two fireplaces! Look, Will, two."

Jack laughed. "You're welcome to sit by the fire all night if you like,

Jimmy. And I'll get you a drink to warm your insides as well."

"You can leave your jackets here," Steven told them, pointing to a hall tree and several hooks overflowing with coats, jackets, hats, and scarves.

Jack left to get a brandy for Will and Jimmy Bou. As soon as Jack was out of earshot, Steven whispered, "What are you doing here?"

"We need to talk with you alone, Steven," said Will quietly. "Your father called the station. I was going to tell you when the phone went dead this morning. There's something you need to know. Right away."

"Come on over here, fellas," Jack called.

Steven, Olivia, Will, and Jimmy Bou joined him by the fire.

"You two are a sight for sore eyes," Olivia said. "I can't believe you came all this way in a blizzard!"

"It wasn't easy. I'll tell you that," said Jimmy, taking the cut crystal glass with amber liquid glowing within. "Thank you." Jimmy took a gulp and sputtered. "Oooh, boy. You weren't kidding when you said it would warm our insides, Jack. I think my throat's on fire."

Everyone laughed.

"Ah, Rider," said Jack, seeing the butler kicking the snow off his boots and entering the room. "We have two more guests for dinner. If you could arrange that…."

"Of course, sir. I wanted you to know I've shoveled the path all the way up to the last cabin."

"Thank you. It looks like we're going to need that cabin after all."

"Certainly, Mr. Jack. I'll see to it right away."

Jack turned to Will and Jimmy Bou. "Cabin F is empty. It's the last one before you reach the stables. You gentlemen are welcome to bunk down there. There are two bedrooms, small but quite comfortable. Rider will make up the beds for you. He'll also get the fire going so the cabin will be warm by the time you turn in."

After Will and Jimmy had thanked Jack and were introduced to the

CHAPTER TWENTY-FOUR

others, Steven said, "Jack, if you don't mind, I'd like a word with my colleagues."

"Of course, I'm going back outside and see what my snow-blowing machine can do. See you later."

As soon as they entered Cabin A, Steven said to Will and Jimmy, "I've talked freely about the case with Olivia. She knows everything I know. And we've discussed as many motives and explanations that we could think of."

"Will," Olivia said excitedly, "it's not as good as your murder board at the station, but wait until you see what I rigged up for Steven."

During their long trek to the Great Camp, Will had prepared himself to face Olivia. He pushed his recent investigation out of his mind and made sure he acted normally. "Swell, Olivia," he said. "Where is it?"

Olivia flung open the door to their HQ and pointed to the makeshift murder board split in two—on the wall and the closet door. "Ta-da!" she cried.

"Wowie, Olivia," said Jimmy Bou. "This is aces!"

"Will, before you fellas read our notes and we talk, tell me what my father said."

Will and Jimmy looked at each other, Jimmy's face sliding into a serious pose.

"Jack was dishonorably discharged from the Navy last year. No one knows what he's been doing or where he's been living for the past year and a half," Will said.

The shock of this news stunned Steven and Olivia. Their eyes widened, and they stared at each other. Neither spoke for a moment.

Finally, Steven asked, "Why?"

"He killed a man."

Chapter Twenty-Five

Great Camp Onontaga, Adirondack Mountains

Margery awoke to darkness. Disoriented, she peered into the night, taking in her environs. She couldn't seem to place this location. She didn't know what day it was. Was it nighttime? Or morning?

Oh, yes. Onontaga. There was her favorite chair by the window. Then, the memory of Julian's death rushed back, overwhelming her. A moan escaped her lips. The realization of what had happened tore at her insides, shredding her heart and crushing her soul. Her baby. Her Julian. Covering her mouth to muffle her cries, Margery shook as she sobbed into her pillow.

Margery wept for the loss of her son—now and all the years before. Why hadn't she spent more time with him? Had he known how much she loved him? Why hadn't she said the words?

Her children had grown up with absent parents. Was it too late, or could she save her relationship with Irene?

When she was drained, Margery swung her legs over the side of the bed and sat up. She had no choice. They were still snowed in in this damned place. Trapped with a killer who was murdering a member of her family every day. They had nowhere to go, no way to escape. *I*

CHAPTER TWENTY-FIVE

swear, she vowed to herself, *if we get out of here alive, I'm never coming back to this place. Onontaga can rot, for all I care.*

Margery reached for the bedside lamp, but the weak light brought little relief to the dark room. She slipped her feet into her shoes and stood. She ran her palms up her stockings to ensure the seams were straight, smoothed the skirt of her black silk dress, and adjusted the narrow belt. She walked to the small dressing table and looked at herself in the mirror on the wall. A stranger stared back. The sparkle was gone. Her face sagged like an old woman's.

Margery thought of Lewis downstairs. Every moment spent with the love of her life was a moment she celebrated and cherished. In over forty years, his presence had never failed to bring a spark of joy. Where was that spark now?

Margery had been fond of Gil. Her father had been right all those years ago, that with work and effort, she would grow to care for him. Her mother had told her to marry a man who loved her more than she loved him. Gil adored her, and they had made a good marriage. Although Gil had worked hard, and she hadn't seen him much, he had more than provided for her and the children. He had given them an aristocratic life. Nothing was beyond their reach. A new fur coat? Of course. The latest model roadster? No problem. A necklace to match her new diamond ring? Gil had only wanted to know: one strand or two?

And Gil had never once objected to the hours she spent on her volunteer work or her visits to the theater with Lewis. Margery wondered if her husband had ever suspected the depth of emotion between her and Lewis. If he had, he'd never said a word.

She knew she'd been a good wife to him. She'd stood by his side, entertained his business associates, acted as his hostess at countless events. And she had never once crossed a line with Lewis. That would have ruined everything. For although she had been tempted, she was too principled to consider it. It had been an unspoken agreement between the two of them since the beginning. Some things were simply taboo.

Enough! Her life with Gil was past. Now, she had the chance to make a new life. Maybe a better life. There was nothing she could have done to prevent Julian's death. And she refused to tarnish her son's memory with an atmosphere of gloom. Time to steel her spine, tilt her chin, and put on a brave face. Time even to celebrate the beautiful boy she had lost.

Margery allowed herself a few more moments of mourning, weeping until her soul was wrung dry, before she forced herself to stop.

She splashed some water on her face, patted her cheeks with a towel, then reached for her wand of mascara, liner pencil, and a tube of lipstick. She still had guests downstairs, and she was going to face them like a Racine should.

"Killed a man?" Steven repeated. "Did my father give you any details?"

"Jack's executive officer witnessed the whole thing," Will said. "Their ship had docked in Manila, in the Philippines, and Jack went ashore. He'd been drinking in a local bar and stumbled out onto the sidewalk. Another sailor, who'd had even more to drink, followed him out, then tripped—they thought accidentally—and pushed Jack out into the road in front of oncoming traffic. Jack barely escaped being killed. He turned around and punched the fella in the face. The man hit his head when he fell onto the concrete sidewalk. He died instantly. Your father wasn't sure if Jack's punch killed him or if it was the man's head hitting the sidewalk. But the result was the same.

"They held a court-martial and convicted him of involuntary manslaughter. Your father had no idea why they didn't throw him in prison. Instead, they sent him packing with a dishonorable discharge. Like I said, no one knows what he's been doing or where he's been

CHAPTER TWENTY-FIVE

living since then."

"Wow," Olivia said as she exhaled forcibly.

"This fills a gap that I've been wondering about. I want to tell you about a theory Olivia and I came up with," Steven said. "Let's sit in the living room. You fellas must be exhausted."

"Yeah, I am a bit tired," Jimmy Bou admitted.

"Steven, I'd like to leave you guys alone so you can discuss things the way you normally do together. I'm going to see if Harry's returned to his cabin. If he hasn't, I'll check the main lodge," Olivia said. "I want to look at those photographs. And I'll try to learn more about his life now."

"We said—" Steven interrupted.

She put her hand on his arm. "I know. But there's no way he's going to hurt me with three policemen thirty feet away. I'll be fine. I'm not worried. Besides, if something happens, I can scream loud enough so that you'll hear me. Don't worry. You talk with Will and Jimmy."

"Maybe Jimmy could—"

"No, you need him here. How many times have you told me that Jimmy Bou came up with a great idea that helped solve the case?"

"Gee, thanks, Olivia." Jimmy blushed.

"It sounds like you're considering Harry Racine as a suspect," Will said. "I brought a whistle with me that Olivia can borrow. You know how shrill they are, Steven. If she gets in trouble, we'll hear her." Will dug into his pocket and handed the silver tube to Olivia.

"Thanks, Will," she said, then looked up at Steven, who was still frowning. "See? You know I'll be okay. You need to discuss the case with Will and Jimmy. The three of you are going to solve it. I'll be back before you know it."

Steven reluctantly let her go.

Olivia knocked on the door to Cabin B. Hearing movement inside, she set her face in a friendly, neutral, and interested mask. When a tousled Harry Racine opened the door, she smiled.

"Hi, Harry. I thought I'd see if you found the box of pictures from the dig at King Tutankhamun's tomb. I figured you might not want to risk bringing them over to the lodge. You know, like dropping them in the snow or something." It sounded pretty feeble to Olivia's ears, but she didn't care. The objective was to sit with him alone and get him talking. She gripped the whistle in her jacket pocket.

"Oh sure, Olivia. Come in. I think I dozed off a bit. Gee, it's dark already."

Harry set about lighting lamps, then motioned for Olivia to join him in one of the leather chairs flanking the fire. He threw on another log, prompting a shower of sparks to fill the hearth, then tilted one that had shifted from the center of the blaze. Olivia noticed a half-empty glass and a book lying open, face down on a nearby Adirondack twig table—one built with legs fashioned from branches.

"What are you reading?" she asked.

He picked up the book and showed her the cover. *"The Sun Also Rises.* Hemingway understands what it was like. You know, the war."

"Yes, I think he probably does."

"Take a seat. I'll get that box," said Harry.

Harry returned with a shoe box stuffed to bursting with sepia-toned photographs. Olivia's face lit up, and she rubbed her hands together.

"Oooh! I can't wait to see these, Harry. I really appreciate you taking the time to show me."

"To tell you the truth, I'm glad for the distraction. It's pretty difficult being a Racine this weekend. Makes me wonder who's next."

Her jaw dropped. "You don't think it's over?"

"I don't know what to think. I can come up with plenty of reasons why somebody would want to do away with my brother. He could be a real bastard." His hand flew to his mouth. "Oh, I apologize. I don't

CHAPTER TWENTY-FIVE

normally use that kind of language in front of a lady."

"It's okay. I've heard worse." *And I've said worse,* she thought. "I was a reporter for several years. You get used to it."

He nodded. "But I have no idea why anybody would want to hurt Julian. He was rather innocuous. Minded his own business. Hated confrontations, so he never got into an argument with anyone. The few times when I was home, and he was around, it was like he was invisible. Never said a peep. The only thing he cared about was that manuscript of his. I can't understand why my brother didn't publish the thing. Gil had more money than Croesus. Even if the book never sold a single copy, Gil could have absorbed the cost. It was his own son, for crying out loud. You'd think he'd be thrilled to do the kid a favor. Gil *knew* how much it meant to Julian." Harry shook his head. "Let's not talk about that. You came over to see the photographs. Shame they aren't in color. But, at least, you'll get an idea of what it was like."

Harry opened the box, and a dozen photos slid off the top of the pile onto the floor.

"You need a bigger container, Harry." Olivia laughed, reaching to pick them up.

"There are a fair number of duplicates in here. And I know which ones they are. You can have them if you'd like."

"I don't know what to say, Harry. Thank you."

He laughed. "Thank me when we find them." He took a handful of precious history and began his commentary.

As Harry talked, Olivia forgot all about the double murder, the killer on the loose, the isolated Great Camp, the snowstorm, and Steven in the cabin next door. Harry captivated her with the story of Howard Carter's discovery of King Tutankhamun's tomb. Words like lapis lazuli, scarabs, funerary mask, and ankh swirled around her mind.

"This is so exciting. How did you go from working with Howard Carter to taking photos for magazines?" Olivia asked.

"I left Howard and the dig in Egypt. On my way home, I stopped in London to see a friend—the fellow who introduced me to Howard in the first place. He was working as an editor for *National Geographic* magazine and was relocating to New York. I showed him some of my photographs, and he hired me on the spot. That man made my career. If it hadn't been for him, I might still be banging on doors looking for work. Later, he introduced me to the editors at several other publications—*Life*, *Scientific American*, and *Travel*.

"The way it works is I let them know where I'm going, and they tell me what kinds of photos they could use, or they tell me what they need for upcoming issues, and I make arrangements to attach myself to an expedition going to that place," Harry explained.

"I have to confess that I love traveling, but I think it takes a special kind of person to endure the type of trips you take," Olivia said. "Do you think what you went through during the war helped prepare you for the harsh conditions of the trips you've taken since then?"

The ghost of a memory washed over the youngest Racine brother's face, and Olivia saw pain in his eyes.

"Oh, Harry! I'm so sorry if I said something I shouldn't have…about the war, I mean. I never know if someone will talk about it." She winced.

"It's okay, Olivia. Yes, the war was difficult, but it happened. And you're right, it did prepare me. The life I chose is hard, but I haven't wanted to be a tourist, staying in nice hotels and eating in expensive restaurants. I believed—and still believe—that in order to take honest and true photographs, I needed to see things as they really are, without the fancy trappings."

"I don't know how you could ever give up this exciting life. To be there when history is being made and have the chance to record everything for posterity is amazing. And you've had the chance to learn how people all over the world live," Olivia exclaimed. "I think

CHAPTER TWENTY-FIVE

I'm envious."

"Yes, but I've been doing this a long time. I don't know how much longer I want to trek through the desert or fight my way through a jungle." He rubbed a knee. "I'm feeling my age these days. The trips are grueling. Extreme temperatures, insects that want to eat you alive, wild animals that would be happy to call you dinner...well, anyway. I don't want to complain. It's been a privilege, but I can see the end in sight."

"I understand what you're saying. I think there comes a time for people to assess their lives and maybe make a change. What do you think you'll do when you no longer take these trips? Photograph things closer to home?"

"Maybe. Honestly, I'd like to stay right here at Onontaga, but in the main lodge, not this miserable little cabin. I've been thinking of writing about my experiences."

"That's a swell idea," she exclaimed. She glanced at the clock on the wall. "Oh, my goodness! It's almost time for dinner." Olivia stood and extended her hand. "Harry, thank you again. It's been lovely listening to your adventures and talking with you."

"You're most welcome. It's been my pleasure. And here, take these pictures. I know I have duplicates." He shoved seven or eight photos into her hand. "And, Olivia, if things don't work out with Steven, let me know." He raised his eyebrows and gave her a smile that came from deep in his eyes. "I think you and I might be kindred spirits."

Chapter Twenty-Six

Olivia paused in front of Cabin A then, curious about the possible portal she had stumbled on, she continued to the corner and faced the space between the cabin and the garage. If Sophie had been there earlier, would she still be here now? Olivia knew it would be cold in 2014, too, and growing more frigid as the night advanced. Sophie wouldn't want to waste gas sitting in the car with the engine running, keeping the heat on to stay warm. What might she have done? Although Great Camp Onontaga wasn't far from Knightsbridge, it was far enough. She couldn't drop in like they stopped by Bailey's Diner or the Three Lords Pub. Would Sophie have gotten a room at a nearby hotel so she could keep returning to check on Olivia? Was she that worried?

Olivia leaned toward the suspected portal and peered into the blackness. She listened. Nothing. No sounds of Sophie's music. No hum of the engine or swish of the windshield wipers. No moonlight reflecting on a glossy SUV fender.

The door to Cabin A opened. Light spilled onto the snow. Men's voices filled the air.

"We'll clean up and meet you in the lodge."

Without looking, Olivia identified Steven's partner, Will.

"I probably shouldn't, but I'm looking forward to tonight, Steven. I bet they put on a really good supper, huh?" said Jimmy Bou.

CHAPTER TWENTY-SIX

Olivia grinned in the darkness. Jimmy was always hungry. She stepped away from the space and met Will and Jimmy at the door.

"Yes, Jimmy, whatever's on the menu, you can be sure dinner is going to be delicious," she said.

"You were gone a long time," said Steven. "I was about to go get you."

"Harry showed me his photographs from the discovery of King Tut's tomb. They were wonderful. He had some exciting stories to tell, too." She edged around the two exiting police officers and stepped into the cabin beside Steven.

"Take your time, fellas." Steven consulted his watch. "I don't think Margery will serve supper much before eight. You've got a good forty-five minutes."

As Will and Jimmy Bou made their way along the path to the last cabin in the row, Steven closed the door and took Olivia in his arms. He hugged her tight. "I was starting to worry."

"You and Sophie." She smiled. "It was fine. I think we were both happy to forget about everything that's been going on this weekend. I got lost in his stories, and I think he did, too. I had to be careful, though. I didn't want him to know I'd been there. He would have wondered how I could afford such an expensive trip in the middle of a depression."

He squeezed her and whispered, "I'm so glad you're back with me, safe and sound. Let's not do that again, okay? We said we'd stay together. I don't know what I would do if something happened to you."

Their kiss lasted for what seemed like a long time. As Olivia melted into Steven, she realized this was what people meant when they used that old cliché "Time stood still."

When they broke apart, Olivia said, "Okay, coming back to reality." She laughed. "Do you think we can dress casually for dinner tonight?"

"Yeah, I don't think even Margery Racine will expect anything fancy after the day we all had. Let's just freshen up and join the others." He turned to enter the bedroom. "Hey, wait! What did you find out from Harry?"

"He wants to settle down at Onontaga. He wants it for himself."

"Does he now?"

"Yes, he said he's getting too old to travel the way he has been. He's had enough."

"He's only in his early forties. That's not old."

"Yeah, but think of the life he's led. All those extreme worlds he's lived in. That's got to take a toll. It wouldn't surprise me if he had health issues. Who knows what diseases he's picked up? Or what's in his system from bug bites?" She shivered. "Something did happen, though, Steven. He got a strange look on his face at one point. It only lasted a second, then he forged ahead with what he was saying. I'm trying to remember what it was."

"Think, Olivia, this could be important."

"I said two things back-to-back. One was about the Great War, and the other had to do with how difficult his trips were. I don't know which one he reacted to."

"I might have a clue. Will told me about an article he saw in the newspaper. You know the trip Harry took on the Amazon River in Brazil last month?"

"Yeah?"

"The guide died."

Olivia gasped. "Was it Harry's fault?"

"Who knows? Maybe. But we can't assume anything because we don't know what happened. The report only said the man had fallen overboard and was attacked by a giant crocodile. It listed Harry's name as one of the people on the expedition."

She exhaled hard. "I can see how upsetting that would be—whether

CHAPTER TWENTY-SIX

or not he was responsible. Obviously, you're going to ask him about it, right?"

"Yes, I'll wait until after supper, then take him aside. Maybe it was an accident. What could he possibly have had against an Amazon River guide?"

After freshening up and changing their clothes—Steven also shaved again—Steven and Olivia walked to the lodge. Holding hands in the moonlight, Olivia wished this had turned out to be the weekend getaway she had thought it might be. No dead bodies. No homicidal maniacs. No murder board in their cozy cabin. She wondered idly if this was what life with Steven would be like. And more importantly, did it matter to her?

And...what the heck was she thinking? *There you go again, Olivia Watson, dreaming about a future you can't have. The cruel question never went away—exactly how would they manage a life together?* Somebody would have to give up their present. She didn't see either of them willing to do that, despite the feelings they had for each other.

When they entered the Great Camp, the atmosphere was subdued. Soft classical music played in the background, music that filled a void but didn't offend.

Will and Jimmy Bou were deep in conversation with Jack and Harry, standing near the sideboard in the dining area where appetizers had been set out. All four were munching on hors d'oeuvres and held a drink in one hand. Irene sat on one of the sofas, gazing into the fire, Victor holding her hand. Neither spoke. Margery and Lewis crossed the room to welcome Steven and Olivia.

"Steven, Olivia, I don't know what to say about involving you both in this terrible situation. All I wanted was for you to enjoy a lovely weekend in the mountains and start the holiday season with us. I am truly sorry it turned out like this," Margery said.

Olivia reached for her hands, stunned that a woman who had lost her husband and son in the past forty-eight hours could muster the composure to think of her guests. "Please, Margery. I'm devastated for you. Don't think about us."

"Margery, I still believe we'll solve this before long," Steven reassured her.

Margery Racine's face fell. "But will I want to hear the answer? I don't know which is worse: that I've lost loved ones or that a loved one made all this happen." She shook her head as if to release sad thoughts and squared her shoulders. "No, tonight I am still your hostess, and you are my guests. We won't be singing Christmas carols, but we're not going to brood all evening. Mrs. Buckley has prepared a lovely dinner, and we will enjoy some interesting conversation. Besides, we have the pleasure of two new guests as well. Steven, you are a lucky man to have such loyal colleagues as Sergeant Taylor and Officer Bourgogne. It's a testament to how your men feel about you."

Lewis placed his hand on the small of Margery's back and, together, they escorted Steven and Olivia into the room. "Can I get you something to drink?" Lewis asked.

"We have some lovely appetizers laid out as well," Margery said, waving in the direction of the dining area.

Olivia marveled at how well dinner went, considering the circumstances.

"Will, did you read the paper yesterday?" asked Jack. "We haven't seen one since we left the city. Any news on the situation between Russia and the Ukraine?"

"Yes, they arrested thirty-seven more people. They're calling it a Russian plot against the Ukraine. That makes one hundred twenty arrests. They're charging them with terrorism."

"Those poor people," Margery said. "Why can't the Russians leave them alone?"

CHAPTER TWENTY-SIX

"Last year, they starved and killed millions of Ukrainian citizens," Steven said. "How can a nation do something like that? It's barbaric."

"Closer to home, the blizzard's been causing some problems," said Jimmy Bou. "A big freighter off the East Coast got in trouble because of the storm. It had to be towed in."

"Is there any good news?" asked Lewis.

"The British want to be better friends with us. One of their admirals wants to invite some naval ships to England in the spring to promote peace and strengthen the ties between the United States and the United Kingdom," Will said.

"Now, that's more like it," said Jimmy, then shared a funny story about a plum pudding one particular Christmas when he'd been a kid. He received good-hearted laughs for his efforts.

Thank goodness for Jimmy Bou, Olivia thought. *He seems to know exactly the kinds of stories that hit the mark—interesting but not trivial, entertaining but nothing to provoke too much laughter. A talent like that is such a gift. I'm glad he and Will came. I know Steven is, too. He relies on both of them.*

The only blemish on the evening was when Irene, who was attempting to eat her corn chowder, came close to breaking down and had to leave the table. Victor pushed back his chair to accompany her, but she put a hand on his shoulder, easing him back onto the seat. "No, darling, I just need to rest awhile. You stay and finish your meal."

After dessert, Steven took Will, Jimmy, and Olivia aside where no one could overhear. "Here's my idea for the evening. I need to ask Rider two questions. I can do that in his room or in the kitchen, depending on whether the cook or the maid is there. Then, I'm going to confront Jack with his Navy discharge. I'd like to know why he's been lying to everybody for over a year. After that, I'll question Harry about the incident in the Amazon." He turned to his partner.

"Will, would you be in on the questioning with me? I need your opinion of these three fellas. It would be a big step if we could narrow our suspects down to two tonight."

"Yes, of course. I'd like to get a sense of who they really are. Jack and Harry were on their best behavior at dinner—as you'd expect. They didn't give much away. And of course, Rider was working so...."

Steven went on. "Jimmy and Olivia, I want you to act as spies. Keep an eye on things and listen to what's being said. You might play cards or a board game. If you position yourselves at the card table, you'll be in the perfect spot to overhear what anyone says."

"Sure, I've always wanted to be a spy." Wiggling her eyebrows at Jimmy, Olivia didn't notice the flash of shock and anger on Will's face.

"Alright, Will and I'll come back here after we finish," said Steven.

The group broke up. Jimmy went to grab a game, and Olivia staked out a claim on the card table.

Steven pushed open the door, and he and Will entered the kitchen. Mrs. Buckley stood at the sink, washing dishes. Corinne Kelly was collecting plates and silverware from a table at the far end of the room, where the staff had had their supper. Rider was nowhere in sight.

"Mrs. Buckley, do you know where Rider is?" Steven asked.

"He took the garbage out, then he was going to clear more of the driveway. He went to get that snow-blowing machine." She brushed her arm across her forehead, pushing back the hair that was sticking to her face. The cook's cheeks were red, and Steven saw steam emanating from the sink. The water must have been scalding.

"Alright, thank you. By the way, your supper was delicious."

"That's nice of you to say, Detective Blackwell. I'm glad you enjoyed it."

After closing the kitchen door behind them, Steven said, "I suppose we'll have to leave him till morning."

"How much of a suspect is Rider? I thought you were leaning toward

CHAPTER TWENTY-SIX

Jack and Harry," Will whispered.

"He isn't, really. And you're right. I am looking at the two brothers. But, for the life of me, I don't know which one it is. We haven't found a shred of physical evidence. I'm speculating based on a few conversations I've had with each of them and on what other people have said. Part of the problem is I keep changing my mind. At one point, I thought something was off with Jack. I was positive he was hiding something or downright lying to me."

"That probably has to do with his dishonorable discharge," said Will.

"Yeah, at least I hope he doesn't have another big secret. Then I thought about Harry and how it takes a lot of courage and a strong, confident personality to go off on those wild trips he takes. That's the character of a killer—bold, daring, determined."

Will nodded.

"And there's Harry's darkroom. He knows better than anybody how to handle the poison." Steven paused. "I'm glad you came, Will. You know how much I value your skills and your opinion. I really need your help on this one."

"You got it. Let's get started. I want to see the other side of Jack and Harry—the part they hide when we're making polite conversation around the dinner table."

When Steven and Will returned to the living room, they saw Jimmy Bou and Olivia off to one side playing Parchisi. It was good to hear Olivia laugh.

Steven approached Jack. "Can we have a word?"

If Jack was surprised, he didn't show it. "Sure."

Chapter Twenty-Seven

Steven closed the heavy door and settled in Gil's chair behind the desk. Will stood to the side. Jack took the wooden visitor's chair.

For several moments, Steven contemplated Jack Racine in silence, his goal to establish boundaries and status.

Jack sat smoking and sipping his Scotch, seemingly at ease. Then he tamped out his cigarette, tossed back the remainder of his drink, and set the empty glass on the desk's blotter. Raising his brows, he said, "So, what are we talking about, Steven? Clearly, you have something in mind."

"I looked into your military record, Jack." Steven stared.

"You found out about my discharge."

"It wasn't just a discharge. Dishonorable discharge after being convicted of involuntary manslaughter. What the hell, Jack?"

Jack Racine made a fist and scowled. "It's this damned left hook. My trainer told me I'd have to be careful with it. And when I was in the ring, I was. I was always very aware of it and of my actions. Even when things got heated. But…." His lip curled, and he slowly shook his head. "Sometimes I lose my temper. That's what happened in the Philippines. A fella pushed me into the street in front of a speeding car. I was lucky. The driver had fast reflexes. He swerved and missed me. I jumped back on the sidewalk because more traffic was racing

CHAPTER TWENTY-SEVEN

toward me.

"But I lost my temper and punched the guy. I don't know if it was the blow that killed him or if he died when his head hit the concrete. It didn't matter, though. He was dead. One of my officers was walking by and saw the whole thing. I have no idea why they didn't throw me in jail. But I got lucky. They dismissed me instead."

"Where have you been living all this time? What have you been doing?" Steven asked.

"My ship dropped anchor in San Diego. I decided to stay in California, as far away from my family as I could get. I've been working on the docks loading ships in Oakland."

"I take it you didn't want your family to know about this?"

"Mostly, I didn't want Gil to know. He would have kicked me out of my quarters in the Fifth Avenue house. He would have distanced himself from me and prohibited everyone in the family from associating with me. Bad for business having a killer in the family."

"No wonder you haven't been home in a long time. I imagine you weren't earning a lot of dough as a stevedore. How did you get to New York at the beginning of the month?"

"Bus. The Greyhound was the only thing I could afford. I figured I'd stay at my apartment as long as I could. I was going to tell Gil I was retiring soon. I have a bank account in the city, so I knew I'd be set with money once I could get to New York. Then I could pretend to leave the Navy and move back to my apartment."

"But it all went wrong, didn't it, Jack? Did Gil learn about the dishonorable discharge? Maybe a piece of mail came to the house, and he opened it to see if it was urgent?"

"What? No."

"Then, to cover your tracks, to keep your secret safe until the time was right, you killed your brother."

"What? Steven, no, I swear I didn't hurt Gil. How can you think that I'd kill my twin?"

"Stranger things have happened, Jack." Steven leaned in closer. "Listen, when this blizzard lets up, and the local cops get here, they're going to want to know every detail about Gil's murder. Then they're going to investigate every minute of your life."

"Steven, I did *not* do this. I suppose you've seen some terrible things in your job, but I could never hurt Gil. Yes, we had our differences, arguments, fights even. But kill him? No. Never."

"What about the Fourth of July when you were eight or nine years old and you stood on the dock watching your twin struggle in the water? If your father hadn't rescued him, he would have drowned."

"What are you talking about?"

"Your family was having lunch on the patio behind Onontaga—right here, Jack—and you and Gil went down to the lake to swim. Gil caught his foot in a rope tied to the dock and kept going under. Rider saw what was happening, and your father ran down to save him."

Jack's mouth opened, then he glared at Steven. "Who told you this? None of that ever happened. Gil was a swell swimmer. And if...I say *if*...he'd ever caught his foot in something, I would have helped him get out. Even if I was mad at him. That's a bunch of malarky."

Steven saw Jack tighten his left fist, and a vein throbbed on his neck as he clenched his jaw. "It's my understanding that you resented your brother for being born first and being the one who inherited everything," Steven said.

"Yeah, that's true when I was a kid. But I grew up and got over it. I wanted to enlist in the Navy—it wasn't a second choice. And I really liked my life onboard ship. I'd already started thinking about where my next assignment would be. I was furious with myself for losing my temper that night in the Philippines. Of course, I felt terrible about what happened to that fella. Steven, the sight of him hitting the

CHAPTER TWENTY-SEVEN

sidewalk is going to haunt me for the rest of my life."

Steven could see Jack reliving the moment—a burst of anger, a wild punch, the sound of impact when his fist hit the man's face, the thud when his head hit the concrete, the sightless eyes as life left his body.

Jack shook his head as if shaking the memory out. "That one terrible night changed my life forever."

"What are your plans now?" Steven asked.

"I'm not sure. Financially, I'll be alright. I've got my apartment in the city for as long as I live. I can come up here to the mountains whenever I want." Jack nailed Steven with a gaze. "I had *no* motive for wanting my brother dead, Steven. I don't want Gil's life. All he ever did was work. I don't want that. And I certainly don't want to work in an office. I'll find a job working outdoors."

"Alright, Jack. Thanks. I'll probably want to talk again later," Steven said.

"Fine." Jack Racine stomped out of his brother's study, leaving the door open.

"He's not very happy with you," Will said.

"I got that impression."

"Who told you about the near drowning?" Will asked.

"Rider."

"Another reason to talk with him. Is there someone else who might corroborate the story?"

"I'd ask Margery, but I think she's gone back to her room. Let's try Aunt Emily. And let's do it now before I question Harry," said Steven.

"Good idea. Want me to get her?"

"No, thanks. I've built up some trust with her over the past few days. I think she'll cooperate better if I ask her."

Steven ushered Emily Racine into the study. When he asked where she would be more comfortable, she chose Gil's easy chair by the fire.

Steven pulled the visitor's chair, abandoned by Jack, close to her so they were almost knee to knee. Will sat behind Gil Racine's desk in what he thought was a non-threatening pose.

"How are you holding up, Miss Racine?" Steven began.

"Not much I can do, is there? We have to keep putting one foot in front of the other, no matter how we feel," she said.

"Yes, that's a practical way of thinking. I can appreciate that. In my job, I've found that, although we can't bring back a loved one, we can get justice. There seems to be a measure of comfort in that."

"Maybe. So, what do you want to know this time?" Aunt Emily asked.

"Someone told me about an incident that happened when Gil and Jack were young boys. I'd like you to tell me if it actually happened."

"I can do that."

Steven recounted the near-drowning episode that Rider had related, and Jack had denied.

"What fool said that?" she demanded. "Absolutely not. That did not happen." She closed her eyes, exhaling with a measure of annoyance. Then she nailed him with a look and said, "Detective Blackwell, my nephew always invited me to come up here with the family in the summer. When the boys were young, I came every year, every time they were here. Believe me, I would remember an incident like that. And especially since you said it occurred on the Fourth of July. I find it's easier to remember things when they're associated with a holiday or a birthday. They stick in my mind." She cleared her throat.

"Gil and Jack were typical brothers, playful, always getting into something," she said. "They'd roughhouse like any other boys, but no matter what quarrels they had, they always, *always* stood up for each other when it mattered. I saw Gil come to Jack's aid and I watched Jack help Gil countless times. Whoever told you that was lying. Pure and simple. Ask Jack. He'll be outraged at the suggestion."

CHAPTER TWENTY-SEVEN

"Thank you. There's something else I'd like to ask, if you don't mind," Steven said.

"Go ahead."

"What can you tell me about the relationship between Gil and Rider?"

"Relationship? Is that what you call it?" She snorted. "Rider is a paid servant. That's all there is to it. Don't get me wrong. He does an excellent job, and he's a nice man. He's worked for our family since he was a kid. But there was no *relationship*, as you call it."

"Can you think of a reason why he might have wanted to harm Gil? Did anything unusual happen recently?"

She considered his question a moment. "There was something about a year and a half ago, but I don't know what it was. I remember going to the house for Easter dinner—see what I mean about remembering things?" She gave him a genuine smile.

Steven returned it.

"When I arrived that Sunday, a man I'd never seen before opened the door. I asked Gil where Rider was, and he said there'd been some problem and Rider would be gone for a while. Maybe he'd return, maybe not." She shrugged. "That's it. Frankly, I didn't concern myself with the goings-on of the staff. I didn't know what it was about and I didn't care. I don't know what you can make out of that. Probably nothing." She stood up. "I hope that's all for now, Detective. Suddenly, I'm very tired."

After the study door closed behind Aunt Emily, Will looked at Steven. "Before you get Harry in here, let's ask Jack if he knows why Rider was absent from his job."

"Good idea."

Steven left the room, then returned with Jack Racine, who seemed to have put aside the detective's earlier insinuations. Steven explained what Aunt Emily said about Rider being gone and asked if Jack had any knowledge of the circumstances.

"Last year, huh? The only thing I can think of is it wouldn't have been too long after the stock market crash in '29," Jack said. "Maybe it had to do with that? A family member who was in trouble? There were a fair number of suicides in those early days after the Crash. Maybe Rider had a family emergency." He shrugged. "Gil and I wrote sporadically, but he never discussed anything to do with the staff. He wrote about the business and family. I imagine Margery knows, though. You should ask her."

Steven thanked him and asked Jack to close the door on his way out. He looked at Will. "He's right. Margery probably deals with the staff. I should have thought of that. What do you think? Try to nail down this information about Rider or convince Harry to tell us what happened in the Amazon jungle?"

"Rider's probably still out with the snow-blowing machine. And I imagine Margery's sleeping. Let's talk with Harry."

It was obvious that Harry Racine had continued drinking throughout the evening. He moved with careful steps, touching the door frame, the wall, and a chair on his way over to his brother's desk, where he dropped onto the unforgiving visitor's seat.

"What can I do for you fellas?" he asked.

"I saw your name in the newspaper recently," said Will. "The article reported an expedition in the Amazon jungle where a river guide fell overboard and was attacked and killed by crocodiles. The journalist mentioned your name as one of the people on the team. We'd like to know more about that incident."

Harry shuddered. He hung his head, shaking it back and forth from side to side, lips pursed. When he looked up, his haunted gaze told them the ghost of that incident had moved in and taken over. "It was horrible. You can't imagine what it's like seeing something like that.

CHAPTER TWENTY-SEVEN

How fast it happens. All you see is a flash of dark green jagged hide. When those crocs have their prey in their jaws, the tail whips back and forth like an airplane propeller. Damned prehistoric beasts."

"It must have been terrible to witness, Harry," Steven said. "Tell us what happened."

"It was a grueling trip. We thought we could avoid the rainy season, but it started early this year. It poured hard for days. The temperatures were near a hundred degrees. The insects were out in droves. Clouds of them swarming all around you. We'd put eucalyptus oil on—that's what the natives use—but the rain kept washing it off. We had a few more days to go and were on our last box of supplies. The guide backed up into it, and the box went overboard. All our remaining food, water, and medicine. I got mad and yelled at him. I should have left it at that. But I pushed him. He lost his balance and went over. The crocs were on him in seconds. We reached out with poles for him to grab onto. We tried to get him back in the boat, but he didn't have a chance. Those bastards were just too fast. We called it an accident when the authorities at the harbor asked about it. Believe me, you don't want to get thrown in a South American jail for manslaughter. It was an accident. But I know I caused it. It was my fault. I'll have to live with it for the rest of my life. I don't mind telling you, it's eating me up."

"It sounds truly horrible, Harry," Steven said. "And I imagine that a lot of booze makes it worse. Why don't you get some sleep? Your family has had a pretty hard time of it this weekend. I'd say you could do with a decent night's rest."

"Yeah, you're right." He threw back the remainder of his drink and stumbled out of the room, empty glass hanging from his fingers.

Will closed the door.

"What do you think?" Steven asked.

"He didn't do it. That's a man consumed with guilt. He's got enough weighing him down for the rest of his life. He wouldn't add to it by killing his brother and nephew. I don't care how badly he wants to live here in Onontaga. He's not our killer."

"I agree, and I also think we're lucky he's been drinking. I'm not sure he would have confessed all of that otherwise." Steven looked at his watch, then arched his back and stretched. He yawned. "After eleven already. What do you say we call it a night, Will?"

"Yeah, I hate to admit it, Steven, but I could use a good night's sleep after the day we had."

A flash of light hung in the window, then passed by.

"Looks like Rider's back with the snow-blowing machine," Steven said. "Jack told me they can only use it for a short while at a time. He must have given the engine several periods of rest. I wonder how much of the access road he cleared."

Chapter Twenty-Eight

Sunday, December 16, 1934

Great Camp Onontaga, Adirondack Mountains

The cabin felt warmer when Steven and Olivia awoke on Sunday. He pulled her closer and nuzzled her neck. "Listen to the silence. I think the storm is over."

"Mmm. Good." She turned over, planting her face in her pillow. "What time is it?" she mumbled.

Steven caught the word *time*. "Six-thirty."

"I'm not ready to get up yet." More mumbling.

"Okay, I'll get in the shower first." As he said the words, Steven wondered when he had adopted Olivia's habit of bathing every day. Nobody in 1934 did that, but he'd found he enjoyed the hot water beating on his back and shoulders, especially when it was cold out.

Twenty minutes later, Steven sat on Olivia's side of the bed and nudged her awake.

"Come on, sleepyhead. Time to get up. We've got a case to solve."

That did it. She sat up, blinking. "I'm up. I'm up. Brr. It's freezing."

"Well, if you wore more clothes to bed, you wouldn't be cold. Although, I have to say, that gets my vote." He grinned, looking at the spaghetti straps on her silky nightgown.

"Ha! Why am I not surprised?" She threw off the covers and ran into the bathroom, closing the door behind her.

Steven went into the extra bedroom to update their murder board, then stood back and analyzed his notes from last night. Why couldn't he see the patterns in this investigation like he always did at home? Every time he thought he had the killer nailed down, he learned something new, and his suspicions flew out the window.

The tortured remorse on Harry's face last night and the anguish in his voice told Steven that Harry might have been an accidental killer, but he was not the cold-blooded murderer who had planned and executed two vicious murders in the same number of days.

Come to think of it, Jack Racine hadn't killed the sailor in the Philippines on purpose either. Did Jack's killing qualify the same as Harry's?

Jack hadn't looked as tortured as Harry, but he had been upset. Steven remembered how he explained the care and attention he always took in the boxing ring. He certainly hadn't meant to kill anyone.

Steven let out an exasperated groan. Olivia popped her head in the door.

"What's wrong?" she said.

"This case! It's making me crazy. Look at what I added this morning. It seems like we're eliminating both Jack and Harry. How can that be, Olivia?"

"Remember you wanted to question Rider again. We still don't know much about him. And, I hate to say it…but maybe we made a mistake about the people we already crossed off the list. Do you think we were too quick to eliminate Lewis?" she asked.

"Lewis?"

"Yes, have you noticed how he's already repositioned himself, not only figuratively, but physically as well? Last night, he acted like *he*

CHAPTER TWENTY-EIGHT

was our host. He led us to the drinks cart, he sat at the head of the table, and he's been making decisions on what everybody should do. He's replaced Gil in every way that's been visible to us. And who knows what goes on behind closed doors?"

Steven considered this. "You might have a point there. I'll tell Will and Jimmy about the change in Lewis's behavior. Let's keep an eye on him today."

Steven sat next to her on the edge of the bed. "All this is pure conjecture." He swept up his hand as if to dismiss everything on the board. "It's nothing but circumstantial evidence—at best. A prosecutor would never go to trial with anything this flimsy. I need hard evidence, one piece of physical proof that clearly points to someone."

Steven studied their notes—the relationships among the players and each one's personality, character, and background. Their possible motives. The opportunities each suspect had had to commit the two murders. He murmured to himself. "The crime scene where Gil was killed. What could the killer have left behind? What could have been taken or transferred?" He closed his eyes—Olivia knew he was picturing the scene—and mumbled, "What could the killer have left or taken from the lake where Julian was killed?"

Olivia copied Steven, observing both scenes in her mind again. She asked herself the same questions, first about Gil, then Julian.

During her tenure as a newspaper reporter, Olivia had mastered a number of skills that aided in recalling information. She relied on techniques using association, repetition, and mnemonics.

Now, she saw in her mind's eye the spot on the ice where the killer had pushed Julian down under the freezing water. She put herself in the killer's place. He'd had to enlarge the fishing hole. That meant some serious tools. Maybe he'd acquired a cut or an abrasion on his hand. Julian had maneuvered one arm up out of the opening. Had he flailed around? If so, could he have scratched the killer's hand or face?

She seemed to remember that the hand out of the water was missing its mitten or glove. Olivia pictured the killer grabbing a metal pole of some kind and pushing it down into Julian's neck. *That's it!*

Olivia and Steven shouted at the same time. *Blood!*

"When the killer pushed the pole into Julian's neck, blood spurted out," Steven said. "It looked like a lot of it was absorbed by Julian's jacket, but the sleeve of the *killer's* jacket must have some blood on it—around the cuff or inside the opening of the sleeve. Why didn't I see it sooner? Finally, Olivia! We've got something to search for. Something concrete to nail this case down."

"I've got another idea, Steven." She told him her thoughts about abrasions or cuts on the killer's hand.

"You're right. That's good." He jumped to his feet. "Are you ready? Let's go."

Lewis knocked softly on Margery's bedroom door. He leaned in and listened. He thought he heard movement inside. "Margery," he whispered and rapped again. A moment later, light seeped out of a narrow slit, and she peeked around the frame. Seeing who it was, she widened the opening and let him into the shadowy room. Lewis pulled her into his arms, aware of the shocking contrast between them—she still in her dressing gown, a pale gray silk with green vines and delicate pink roses trailing down the lapels, and he already dressed in dark corduroy pants, a brown-and-white plaid flannel shirt, and a cream-colored, cable-knit sweater. He ran his hand over her hair, cupping the back of her head.

"How are you this morning?" he asked, looking deep into her eyes.

Margery saw the wrinkles at the corners of his eyes and marveled that she'd never noticed the crow's feet. If asked, she would have said she knew every detail about him.

"I slept. Things look better the morning after a proper night's sleep.

CHAPTER TWENTY-EIGHT

I'll be alright about losing Gil. Given the circumstances, I think we did our best all these years. You know we ended up as good friends and partners because of the children." She heaved a sigh. "But, losing Julian...." Her voice broke. "Does a mother ever get over losing a child? Even in a case like ours where we weren't close. Do you think he knew I loved him, Lewis?"

"I'm sure he did."

"I've been a terrible mother."

"You did everything you could, Margery. You always tried to do what was right."

"Hmm, maybe. Well, we have to look forward, don't we? So, I'll put one foot in front of the other, fix a friendly smile on my face, and take it one day at a time. What else can I do?" She rested her head on his shoulder, tightened her arms around him, and sighed. "Thank God I have you, Lewis. I can't imagine my life without you."

"We've been lucky to have each other, my dear. I have to admit that there were times when I felt guilty because of Gil. After all, he was my friend, and he loved you. Although I do believe he knew he wasn't capable of giving you the time and attention you needed. He never said anything, but there were moments when I think he suspected the truth about us."

"Lewis, I'll be happy when we don't have to hide anymore."

"Me, too. I think we should give it six months or maybe a year, then we can ease into *going public*, as they say."

"I agree. Now, let me get dressed. I'll meet you downstairs for breakfast."

He kissed her on the cheek and left her alone in her room.

Before Steven and Olivia could button their jackets, they heard a knock on the door. Steven opened it and found Will and Jimmy Bou on their doorstep.

"Phew," Jimmy said, spying Steven and Olivia ready to leave. "I'm glad we didn't wake you."

"Not a chance," Steven said. "We were on our way to get you. Come in. I have something to tell you." He closed the door behind them. "Listen to this, fellas. I think we've got a way to get some physical evidence." He told them about the idea of blood on the killer's sleeve and about the possibility of damage to the killer's hand.

"That's a swell thought. I bet the killer didn't even notice if there was blood *inside* his sleeve. We're going to find him today, Steven," said Jimmy with his usual optimism.

Chapter Twenty-Nine

When Steven, Olivia, Will, and Jimmy Bou entered the lodge, most of the family and their guests were in the dining room having breakfast.

Irene looked like the tragedies of the past three days had swallowed her up, leaving her weighed down with grief. Black smudges circled her dark eyes. Her once-pink complexion looked pasty and dull. Her body appeared weak, as though ravaged by illness. Irene moved with a lethargy that reminded Olivia of a slow-motion movie.

Sitting next to Irene, Victor paid more attention to her than he did to his own breakfast. One small bite from a piece of toast and a serving of scrambled eggs left cooling on his plate told Olivia that Victor hadn't eaten much. She watched him as he watched Irene, wondering if he feared Irene might topple off the chair. She didn't appear firmly anchored on her seat.

At one end of the table, her daughter on her left, Margery sat straight and tall, taking small bites of an omelet while she conversed softly with Lewis, who sat at her right. At the other end, brothers Jack and Harry were deep in conversation. Neither had taken breakfast. Both drank large cups of coffee as they whispered, their heads close together.

The new arrivals greeted everyone, served themselves at the buffet, then settled in the empty chairs—Olivia between Harry and Jimmy Bou, who was talking with Aunt Emily. Steven chose the seat next to

Jack, and Will sat on Steven's other side.

Steven caught the end of a sentence. Jack had said, "But who?"

They made small talk as they ate, and all three policemen and Olivia checked the hands of the men at the table for cuts and abrasions. They noticed nothing suspicious.

Steven sighed to himself. *There had better be some evidence on somebody's jacket or we're done for.*

After he'd finished eating, Steven, under the pretense of getting something out of his jacket pocket, returned to the hooks and coat tree near the front door and inspected the sleeves of all the men's jackets.

He found nothing.

Devastated, he stared at the mass of abandoned coats, hats, and scarves. Now, what was he going to do? He thought back to when he'd seen each of the men outside or getting ready to go out. Did anyone have a second jacket? Could the killer have noticed blood on his sleeve, thrown the coat in the garbage, then worn an extra jacket that he kept here at the Great Camp? Had someone travelled with a second jacket or coat?

It was time to search their rooms.

Until now, Steven had held off because it had seemed like a step too far. This wasn't his investigation. He had no legal jurisdiction here at Onontaga. He didn't want to do anything that could compromise a case when it got to court—New York State had carefully articulated laws about search and seizure.

Margery Racine had publically implored Steven to look into the murder of her husband, but he couldn't take the chance that a piece of critical evidence found in someone's private quarters might be excluded from a jury. However, now there had been a second murder and a brutal one at that, and he needed to increase the scope and intensity of his investigation.

CHAPTER TWENTY-NINE

He went to the sideboard and extracted paper and pencils from a drawer, then turned to the dining table and cleared his throat to draw everyone's attention.

"I apologize for disturbing your breakfast, but while you're all here, I need your cooperation with something."

Conversation halted, and everyone stared.

"I've reached the point where I need to search your rooms. I've held off as long as possible out of respect for your privacy, but I can't wait any longer. What happened to Julian changes everything. I'm going to give each of you a piece of paper and pencil. I want you to write out a simple sentence that gives me and my officers permission to examine your bedroom or cabin, your car, and everything in them. Please sign and date it. Are there any questions?"

No one said a word.

Steven thought they were so stunned no one could think of anything to ask.

After a whispered word with Lewis, Margery stood up. "We will all comply, Detective Blackwell. You and your men have our full cooperation." She stared at each individual around the table. There was steel in her voice when she said, "Isn't that right?"

"Those of you who have keys to your rooms or cabins, may I please have them?" Steven added. "And if you locked your car, I'll need that key, as well."

After he had gathered the keys and signed permissions, Steven led Will, Jimmy Bou, and Olivia to Gil's study.

"As you probably guessed, I didn't find blood on any of the jackets by the door. I hope I haven't left this too late. I didn't want to take the chance of compromising evidence because we're not conducting an official investigation. I don't have jurisdiction here."

"I would have done the same thing, Steven," Will said. "You're trying to play it by the book even though there's no book in this case. With Mrs. Racine's little speech and all the signed papers, I'm sure we'll be alright."

"Thanks, Will. I'll keep these papers secure," Steven said, folding them and placing them in his trousers pocket.

"Are you going to search the staff quarters too, Steven?" Jimmy Bou asked.

"Yes, but we'll leave that for last. Jimmy, would you search Cabin B? That's where Harry Racine stays all the time, so your search might take a while. There's a good chance you'll find an extra jacket or coat there. I don't have to tell you to be thorough."

"Nope, I've got it."

"Jimmy, check Cabin D as well." Steven handed him the key. "It's the one Harry uses as a darkroom. Olivia and I went in after Gil was killed. That's when we found the potassium cyanide. Wear your heaviest gloves, and don't touch anything. Especially, don't get too close to that cyanide container—it's marked with the chemical symbols KCN and a skull and crossbones. See if someone hung a jacket behind the door or maybe stuffed it behind the containers of chemicals. They may have thought no one would go back in there."

Steven turned to his partner. "Will, would you take Cabins C and E? Victor's staying in C. I'm afraid E is going to be an unpleasant job—we're using it as a temporary morgue. We needed a place to keep Gil's body cold. Then, when Julian was killed, we put him in there, too. They're both in one of the bedrooms." He stuck his hand in a pocket. "Here's the key to Cabin E."

"It'll be fine, Steven. Thanks."

"Jimmy, when you finish your two, check to see if Will needs a hand." Jimmy saluted his boss.

"I'm going to search Jack's and Lewis's rooms here in the main lodge." Steven looked at Olivia. "Would you position yourself someplace in

CHAPTER TWENTY-NINE

the main area where you can keep an eye on everybody coming and going? I don't want someone getting rid of a coat when we're looking the other way."

Jimmy Bou decided to start with Harry Racine's darkroom. The door swung open when he turned the key. He flicked on a light, and the rough cabin sprang into view. Jimmy checked behind the door. The hook screwed into the wood held nothing. He crossed the room to a large counter where a variety of glass jars, bottles, and other containers stood underneath. Jimmy read the labels and saw all but two dealt with developing photographs. He had no trouble spotting the skull and crossbones and stayed far away.

Stretching his neck to peer behind the row of containers, he saw nothing but a few rags. He looked around and decided there was no other place that might conceal a jacket with a bloody sleeve. He turned off the light and exited Cabin D, locking the door behind him.

Jimmy entered Cabin B and turned on a lamp near the entrance. For a cabin in the woods, it was pretty sweet. Thick rugs covered the plank floors, heavy drapes kept the cold from seeping through the windows, and a fire warmed the room. Jimmy stuffed his heavy mittens and knit hat—handmade gifts from his mother last Christmas—in his pockets, unwound his long scarf, and removed his jacket. He set everything on a chair near the stone hearth.

"Okay," he said out loud to himself, rubbing his hands together to get the blood circulating. "Let's start in the main bedroom."

For the next twenty minutes, Jimmy Bou examined every conceivable spot—in drawers, on shelves, in a heavy trunk at the foot of the bed, under the bed, behind the door, under a thick cushion on a deep-seated chair. He grabbed every hanger holding a piece of clothing from the bar in the closet and checked carefully. He found a rich brown leather jacket that he wished were his and a heavy suede winter jacket with a thick lining. He discovered no blood.

Jimmy checked the second bedroom, living room, tiny kitchen area, and bathroom. Nothing pointed the finger at Harry.

It looks like it's not him. I'm glad. I like Harry.

He donned his outer gear and went to help Will.

Sergeant Will Taylor performed the same tasks in Victor's Cabin C as Jimmy had done in Cabin B, and with the same results. McAllister had brought a long, black wool dress coat, or perhaps he had worn it on the trip up to the mountains, but of course, it was pristine. If you were going out on a frozen lake in the middle of the night to kill somebody, you wouldn't wear your party clothes.

After a thorough search of Cabin C, Will hiked up the lane to the makeshift mortuary in Cabin E. The key turned smoothly. When he opened the door, he noticed the temperature had stabilized—chilly but not freezing.

Will began by doing a sweep of the living area—nothing—followed by the small kitchenette and bathroom. Nothing there either. He slowed his search in the empty bedroom. Closet, dressers, trunk, and bed held no bloodstained clothing. Will was about to enter the second bedroom where the bodies of the two victims lay, one on each bed, when he heard the outer door open. He turned to see Jimmy Bou stomping snow off his boots.

"I finished, Will. Can you use a hand?"

"Good timing, Jimmy. Yes, I'm trying to think like a killer looking for a place to hide my bloody jacket until I can escape. I thought that a likely spot might be *underneath* one of the corpses in here."

"Holy cow, Will. That's diabolical. I like it."

Will rolled his eyes. "Let's see if they're still in full rigor. It's been two and a half days since Gil Racine was killed, so rigor mortis should have passed off by now. Unfortunately, half of Julian's body was frozen. I

CHAPTER TWENTY-NINE

don't know how to calculate that."

Will approached the first body. "This man looks older; must be Gil." He put his hands under Gil's hip and shoulder, lifting him slightly off the bed, and bent to look. "Nothing under his body. He's loosened up, Jimmy. Go around to the other side of the bed. I'll tip him toward you. Hold him in that position while I look under the covers and the mattress for the jacket. Then we'll do the same thing on your side."

Jimmy walked to the far side of the bed and supported Gil Racine's body as Will searched.

Will shook his head. "Nothing here." They eased the corpse down. "Okay, Jimmy, tip him over toward me." Will supported the victim while Jimmy searched, but to no avail.

"That was a swell idea, Will. Maybe we'll find something under Julian."

The two police officers turned to the second bed. They discovered Julian's arms and legs were in a state of partial rigor mortis, but his torso was still largely frozen.

Jimmy Bou shook his head. "What a sad end for this guy."

They repeated the procedure, finding it easier to tilt Julian's stiff body, but found nothing hidden under the second corpse.

"Now that we've got that rather distasteful task done, let's do a normal search, Jimmy. There's only this room left. I already checked everywhere else."

Both policemen came up empty-handed.

In the upstairs bedrooms of the Great Camp, Steven wrestled with the same reality as Will and Jimmy. No matter how ridiculous the idea, he searched hiding places large and small, sure the jacket had to be somewhere in the lodge or one of the cabins.

After a meticulous examination of the Eastern Hemlock room, where Jack was staying, and Lewis's Black Spruce bedroom, Steven was forced to accept there was nothing to find. He headed down the hall toward the staircase and was passing the Balsam Fir room, which had been Julian's, when a thought struck him.

What if the killer hid the jacket in Julian's room?

The act of hiding the evidence in the victim's room smacked of the utmost cruelty, and Steven wasn't sure if he wanted to find the bloody jacket in Julian's room or not. Anger coursing through him, he yanked the door open. He spent the next twenty minutes searching and came up empty.

Argh! he thought. *Where is that jacket?* Because he knew without a doubt that it had to be somewhere.

Steven returned to the great room where Olivia was keeping watch. She was curled up in an armchair, pretending to read, but Steven saw her look up every few seconds. He knew from that spot she'd be able to hear everything.

"Hey," he said, approaching her. "Let's get some fresh air."

They grabbed their jackets and settled on the porch steps to wait for Will and Jimmy Bou. Only a few minutes passed before they saw both policemen heading down the path.

Steven jumped up. "Come on." He hurried up the trail to meet them, and they all trooped into Cabin A.

"Well?" he asked, dreading the answer he could already see in their faces.

Will and Jimmy shook their heads. "Nothing," Will said.

"Can I say something?" said Olivia.

They all looked at her.

"Of course," said Jimmy, eager to hear Olivia's thoughts.

Olivia held up her hands and began counting off on her fingers the points she'd been thinking about since the men had left. "First, it's a dirty job, but no one's checked the big garbage cans by the back door

CHAPTER TWENTY-NINE

yet. Second, all the cars are in the garage next door." She waved her thumb toward the building next to Cabin A. "I don't think the killer would put the jacket in Steven's car, but there are four or five others in there. And there's the snow-blowing machine. I noticed a tarp on the back. Anything could be hidden under that."

Jimmy's eyes lit up, and he was nodding his head so hard Olivia thought he was going to give himself whiplash. She ignored him and concentrated on what she was saying.

"And my last point is, don't forget what Rider told us—"

"Yes!" Steven exclaimed, interrupting her. "I'm sorry, Olivia. I was just going to say that." He looked at his partner and Jimmy Bou. "With our focus on the searches this morning, I forgot to tell you. Rider related an incident when Gil and Jack were young boys. They were swimming in the lake here and Gil kept going under." Steven shared Rider's story. "But here's the thing…when I asked Jack about it, he was outraged. He swore it never happened. I asked Aunt Emily, and she was angry and annoyed. I think Rider lied to us."

"But we have no idea why he lied," Olivia said. "And we haven't come up with a motive for Rider to have killed Gil or Julian."

"We know a little about Rider's background." Steven told Will and Jimmy what he and Olivia had learned during their interview with the butler. "Without any more specifics, let's start with the age-old motive of money. The man has worked his entire life for the Racine family. I wonder how much he's earned—and managed to save," Steven said.

"And how much he still has in the bank since the Crash," said Jimmy.

"Steven, Rider's a big man. He must be six feet, and he looks solid," said Will. "Let's the two of us go together. We can question him and check his jacket and his room."

"Good idea, Will." He turned to Olivia and Jimmy. "Would you two go back to the main lodge? Wander around among people talking. Eavesdrop. Listen for anything that might help. If you find an opening in a conversation, try to learn more about him. And remember, we have to keep an open mind. We don't know Rider is our killer. The only thing we suspect is that he lied, and there could be any number of reasons why. Because he's a liar doesn't mean he's a killer."

Chapter Thirty

Steven and Will entered the kitchen and saw Rider enjoying a cup of coffee and a cigarette at the pine table at the far end of the room. Scattered plates, cups, and cutlery indicated the staff had recently eaten breakfast. Corinne was at the sink, washing dishes. Mrs. Buckley was nowhere to be seen.

"Rider, excuse us for interrupting," said Steven, intending to put the butler at ease and misdirect him from the serious interrogation that was looming. "We'd like to ask you a few more questions."

"Certainly, Detective. Just having a smoke before I do some more snowblowing. We'll get that road cleared yet." He gave a small smile. "Corinne," he shouted down to the far end of the room, "go check the dining area to see if any of the family or our guests need something. Stay there until I come and get you." He turned back to the police officers. "Better to speak alone," he said, dipping his head as if to confirm that he'd made a true statement.

"By the way, you've met my partner, Sergeant Taylor, haven't you?" Steven asked, taking the chair next to Rider with Will sitting across the table.

The butler nodded, then blew a lungful of smoke up to the ceiling.

"I'd like to ask about two things you told me earlier, Rider," Steven said. "First, do you have plans to retire in the near future?"

"What a strange question, Detective."

"Nevertheless, if you wouldn't mind."

"Yes, I'm hoping to stop working in the next few years. My sister is a recent widow. I'd like to go live with her in Massachusetts."

Steven leaned forward. "I understand this is uncomfortable, Rider, and an intrusion into your private affairs. However, I need to know if you'll be able to afford to retire."

The butler scowled. His face reddened, and he hesitated before speaking. "I'll have to wait some time until I'm able to help my sister. I cannot be a burden on her."

Steven knew Rider was a proud man. And proud men did not talk about money with strangers. Especially inquisitive police officers.

Steven moved to the edge of his chair, narrowing the space between them. "Thank you. And my second question…do you remember the incident you told me about? The day Jack was watching Gil struggle in the water when they were kids?"

"Yes, of course." He crossed his arms over his chest and sat straighter.

"Are you certain there were no other incidents like that where Jack somehow threatened his brother?"

"Absolutely. Just that one time."

"Alright…there's a problem with that, though…when I asked Jack about it, he swore it never happened."

"Well, he would, wouldn't he? It was a terrible thing to do. Or maybe he forgot. They were only children. It was a long time ago."

Maintaining eye contact, Steven moved his chair closer, nodding as if he agreed with the assessment. "Yes, that's true…but I also asked Emily Racine, and she was positive it never happened. She was quite upset at the idea."

"She probably wasn't here that day. She came and went, you know," Rider said, shifting to one side, as if trying to get away from Steven's encroachment on his private space.

"So, you're absolutely sure what you told me is accurate? Jack stood

CHAPTER THIRTY

by and let his brother struggle in the water? And if their father had not rushed down to the lake, Gil likely would have drowned?"

"Yes, Detective. I would never make up something like that." He stubbed out his cigarette in a small tin ashtray.

"Alright, Rider, we'll let you get on with your duties," Steven said.

"Thank you."

Steven and Will stood, turned away from the butler, and headed toward the door. When they were at a safe distance, Will leaned in and whispered, "He's lying."

"I know," Steven whispered back.

To the side of the doorway was a three-foot-long strip of wood nailed to the wall with several hooks screwed into it. On one of those hooks hung the dark green jacket Rider had been wearing all weekend.

Steven and Will worked like a well-oiled machine, instinctively knowing what to do.

Will turned back toward Rider and said, "Oh, Mr. Rider, one more thing before we leave...," while Steven grabbed the right shoulder of the garment and bent the sleeve to reveal the cuff and the interior. All around the inside, reaching two or three inches up, was a large, dark brown stain. Blood.

Steven cleared his throat. Will looked back at his partner, and Steven gave an almost imperceptible nod.

Rider watched the two policemen as they walked away from him. He saw them whisper something, but was too far away to hear. He felt inside his tuxedo jacket pocket, reassuring himself the gun was still there, glad he'd thought of it. Last night, he'd gone to the hidden compartment near the back door where Gil Racine had always kept an assortment of rifles and handguns for protection against black bear and other wild animals.

Rider focused on what Steven was doing at the coat rack and wasn't paying attention to what Will was saying. Over Will's shoulder, he saw Steven examine the sleeve of his jacket and nod.

They know, he thought.

Rider certainly wasn't going to sit around waiting for confirmation.

In one smooth movement, he stood, grabbed the back of the wooden chair he'd been sitting on, threw it in the aisle between the table and the wall, and ran out the back door. In the small vestibule, he shoved a broom handle under the inner doorknob and fled through the outer door, using a shovel to jam that door as well. He took precious seconds to kick the bottom of the tool, making sure it was wedged in securely.

Steven and Will reacted the moment the butler launched himself out of the chair.

"I'll take the back," said Will, already in pursuit.

"I'll go around the front," Steven shouted and fled into the corridor.

It took Will less than a minute to crash through the first door. The second one required two more assaults before the shovel popped out and lay on the snow-covered ground.

"Help. Help."

Will looked around and saw Mrs. Buckley lying on her back in a four-foot high drift, arms and legs flailing. She was not wearing a coat, although winter boots protected her feet. He rushed over to her.

"Mrs. Buckley, what are you doing out here? Take my hands."

Will grabbed her hands and, with one smooth motion, pulled her out of the snowbank.

"I went to the smokehouse to get a ham for dinner tonight. What's going on? Rider ran out the back, slammed into me, and pushed me off my feet. Thank goodness you came along. I don't want to think about how fast I would have frozen." She dusted the snow off her dress, apron, and cardigan sweater. "Now, where did my ham go?"

Will was already running away from her. "Get in the house and lock

CHAPTER THIRTY

the doors," he shouted. "Rider is the killer."

Her hand flew to her chest as she inhaled so deeply that she swayed. "Good lord!" she shouted and ran into the house, locking both doors behind her and leaving the ham where it had flown. "Dinner be damned."

Will took advantage of his lean, muscular physique and long legs to make up for the time he'd lost helping Mrs. Buckley. He flew down the cleared path that ran behind the lodge.

In his attempt to escape, Rider had grabbed everything he passed and thrown it in his wake. Will leapt over two metal garbage cans, several long-handled tools, and numerous logs that Rider had flung from piles of firewood at the back of the Great Camp.

As Will approached the corner, he heard a cry. He put forth a burst of energy, rounded the corner of the building, and saw Jimmy Bou lying on his back in the snow, the area around his head covered in blood.

As Rider escaped out the back entry, Steven ran down the hallway and into the main living area, heading for the front door. Crossing the great room, he saw Aunt Emily and Olivia sitting alone on a sofa near the fire.

As he hurried by, he yelled, "It's Rider. He's trying to get away."

Olivia's jaw dropped. Aunt Emily gasped.

"Olivia, where's Jimmy?"

"He went to the garage to check the cars for the jacket."

"Damn! Stay here and lock the door behind me."

Steven took a few seconds to pull on his winter boots, which had better treads than the smooth-soled shoes he wore inside. He grabbed his jacket and raced out the front door.

He turned left, toward the row of cabins, and sprinted up the path, legs pumping, running full out. When Steven passed the gap between the Great Camp and the garage, he glanced toward the back and saw Will leaning over Jimmy Bou. He trusted his partner to do what was necessary and ran on.

As he cleared the corner, Steven looked into the space between the garage and Cabin A, the spot that Olivia was convinced was a newly discovered portal. He caught sight of Rider's foot as the butler ran behind the cabins.

Where does he think he's going? Steven thought. *There's nothing but forest out there.*

He turned into the space between Cabins A and B. This was slower going because the snow was almost up to his knees, but it was a short distance. As soon as he rounded the corner at the back, he'd be able to keep Rider in view as he chased after him.

Olivia had no intention of staying in the Great Camp while Steven, Will, and Jimmy Bou were out there risking their lives. She had skills, too, and she wasn't afraid to use them.

She ran to the coats and jackets hanging near the front door, quickly exchanged her shoes for boots, and grabbed a jacket, not caring if it was hers or not.

"Lock this door," she shouted to Aunt Emily. "Don't let Rider in if he comes knocking. No matter what!"

By the time Olivia reached the porch, the path was empty. Looking left and right, she stepped into the driveway and crept toward the garage. She thought she heard a runner's heavy breathing, but it seemed far away. Planning to give Jimmy Bou a heads-up, Olivia pulled the handle on one of the two heavy doors. The hinges creaked as it swung open.

Olivia peered into the dark, tomb-like structure. She hesitated to say anything in case Rider was hiding in one of the murky corners or behind one of the cars. She took several cautious steps into the

CHAPTER THIRTY

building then stopped. Dust motes floated high above her in the space. She loosened her outer clothing and loosened her body. She did a couple of squats, twisted her spine, jumped straight up, and landed softly. If she had to use her kickboxing skills, she was ready. She focused her mind on defense and stepped farther into the shadowy garage.

"Jimmy, can you hear me? Are you okay?" Will said to the young officer.

Jimmy Bou groaned and opened his eyes. "Will?" He squinted up at his friend. "What happened?"

"That's what I want to know."

Jimmy squeezed his eyes shut and placed a hand on his forehead. He blinked several times, then tried to sit up but fell back onto the ground. "Oh, dizzy, Will."

Will knelt next to him. "I'd say you had a run-in with Rider. Let's see if you can sit up. I want to check the back of your head. There's a lot of blood here. Head wounds bleed quite a bit, so I need to see how serious this is. I want to make sure you're going to be alright, then I have to help Steven. Rider's the killer, Jimmy."

"Rider? Yeah. I was coming out the back door of the garage, and he hit me with something hard. Maybe a gun. Be careful. Say you'll be careful, Will."

"We'll be careful, Jimmy. Come on. Let's get you sitting up. There, that's good. Now, can you stay like that while I check your head?"

Will checked all around Jimmy Bou's head until he found a gash. Taking a handful of pristine snow, he wiped the area clean. Jimmy winced. "Ow."

"That's not too bad. You'll probably have a headache for a while, though. I'll help you stand up. I bet Mrs. Buckley has a first aid kit in her kitchen."

After depositing Jimmy Bou on a chair in the kitchen, secure in knowing Mrs. Buckley, who was already making a fuss over him, had Jimmy's injury in hand, Will left by the back door for the second time.

Steven reached the end of the gap between Cabins A and B and looked to the right, the direction in which he'd seen Rider run. The space was empty. Bewildered, he stopped. Did any of the cabins have back doors? Not that he knew. Rider must have turned into the area between two of the buildings, but which two?

Peering ahead, Steven saw that the snow was disturbed, as if someone had plowed through it. Closer to the Great Camp, he had noticed deer prints near some bushes that hugged the walls, and there had been prints near the garbage cans that he couldn't identify. Raccoons maybe. He suspected most of the woodland animals that didn't hibernate stayed well away from the camp, closer to their natural habitats, but you never knew.

Steven moved forward, the deep snow slowing him down. Prints from a large shoe told him Rider had run to the end of the row of cabins, but Steven wasn't going to take any chances. As he reached the corner of Cabin B, he carefully peeked around to the side. Nothing. As though wading in thigh-high water, he pushed through the snow along the back of Cabin C. His loaded gun firmly in hand, Steven peered around the far end of that cabin as well. No one was there.

By the time he reached Cabin E, where the two bodies were being kept, Steven was on high alert. He had examined the back wall of each building as he passed by and had discovered no doors. He checked the areas leading into the woods. The freshly fallen snow was marred only by the tracks of rabbits, deer, foxes, and other woodland animals. He saw no man-made footprints.

When Steven reached Cabin F, he spied a nearly undetectable door built into its back wall. He slowed his breathing, focused his

CHAPTER THIRTY

energy and concentration on surprising and apprehending a killer. He gripped the doorknob and turned. It offered no resistance.

Slowly, he opened the door.

Olivia stood motionless for what seemed like ages. Hearing nothing but the rustle of mice, she began moving around the garage. She crept around Steven's jungle green Chevy, which had been backed in and was facing the doors. Nothing at the rear. No one crouched down, hiding behind the opposite side. She opened the driver's door and peered inside. Empty.

She performed the same experiment on each vehicle—a heavy maroon automobile, a fancy roadster, a red four-door, a white Cadillac, and a black sedan. Each one was empty. Olivia exhaled. *Phew!* For all her determination and bravado, she had no desire to engage in hand-to-hand combat with the six-foot-plus Rider.

After checking the snow-blowing machine, which stood off to the left, Olivia knew for certain the butler was not hiding in the garage. Jimmy Bou had come and gone as well. She decided to leave the garage, then figure out her strategy based on what she saw or didn't see outside.

Olivia closed the heavy door behind her, then crept up the path alongside the cabins. Suddenly, she realized she had made herself an easy target, and it would be smarter not to remain out in the open. She stepped off the path into the area between the garage and Cabin A.

Based on her previous experience, Olivia estimated she stood on the threshold of the portal. She stopped and wondered what she should do next. What could she do to help? The last thing she wanted was to get in the way or, heaven forbid, become Rider's hostage. She needed to remain vigilant. Should she go back to the lodge and wait for Steven, Will, and Jimmy to catch the killer? Was there any advantage in her staying here? If Rider ran down the path, he wouldn't see her, although she would likely hear him. Could she trip him, causing him to fall so that a policeman in pursuit could capture him? Realistically, what was she *doing* here?

Steven tiptoed through the back room in Cabin F, expecting to encounter Rider around the next corner. As he exited what appeared to be Jimmy Bou's bedroom, Rider jumped him from behind. Steven fell hard, the impact sending his gun flying down the hallway, sliding across the wooden floor and into the bathroom. The two men wrestled—the butler heavier and taller, holding the advantage. Steven used every skill and maneuver he'd learned to free himself. Nothing worked.

All of a sudden, Steven felt a piercing blow. He saw stars, and his world went black.

After bashing the detective on the head with his gun, Rider got up. Breathing hard, he bent over and put his hands on his knees, his gun dangling from a finger. Damn it! None of this was supposed to happen. What the hell was he going to do now? He'd assaulted two policemen, and he still hadn't reached the garage.

Rider's final plan had been to get one of the cars and tough it out. Having cleared some of the access road with the snow-blowing machine, he intended to ram the heavy vehicle through any remaining snow drifts and head for the main road. From there, he'd head north into the mountains, where, eventually, he would find his way across the Canadian border. Exactly where he'd be able to cross, he hadn't figured out yet. But that didn't matter. He was running on adrenalin and flying by the seat of his pants.

He hit Steven once more to be sure the cop was out cold, then peeked out the front door of Cabin F. The way was clear.

CHAPTER THIRTY

He closed the door behind him and fled toward the garage.

After leaving Jimmy Bou in Mrs. Buckley's capable hands, Will returned to where he'd found him. The previously smooth snow cover resembled the surface of a lake after a motorboat had churned up the water. But Will was an expert tracker, and he spied two distinct sets of footprints leading to the last cabin, telling him Steven had chased after Rider *behind* the cabins. Will chose to go around the *front*. He knew the butler must still be nearby. If Rider's plan was to get away in one of the cars—and that was the only thing that made sense—he hadn't escaped yet. Will would have heard the engine start in the midst of the quiet forest.

Before stepping onto the path and out into the open, making himself a target, Will listened. Trees creaked in the wind. Branches groaned from the weight of the snow. Nearby in the woods, a deer snorted.

Hearing nothing alarming, Will rounded the garage, intending to move along the path and check each cabin in case Rider was sheltering inside one of them.

"Will," a voice whispered.

Taken by surprise, Will spun to his left and saw Olivia standing between the garage and Cabin A.

"Olivia!" he whispered back, stepping off the path and facing her. "What are you doing? You need to go back to the lodge. Rider's got a gun. It's too dangerous for you out here."

Olivia gasped. "Rider's got a gun? I came to tell Jimmy what was going on. He went to the garage to search the cars for a bloody jacket. He doesn't know about Rider."

"He knows now," said Will. "Jimmy left the garage by a back door at exactly the wrong moment and ran right into Rider. Rider hit him on the head with his gun and knocked him out."

"Is Jimmy okay?"

"Yeah, I found him as he was coming to. He's alright, although he's dizzy. He's in the kitchen now. Mrs. Buckley is taking care of him."

"That's good."

Suddenly, Olivia's eyes widened, and her jaw went slack. Will felt the muzzle of a gun on the back of his head.

"Don't move," Rider growled. "Looks like you're the last policeman standing, Sergeant."

Olivia's only thought was saving Will. She reached out and grasped his hands. His eyes narrowed, and he frowned.

"What...?"

"Trust me, Will, please," she pleaded, eyes wide.

"Olivia...." Will automatically started to shake his head but stopped when he felt the butt of the gun push further into his skull.

"I wouldn't move if I were you," said Rider. "And you," he nodded to Olivia, "shut up."

Olivia squeezed Will's hands and mouthed, "Trust me."

She stepped back and pulled hard. Surprised by the movement, Will followed her without thinking.

Chapter Thirty-One

Steven rolled over on the floor of Cabin F and groaned in pain. He put his hand on the spot where Rider had hit him and came away with a modest amount of blood. *Not too bad*, he thought.

He struggled to his knees then, holding onto the door frame, he got to his feet. A wave of dizziness washed over him. Using the wall for support, he staggered into the bathroom, where he saw his gun on the floor, bent, and picked it up. That was a mistake. An intense wave of vertigo threatened to render him unconscious. He gripped the edge of the sink and breathed deeply.

Not your finest moment, Blackwell, he chided himself.

He waited until the dizziness passed. Then he turned on the tap and splashed liberal amounts of bracing cold water on his face and the back of his neck. He quickly checked the spot on the side of his head that had met Rider's gun. He'd had worse. Already, the bleeding had stopped. He wondered how long he'd been out.

He sat on the toilet seat cover, dropped his head between his knees, waited a moment, and then looked up, testing the sensation. The wooziness seemed to be over.

He stood up, looked from left to right, then back to the left again. Nope. He seemed okay.

Steven exited the bathroom, crossed the living room, and eased the front door open. He peered out and observed the path toward the

Great Camp.

Rider stood near the far corner of Cabin A. His arm was raised, his elbow straight, both feet planted firmly on the ground. It was the stance of a man holding a gun to someone's head.

December 14, 2014

Great Camp Onontaga, Adirondack Mountains

When Olivia pulled Will, she rapidly took several more steps backward to make sure she'd crossed the portal's threshold, and both of them had traveled forward in time to her 2014. Rider instantly disappeared. Sunny blue skies replaced the gloomy gray day, and the nearly four feet of snow in 1934 shrunk to less than a foot, a noticeable difference.

Thank God she'd done it. At first, she was so relieved that she'd saved Will—and probably herself, too—that Olivia didn't notice his reaction.

The sound of a motor broke the silence, interrupting her thoughts. Olivia peeked around Will as Sophie's SUV appeared on the path.

Sophie pulled up to the front of Cabin A and spotted Olivia. She left the engine running and her music blaring, jumped out of the vehicle, leaving the door ajar, and ran toward Olivia and Will.

"Olivia!" she shouted, rushing over to hug her best friend. "What are you doing here? Are you okay? Where's Steven? Who's this?"

As soon as Olivia let go of Will's hands, he looked around wildly. What was she talking about? *Trust me.* What did that mean?

Suddenly, he realized the pressure of the gun barrel on the back of his head was gone. Will whirled around. Rider had vanished. What was going on?

CHAPTER THIRTY-ONE

And what happened to the weather? It had been another cloudy day, but now the sun was shining in a clear blue sky. And the snow. Where did all the snow go? A moment ago, it was nearly up to his knees. Now, it barely touched the top of his short boots.

Will ventured out from the space between the buildings and looked up and down the lane. It was empty...except for an enormous vehicle barreling down on him. He leapt aside.

What was this strange thing? And who was this red-headed woman jumping out and hugging Olivia? What was that noise?

What the hell is going on?

Olivia kept the hug short. "Sophie, I'm so happy to see you, but I need you to hang on for a second. This is Steven's partner, and he has no idea what just happened to him."

Sophie went to sit in her car. She closed the door, cutting off the sound of her CD player.

Olivia turned to Will. "Steven and I were going to tell you at some point, Will." She stopped, unsure how to continue. "We actually talked about it not too long ago. I mean, we probably would have told you any day now. Maybe have you over for dinner and show you then."

Will stood as still as a stone statue and glared at her.

She took a deep breath. "Alright, first, let me say that I did not do this lightly. And second, you're not in any danger. I did this to save you from Rider shooting you. And Steven can get you back."

Thunder rolled over Will's face. "What the hell just happened, Olivia? And what do you mean you were going to tell me? Steven is going to get me back from *where*, exactly?"

Olivia took another deep breath. "Did you ever wonder about me, Will? Did I ever seem different from other women in 1934?"

"Funny you should say that," he spat. "Yes, I *have* wondered about you. As a matter of fact, I checked with Syracuse University and the

265

Syracuse Journal offices this past week. You never graduated from journalism school, Olivia. There is no record of you ever working on the newspaper."

"You're sort of right, Will. There wouldn't be any records in 1934. Because I graduated from S.U. in 2004 and I worked at the paper from 2004 to 2009."

Will eyed her as if she had lost her mind.

"Last winter, Steven and I discovered a portal in the house where we live. He lives there in your time, but I live there in 2014. This whole year, we've been experimenting, traveling back and forth from 1934 to my time. We learned how to time travel, Will."

Will stared. If looks could trigger the weather, Olivia would be standing in the midst of a cyclone.

"I accidentally stumbled on this spot between the garage and our cabin the other day. Steven knows about it. When he realizes we've disappeared, he'll come and get us. He can easily bring us back to 1934."

"You're insane."

Olivia chuckled. "Yeah, I know it's hard to take in, but I can prove it…right now…if you give me a chance."

"Saying for a minute that I actually believe you, why can't we just walk back into what you call my time, 1934?"

"It doesn't work that way, Will. Steven and I found out we can easily travel to our own time. That's why I was able to bring you here. But, to go into each other's time, we need to physically touch the other person. We hold hands when he brings me into 1934 or when I bring him into 2014. That's why I took your hands."

"Who's that woman, and what is she driving?" Will asked.

"That's Sophie. She's one of my best friends. Sophie always worries when I travel to 1934. She probably came up here to check in case I got pulled back into 2014. This is the first time I stayed overnight in

CHAPTER THIRTY-ONE

1934 in a place other than Steven's house. I think Sophie was anxious about which year I'd wake up in.

"Her car is called an SUV. They're popular because people can haul a lot of stuff." Olivia rubbed her icy hands together, then shoved them in her pockets. "So listen, Will, when I first met Steven and suggested this might be what we were experiencing—we can tell you more about that later—he told me he wanted to see some evidence. Concrete physical proof. How about it? Will you let me prove it?"

"Sure, proof is an excellent idea." He still glared at her.

Olivia had come to know Will over the past year. She knew he was smart and wasn't easily fooled or taken in. He was proud and didn't like being tricked. Steven had also told her Will had a photographic memory.

"Okay, here's my proof. One:..." She ticked off the numbers on her fingers. "In 1934, it was dark and gray today. We took one step, and it's blue skies and sunshine. Two: there was well over three feet of snow in 1934. Look around you, barely a foot. Three: there were loads of footprints all around the cabins. See if you can find any at all here. Four: you know you've never seen anything like Sophie's SUV. That's because they didn't exist in the 1930s. Five: let's ask Sophie to show you her license and car registration. You'll see the dates are in the two thousands. Six: where do you think Rider disappeared to? One minute he was there, the next he vanished. What's your explanation for that?" She started to turn, then stopped. "Oh, and by the way, you're welcome for saving your life."

She spun around and walked to Sophie's car. Sophie had turned off the engine and was reading the newspaper while waiting.

"Sophie, can I see your wallet, please? I'm trying to convince Will of what just happened."

"Sure." Sophie reached across the bucket seats and grabbed her purse. She took out her wallet and handed it to Olivia.

"And the paper, too, please."

Sophie handed her the *Knightsbridge Gazette*. It was dated Sunday, December 14, 2014.

"Thanks. Come here, Will," Olivia said. She handed him the newspaper, then began taking out Sophie's license, car registration, two credit cards, YMCA membership, and health insurance card. All had dates beginning with 20….

"Today's December 16th, not 14th," Will said in what Olivia thought was a feeble attempt at crushing her evidence.

"I know. The days are always the same, but the dates are usually one or two numbers off. We figured it has to do with leap years. That's our best guess. But, look at the year, Will, and for that matter, look at the contents of the paper. Go to the ads and check out the grocery prices. And the stuff for sale for Christmas shopping. Do you really think Sophie showed up here with a manufactured newspaper on the off chance I'd bring you into our time?"

Will scanned several pages of the newspaper, then set it on the SUV's hood and picked up one document after another from Sophie's wallet. As he read the printed information, he also noted that each document looked different from those with which he was familiar. His license was nothing like this one, nor was his YMCA card.

While Will examined the treasure trove of proof, Olivia kept her eye on the space between the garage and Cabin A.

At last, Steven appeared.

"Steven," she cried and ran to the portal. "Oh, my God, are you okay?" Relief flooded her when she saw Rider face down on the ground, his hands cuffed behind his back.

"Is Will with you, Olivia?"

At the sound of his partner's voice, Will spun around and hurried to him.

"What the heck is going on, Steven?"

CHAPTER THIRTY-ONE

Steven reached out his hand. "Come on, partner." Will took it, and Steven backed up, returning him to 1934. "Olivia, hurry."

Unable to see or hear Steven, Sophie started. "Oh! Will just disappeared. Steven must be on the other side."

"Yes, and he caught the killer," said Olivia. "Everything's okay now, Sophie." She gathered her friend's belongings and returned them to her. They hugged.

"I'll see you at home as soon as I can get out of here, Sophie. We've been snowed in."

Sophie gave her one last squeeze. "Be careful." Her brow still furrowed as worry lines crisscrossed her pale face.

"It's over. I'll be okay. I'll text you and Liz the minute I get home."

Olivia gave her a final hug and walked to Steven. He reached out his hand. Olivia took it, and he brought her back into the past.

Chapter Thirty-Two

Sunday, December 16, 1934

Great Camp Onontaga, Adirondack Mountains

When Will stepped back into 1934, he saw what Olivia had already noticed—Rider lying face-down in the snow with his hands behind his back.

At Will's questioning look, Steven said, "When Olivia pulled you into her time, and the two of you disappeared, Rider was completely thrown. He was so focused on trying to figure out what had happened that he never noticed me sneak up behind him. I knocked him out with my gun. It's a surface wound. He'll be fine." He looked at his partner. "Will, Olivia and I have a lot to explain to you. After we take care of Rider, when we get home, I promise we'll tell you everything. I want to keep Jimmy out of it, though. I'm not ready for him to know yet. Maybe someday, but not today."

"We'd better come up with a believable story, Steven. He's going to want to know what happened while he was sitting in the kitchen with Mrs. Buckley, especially how you captured Rider," Olivia said.

Rider groaned, and they all looked down. The butler was coming to.

CHAPTER THIRTY-TWO

"What happened? What's going on?" He twisted his neck to peer up at Olivia and Will. "Where the heck did you go? One minute, the two of you were here, then you disappeared."

"You're imagining things, Rider," said Steven. "I knocked you out. You must have been dreaming."

"I don't think so."

"Well, you can see we're still here, Rider," said Olivia. "You must have imagined it."

Steven grabbed the butler's arm and hauled him to his feet. "What's your first name?"

"Gerald."

"Gerald Rider, I'm arresting you for the murders of Gil Racine and Julian Racine, for the assault on police officers Jimmy Bourgogne and myself, and for the menacing of Sergeant Will Taylor."

At this moment, Jimmy Bou, his head bandaged, exited the Great Camp and hurried to Steven, Will, and Olivia.

Sneering at Rider, he said, "If I wasn't such a good cop, I'd punch you in the nose, you creep." He turned to the others. "Are you guys alright?"

"We're fine, Jimmy. How's your head?" Steven asked.

"I'm okay. Mrs. Buckley did a swell job patching me up."

A siren shattered the quiet of the forest, and everyone turned toward the sound. Moments later, two Hamilton County Sheriff's cars sped up the road, then screeched to a halt a few feet away.

"Aunt Emily called the cops," Jimmy said helpfully. "I like that lady. She's got guts."

"She sure does," Steven agreed.

Four sheriffs exited the black Fords and approached the group.

Steven stepped forward. "Officer, I'm Detective Steven Blackwell with the Knightsbridge Police. This is my partner, Sergeant Will Taylor. And this man," he pulled Rider toward the policemen, "is the Racine family's butler, Gerald Rider. He murdered Gil Racine Thursday night. On Friday, he killed Gil's son, Julian—I have concrete proof. Within the past hour, he assaulted me and my junior officer Jimmy Bourgogne, and held a gun to my partner's head, threatening to shoot."

A husky man sporting a bushy beard stuck out his hand. "Glad to meet you, Detective. Thanks for the call the other night. I'm sorry we weren't able to get here sooner. I'm Lieutenant John Delaney. This is my partner, Lou Banks." He indicated the tall man by his side. Everyone shook hands. "We've been ready to come as soon as the roads were plowed. Looks like good timing, huh, Detective?"

Delaney turned to the two officers waiting behind them. "Johnson, Michaels, take our suspect and put him in the car, will you? Keep an eye on him."

"Can you fellas come down to headquarters and give us your statements?" Delaney looked at Steven, Will, and Jimmy. "I'd like to get this man in a cell and processed right away. And, Detective Blackwell, I'd like you in the room when we question our suspect. What do you say? Want to assist?"

"Sure. By the way, that proof I mentioned before is in the kitchen—the suspect's jacket with the second victim's blood inside the right sleeve. Why don't we all go inside? I'll show you where the jacket is, and I can introduce you to Margery Racine. She's Gil's widow and Julian's mother. I know you'll have plenty questions for her and the rest of the family and guests later on."

"Right. Banks, grab an evidence bag from the car."

"By the way, Lieutenant...," Steven began.

"John, please."

"John, one of the guests is a doctor friend of Gil Racine. He pronounced Racine dead Thursday night. He'd brought his medical bag with him, so I asked if he'd be able to get me some blood, hair, and

CHAPTER THIRTY-TWO

nail samples. I've followed protocol and have them in my cabin. I'll hand them over when we get to your HQ."

"Swell! Seems you thought of everything."

Steven turned to Will, Jimmy Bou, and Olivia. "I'm going to tell Margery—or Lewis, if she's not available—what's going on. Then I want to wash off this blood, change my shirt, and make myself presentable. Will and Jimmy, I'll drop you off where you left the car yesterday. It sounds like the roads are cleared enough so we can all go home after we finish with the sheriff. What do you want to do? Go back home or stay here for supper?"

Will looked at his watch. "It's still early, Steven. We should be done by two. I'd rather go home. Jimmy, what do you think?"

"Yeah, I want to go home. Thanks for asking me, Will."

"Okay, that's settled. We'll get our things from the cabin, load everything in your trunk, then transfer our gear to the car down the road," Will told Steven.

"Let's meet in the lodge in fifteen minutes," Steven told his partner.

"Don't forget your snowshoes and poles on the porch," Olivia reminded them.

"Olivia, what do you want to do?" Steven asked.

"Go home as soon as possible. While you're cleaning up, I'll pack up my stuff then I can help you with yours. Do you want to give the lieutenant our makeshift murder board? We can roll it up."

"Yes, I don't want any of the Racine family to read our notes."

After introducing John Delaney and Lou Banks to Margery, Lewis, Jack, Harry, and Victor—Irene and Aunt Emily were both napping—Steven explained what had happened since Rider had fled the kitchen.

"We don't know yet why he did it, but he went quietly. He knows we've got him dead to rights. Lieutenant Delaney's going to question him now. I'll sit in and help when I can. Hopefully, Rider will talk. Lieutenant Delaney will keep you updated. It's his case now, Margery."

Margery Racine rose from the couch, where she'd been sitting with Lewis, and approached Steven. She took both of his hands in hers. "Thank you from the bottom of my heart, Steven. I'll never be able to tell you how much I appreciate everything you did over these past horrible days."

"I'm so sorry about Gil and Julian. I'm glad you have Lewis's support. Each day will get a little easier." He leaned over and kissed her cheek, then explained the plans they'd made and their intentions to return to Knightsbridge. "We'll head home directly from police headquarters. Despite the terrible things that happened this weekend, you've been a gracious hostess—as well as a courageous woman under extraordinary circumstances—and I thank you for having us, Margery."

Olivia expressed her gratitude as well, and they left to pack.

Steven closed the door to Cabin A behind them. He leaned against the rough wood, dropped his head, and closed his eyes. He let out a deep sigh. "Thank God it's over and no one else got hurt." He looked at Olivia, then reached for her hand. "If you hadn't found that portal, Will would be dead. And probably you, too. I doubt Rider would have stopped at one. He was in a panic. He'd have wanted to get rid of any witnesses." He pulled her in and wrapped his arms around her. "Lately, I've wondered if I should get a different job. I've never put anyone I loved at risk before. I'm not sure about this job anymore."

Olivia held him tightly. "Let's not think about that now. Like you said, it's over, and nobody else got badly hurt. You and Jimmy will mend. I can't wait to get home, Steven. I think we should turn off the phones and lock ourselves in for a few days. I need to decompress from this weekend."

Steven laughed. "I like the way you think." He kissed her forehead

CHAPTER THIRTY-TWO

and pushed away from the wall. "I'm going to clean up and get this over with. I want to go home, too."

The caravan—Steven and Olivia in his car and Will and Jimmy Bou in the department Ford following Delaney and Banks, trailed by the two officers with Rider in a fourth vehicle—turned into a small parking area behind a plain brick building. The only clue to its function was a weathered sign out front, which read "Hamilton County Sheriff."

Steven pulled up next to John Delaney's vehicle, cut the engine, and they exited his Chevy. Following right behind, Will and Jimmy did the same. They made their way along a narrow, shoveled path to the entrance and trooped in, knocking snow off their boots as they entered. Lieutenant Lou Banks led them down a long corridor to an office. The notification CID—Criminal Investigation Division—was etched into the glass on the top part of the door.

"Hasn't said a peep," Banks told them. "We've got him in Interview 1. If it's okay with you, Delaney, I'll take Sergeant Taylor's and Officer Bourgogne's statements in here while you're in with Detective Blackwell and our suspect. Miss Watson, would you mind waiting in the lobby?"

"Yeah, that's good. Get Miss Watson some coffee." Delaney turned to the three Knightsbridge policemen. "Would you fellas like a cup of coffee? Still pretty cold out there. As a matter of fact, it's cold in *here*, too." Delaney stuck his head out the door and yelled down the hall. "Hey, Kessler, see if you can get some heat in this place, will you?"

Steven and John Delaney left Will and Jimmy with Lou Banks and headed to Interview 1.

It was a small, simple room resembling the interview rooms at the Knightsbridge Police station–two metal-framed chairs facing each other across a battered wooden table, an extra chair in a corner, a window high on the wall that let in little to no light, and a bare bulb hanging from the ceiling. Delaney asked the officer on guard to wait outside the door while he pulled the extra chair over for Steven.

Delaney and Steven settled on one side of the table facing Rider. Rider sat straight with his back to the door, his head down, and his hands folded in his lap. When the policemen had first entered the room, Rider had looked up, then returned to staring at his knees.

Steven observed Rider, waiting to see if the Racines' butler would speak first.

He did.

Ignoring the county sheriff, Rider locked eyes with Steven. "I'm sorry." He spoke slowly but deliberately. "I did all those horrible things, and I don't feel any better. All I did was make Mrs. Racine feel as terrible as I have for the past year and a half."

Rider's shoulders and face sagged, and, for the first time, Steven thought he looked his age. The man's eyes and the lines carved in his brow displayed a long, hard life.

"What happened a year and a half ago, Rider?" Steven asked.

"My son was killed."

"Oh, I had the impression he died in the war."

"No, Jack Racine killed him at a bar in the Philippines."

Steven's jaw dropped. "The sailor that Jack punched, who then died, was your son?"

Rider nodded. "I wanted Jack to suffer like I have. I know he didn't mean to do it…he never even saw my son before that night…but the feeling of revenge was too strong. I wanted to take away the person closest to him, his twin. I wanted him to hurt. But in the end, it didn't make me feel any better. All I did was hurt Mrs. Racine. And she never did anything to me." He cleared his throat.

"I never meant to kill Julian. He walked in on me when I was spreading the poison on the keys. When your friend Miss Watson recognized the potassium cyanide, Julian realized what I had done. I

CHAPTER THIRTY-TWO

needed to move fast. I'm really sorry about what I did to Julian. And I'm sorry I hurt you and your friends, Detective. I had one bit of bad luck after another." He shook his head. "It's all over for me now. I know that. Will they let me have my photographs in prison, do you think? Just the two—the one of my wife and the one of my son—just the two. That's all I need."

Steven waited a moment, then asked the butler what he'd used to push Julian under the water and keep him there. Rider refused to say another word. When Lieutenant Delaney officially charged him, when an officer took his arm to escort him to a cell, when he stopped in the middle of the corridor and turned to look back at Steven, all the way down the hallway and out of sight, Rider never said another word.

Their statements to the Hamilton County Sheriff's Department didn't take long. Shortly before four-thirty, Will parked in front of Jimmy's house. Both were happy to be home. Steven and Olivia arrived in Knightsbridge after five, having driven the last hour in the dark. On the way home, they'd decided to stop at Bailey's for supper, then go into Olivia's time to cuddle up on the couch in front of the Christmas tree and watch a movie in their pajamas.

As Steven pulled into the driveway, Olivia exclaimed, "I've never been so happy to see this house. And by the way, I wasn't kidding when I said I want to hide out here for a few days."

Steven chuckled. "I called the chief before I left the station and asked if I could take tomorrow and Tuesday off. This case took a toll on me, too, Olivia. He said yes. I also made plans with Will for him to come over so we can tell him everything and show him how our doorway works. We just have to pick a day. Is that alright with you?"

"Yes, definitely. I trust Will, and you know how much I like him. Besides, I think it's time someone in your world knows about us."

Chapter Thirty-Three

Wednesday, December 19, 1934

Knightsbridge, New York

The doorbell rang at six o'clock. Steven rose from the couch where he'd been relaxing and went into the hallway to answer it. Shoulders hunched up in the cold, wool fedora tilted on his head, his partner, Will Taylor, stood on the porch, stomping his feet to knock snow off his boots.

"Come in, Will. You can hang your coat and hat on the rack here," Steven said, gesturing to the hall tree near the door. "Let's sit in the kitchen. Would you like a beer?"

"Sure, thanks."

After they'd settled at the table, Steven said, "Do you remember last February when we were on the Chambers' murder?"

"Sure!" Will's brows rose on his high forehead. "That was a rough investigation."

"Exactly. We were all so tired we were dizzy from the long hours, day after day after day. There were times when I thought we might not solve it." Steven took a swig of his beer. "Do you also remember that my mother died the month before?"

CHAPTER THIRTY-THREE

"Of course I do," Will said softly.

"Well, toward the end of the investigation, I started having what I thought were hallucinations. Every night when I walked past my mother's bedroom door, I saw a woman sleeping in her bed."

Will's jaw dropped, but he refrained from speaking.

"I thought the exhaustion from the case and the grief over my mother's death were making me go crazy. I decided that as soon as the case was over, I'd get myself to a doctor and see what was going on."

Unwilling to interrupt, Will said nothing.

Steven went on. "One night, this woman—who I thought only existed in my mind—sat up in bed and spoke. I'll never forget it. All she said was hello, but you could have knocked me over. And, without thinking, it just came out. I said, 'Are you real?' She laughed, and I guess that sort of broke the ice. So, we started talking. She said her name was Olivia, and she lived in 2014. She had recently learned about one of Einstein's theories. He believed time could fold over to reveal another time. She said maybe that was what was happening to us."

Even if Will had wanted to speak, he wouldn't have been able to find the words. This was too unbelievable. Yet, he knew Steven, and if there was one thing that Detective Sergeant Steven Blackwell was not, it was fanciful or gullible.

Steven went on to explain how he and Olivia proved to each other that they were who they said they were, how they experimented and discovered they could move into each other's time, how they began spending evenings together, and how they became friends.

"Can I show you, Will? Olivia's expecting us," Steven said.

As if in a daze and still not knowing what to say, Will simply nodded. He set his beer on the table, rose, and followed Steven up the stairs.

They walked down the dark hallway, covered in navy blue wallpaper, toward the empty bedroom at the front of the house. Steven instructed Will to stay on their side of the doorway. "Stand here, Will. You'll see how it works," he said.

As they waited, Will took in Evangeline Blackwell's elegant Art Deco boudoir. He admired the small reading nook set up in front of the bow window with a view of the trees that lined the street outside. He imagined himself reading the evening paper, sitting in the comfortable-looking midnight blue chair with his feet propped up on the caramel-colored leather hassock.

Suddenly, as if by magic, Olivia appeared out of nowhere. It was like she'd been walking through a mist that lifted to reveal a human figure. Stunned, Will watched the room transform before his eyes. A small sofa and coffee table piled high with newspapers and magazines materialized in the reading nook, replacing the welcoming vignette. The blue drapes faded away; sheer curtains hung in their place. The white walls turned into Olivia's pale blue ones.

Olivia approached the doorway. "Hi, Will." She smiled. "I know Steven told you everything, but I bet you still have a lot of questions."

"I don't know where to begin," he stammered. Will Taylor had never stammered in his life.

"Would you like to see some more of the future?" Olivia asked.

Will turned to Steven.

"Olivia's prepared supper. What do you say, partner?"

Will gulped. "Sure."

Olivia reached out her hand. Will took it, and she brought him over the threshold into the 21st century. Then Olivia took Steven's hand, and he followed, grinning.

Chapter Thirty-Four

Christmas Day, 1934 and 2014

Knightsbridge, New York

The week passed in a flurry of holiday activities. Olivia met Sophie and Liz for breakfast at Sophie's *Pâtisserie-Café* one morning and for dinner at The Three Lords pub one evening. She finished her Christmas shopping, wrapped gifts, and displayed them under the tree. She whipped up batches of cut-outs and commandeered Steven to help frost and decorate them. He said that was a first and they should make it an annual tradition. Olivia proposed a second tradition, and Steven agreed to fill and hang stockings for each other. Throughout the week, they opened the front door to carolers, both in his time and in hers, inviting them inside and offering punch and Christmas cookies after enjoying a song.

One day, Olivia received a phone call from her parents in California, informing her that her mother had fallen and broken her leg; they couldn't come for Christmas. They made plans to reschedule as soon as Mom was on her feet again. Liz and her husband, Joe, jumped in with an invitation to arrive early and spend the afternoon at their house since they were all having Christmas dinner together, anyway.

In Steven's time, Christmas morning arrived crisp and cold but with clear blue skies. Snow still covered the ground, and a new dusting on Christmas Eve sparkled in the sunshine. Steven had asked Olivia to attend Christmas services with him.

"I feel bad for the Racines this Christmas," she said in the car on the way to church. "I wonder how they're doing."

"Margery called to wish us a Merry Christmas yesterday. I haven't had a chance to tell you."

"That was thoughtful. What else did she say?" Olivia asked.

"They had the reading of the will. It was pretty much like we figured. Margery can stay in the Fifth Avenue house for as long as she wants and has plenty of money for the rest of her life. The same for Irene. Harry gets Onontaga. Jack and Harry inherit the two companies, with the stipulation that they have to spend time learning the business before they can take over."

"Well, that sounds good."

"And I left the best for last," said Steven, eyes twinkling.

"What?"

"Irene and Victor are engaged."

"Wow! No kidding."

"Yup, Margery said Victor won everybody over the way he acted at Onontaga, and she didn't want to stand in the way of Irene's happiness."

"It looks like some things have changed for the better for the Racines. I'm happy for Irene."

"Jack got on the phone after Margery finished," Steven said. "He's really cut up. The news that the man he killed was Rider's son shocked him. I think it's going to take quite a long time for him to get over that."

CHAPTER THIRTY-FOUR

When Steven parked along the curb in front of the First Methodist Church, he saw friends and neighbors in their holiday best filling the sidewalk, calling out to one another as they strolled to the front door. He and Olivia entered the packed church and found two seats halfway down the aisle next to Steven's childhood friend Artie and his family. After the congregation had sung the last hymn and the minister left the church, Olivia told Steven that she'd thoroughly enjoyed the service, especially the singing and music.

Weeks before, Olivia had invited Steven into her time for a special Christmas breakfast. She'd already prepped Giada De Laurentiis's berry strata and, when they returned home she pulled the casserole dish from the refrigerator and turned on the oven. They went upstairs—Olivia stopping in the living room to light the tree and put on a Christmas CD—to change out of their 1934 clothes and into something festive but more casual for the holiday in 2014.

Steven exchanged his Sunday suit for a pair of charcoal gray trousers, crisp white shirt, and cable-knit pullover. He also retrieved what he called his house slippers. Olivia chose a pair of cuffed gray plaid trousers and a red silk blouse. She added a chunky gold necklace, then opened the bedroom door to where Steven waited. Reaching out, she took his hand and brought him into the room. They turned around, walked back out the door, and down her 21st-century pale green hallway.

The bell on the stove dinged, and Olivia popped the strata into the oven and set the timer.

"I'm going to make a pitcher of mimosas," she said.

"What are mimosas?" he asked.

"It's a cocktail. Orange juice and champagne."

"In the morning?"

Olivia laughed. "A lot of people make them for special occasions.

Besides, we'll be having a big breakfast to offset any effects of the alcohol. Don't worry. Besides, it's a holiday!"

Olivia set about making the drinks, brewing coffee, and frying sausages—something she never ate but Steven liked. Before church, she'd set the table with what she thought of as the *fancy* things she'd inherited from her grandmother—a white linen tablecloth, matching napkins, and goblets. Now, she placed the pitcher of drinks on the table. She poured the coffee in a thermal carafe decorated with a Christmas theme and set it to the side.

"Would you pour us a mimosa?" she asked while serving portions of the berry strata and the sausages for him.

Sitting across the table, Olivia raised her glass. "Here's to our first Christmas together."

Steven touched his glass to hers, the sound of crystal echoing in the room.

"And here's to many more Christmases together," he said, touching her glass again, then taking a drink. "Oh, this is aces! We're going to have to make this another tradition."

Olivia laughed, then set her drink down, reached across the table, and took his hand. "I am so happy." She beamed at him.

He squeezed her hand. "Me, too. Now, let's eat."

After breakfast, they settled on the couch in front of the Christmas tree, whose scent filled the room. Both drifted into thoughts of their own and, for a few minutes, the only sounds were of carols playing softly in the background.

Suddenly, Olivia laughed. Steven turned to look at her.

"What?" he asked.

"I remembered another tradition I forgot to tell you about."

"I'm all ears."

"It started when Liz, Sophie, and I were kids. When each of our families decorated their Christmas tree, the other two of us went to

CHAPTER THIRTY-FOUR

help, then stayed overnight for a pajama party. One year, when we were around eight, Sophie made a mistake and grabbed the top from one pair of pajamas and the pants from another set. She spent the weekend in plaid bottoms and a striped top. We all thought it was hilarious. We laughed like crazy. But we loved it. So, a tradition was born. From then on, we purposely brought mismatched pajamas for the annual tree decorating."

"Yeah, that's a fun story, but I'm not sure I want to join that particular tradition."

"Suit yourself." Olivia grinned. "But, just so you know, tonight, when we get back from Liz's, I'm putting on mismatched pajamas for our Christmas movie."

The afternoon and evening flew by with great joy. By the time everyone had arrived at Liz and her husband Joe's house, the temperature had plummeted again, but their home was toasty warm with the crackling fire and the laughter of family and friends. They enjoyed a sumptuous dinner prepared by Liz and her mom, and cheesecakes to-die-for that Sophie and her boyfriend, Luc, had whipped up. Later that night, when Steven and Olivia pulled into their driveway, Olivia told him it had been one of the best Christmases ever. They went upstairs, agreeing to meet after they changed into their pajamas. Then, they'd get comfortable in her living room and watch a movie. Being a fan of Ralphie, Olivia was eager to share *A Christmas Story* with him.

Feeling so happy she could burst, Olivia stood at her bedroom door, waiting for Steven to disappear into his room. Instead, he stopped in the middle of his hallway.

That was when she noticed the light.

A light escaped under the door of what had been his mother's art studio. As Steven stood listening for movement behind the door, he heard Olivia whisper, "Be careful."

Steven inched toward the room and pushed the door slightly so more light spilled out. Standing at the threshold, he heard a creaking like the sound his mother's easel used to make scraping the floor when she moved it near the window to catch more of the sun. He inhaled…and smelled her perfume. He opened the door wider, took a step, and gasped.

A younger version of Evangeline Blackwell turned to face him. The smile he had missed so achingly for nearly a year beamed at him.

"Mom?" His voice cracked, and he could barely get the word out.

"I need you to come to Paris," whispered Steven's mother.

Not…the end.

A Note from the Author

(1) The Racine Great Camp Onontaga was named after the Onondaga Indians, the name meaning "on the mountain." The Onondaga are one of the five original tribes composing the Haudenosaunee (Iroquois) Nation. Onontaga was loosely based on Great Camp Sagamore.

(2) The now legendary Adirondack Great Camps came into existence in the late 1800s in an explosion of building, lasting until the 1920s, by America's wealthiest families, such as the Vanderbilts and the Rockefellers. William West Durant is considered the "Father of the Great Camps", whose architectural style reflects a philosophy of building as one in nature. There are several criteria which make a Great Camp: 1. The complex is composed of 10 or more buildings. 2. They're built on the shore of a lake. 3. One family owns the entire complex. 4. All buildings are constructed using natural materials from the area. 5. The builders use bark and local stone to create artistic patterns and designs unique to the Great Camps. 6. The camps are self-sufficient. 7. Each building is conceived with a single-use purpose.
    In *RSVP to Murder*, I broke Rule #7 and made the buildings multi-use to suit the story.
    Source: *Adirondack Great Camps Part 1: Durant and Raquette Lake*. DVD 1996. Media M Productions. New York.

(3) Broncho Billy (1880-1971): Broncho Billy was the first star of Western movies. The 1980 film called *Bronco Billy*, starring Clint

Eastwood, tells the story of his life.

(4) The Shubert Brothers—Lee, Sam, and Jacob—emigrated to the United States with their parents from what is now Lithuania. The family settled in Syracuse, New York, joining a growing Jewish community from their home in the then Russian Empire. Over the years, the brothers became a dominating force in the theatrical world, owning some 50 theatres around the globe by 1905. They are credited with building "Broadway as we know it."

Source: Article in the *Syracuse Post Standard* by the Onondaga Historical Association.

(5) Moving the Truax Hotel: The story Jimmy Bou tells Will is true!
Source: http://www.Syracuse.com, July 2, 2914.

Acknowledgements

The idea of an author sitting alone and writing a novel in a romantic Parisian attic or atmospheric old house on the ocean's shore is itself the stuff of fiction. Writers need help. That's all there is to it.

I've been extremely lucky in getting help from both strangers and friends. Each has contributed to making this a better book. My heartfelt thanks go to:

Andrew Sadowski for helping me figure out how to poison my victim.

Denise Donato for the fantastic title. I love it!

Beta readers Mickey Hunter, Marylou Murry, MaryAnn Shovlowsky, and Sue Watchko for reading my manuscript and offering such wonderful comments. You guys always make it better!!

Jon Anderson for generously sharing his vast knowledge of police procedures as well as the history of policing, and for reading an early draft and giving me fantastic comments and ideas. Any procedural mistakes are my own.

Luci Zahray for her invaluable help with poisons.

Scott Case for taking his time to answer all my questions about bridling horses and horse-drawn sleighs…and for the awesome sleigh ride!

Nick Brandreth, Historic Process Specialist at The Eastman Museum, Rochester, NY; Commanding Officer Toolan at the Navy Reserve Center, Syracuse, NY; Kevin Donohue at St. Patrick's Cathedral, New York City, NY. The details are always important.

Tina deBellegarde for helping me proof *RSVP*, for her fabulous comments, and for a list too long of other book-related things that keep us on the phone every day!

Shawn Reilly Simmons at Level Best Books for her always insightful notes and for the stunning cover. I absolutely love it.

Deb Well at Level Best Books for her help.

My partners-in-crime Jen Collins Moore, Tina deBellegarde, and Lida Sideris for things too many to name.

And to you, dear reader, for your interest in Steven and Olivia and for reading my books.

Thank you, all!!

About the Author

A former language teacher and business owner, Carol Pouliot writes the acclaimed Blackwell and Watson Time-Travel Mysteries. With their fast pace and unexpected twists and turns, the books have earned praise from readers and mystery authors alike. Carol is a founding member of Sleuths and Sidekicks, Co-chair of the Murderous March Mystery Conference, and President of the Upper Hudson Chapter of Sisters in Crime. When not writing, Carol can be found packing her suitcase and reaching for her passport for her next travel adventure. Learn more and sign up for Carol's newsletter at http://www.carolpouliot.com and https://www.sleuthsandsidekicks.com/

SOCIAL MEDIA HANDLES:
    https://www.facebook.com/WriterCarolPouliot/?view_public_for=101607075003213
    https://www.goodreads.com/author/show/15907927.Carol_Pouliot
    https://www.instagram.com/carolpouliotmysterywriter/?hl=en
    https://www.bookbub.com/authors/carol-pouliot
    https://www.pinterest.com/cpouliot13/

AUTHOR WEBSITE:
   https://www.carolpouliot.com/

AUTHOR BLOG:
   https://www.sleuthsandsidekicks.com/

Also by Carol Pouliot

Doorway to Murder A Blackwell and Watson Time-Travel Mystery (Book 1)

Threshold of Deceit A Blackwell and Watson Time-Travel Mystery (Book 2)

Death Rang the Bell A Blackwell and Watson Time-Travel Mystery (Book 3)